BY
  THE
TIME
    YOU
READ
    THIS

OTHER TITLES BY BRIANNA LABUSKES

Raisa Susanto Novels

The Truth You Told

The Lies You Wrote

Dr. Gretchen White Novels

See It End

What Can't Be Seen

A Familiar Sight

Stand-Alone Novels

Her Final Words

Black Rock Bay

Girls of Glass

It Ends with Her

PRAISE FOR BRIANNA LABUSKES

What Can't Be Seen

"The book's well-constructed plot matches its three-dimensional characters. Psychological-thriller fans will be eager for more."

—*Publishers Weekly*

A Familiar Sight

"A horrific brew for readers willing to immerse themselves in it."

—*Kirkus Reviews*

"A strong plot and unforgettable characters make this a winner. Labuskes is on a roll."

—*Publishers Weekly*

"*A Familiar Sight* has everything I crave in a thriller: a shocking, addictive female lead; unexpected twists that snapped off the page; and an ending that made me gasp out loud. I never saw it coming, but it was perfectly in sync with the razor-sharp balance between creepy and compelling that Labuskes carries throughout the novel. This is a one-sitting read."

—Jess Lourey, Amazon Charts bestselling author

Her Final Words

"Labuskes skillfully ratchets up the suspense. Readers will eagerly await her next."

—*Publishers Weekly*

"Labuskes offers an intense mystery with an excellent character in Lucy, who methodically uncovers layers of deceit while trusting no one."
—*Library Journal*

Girls of Glass

"Excellent . . . Readers who enjoy having their expectations upset will be richly rewarded."
—*Publishers Weekly* (starred review)

It Ends with Her

"Once in a while a character comes along who gets under your skin and refuses to let go. This is the case with Brianna Labuskes's Clarke Sinclair—a cantankerous, rebellious, and somehow endearingly likable FBI agent with a troubled past. I was immediately pulled into Clarke's broken, shadow-filled world and her quest for justice and redemption. A stunning thriller, *It Ends with Her* is not to be missed."
—Heather Gudenkauf, *New York Times* bestselling author

"*It Ends with Her* is a gritty, riveting roller-coaster ride of a book. Brianna Labuskes has created a layered, gripping story around a cast of characters that readers will cheer for. Her crisp prose and quick plot kept me reading with my heart in my throat. Highly recommended for fans of smart thrillers with captivating heroines."
—Nicole Baart, author of *Little Broken Things*

"An engrossing psychological thriller filled with twists and turns. I couldn't put it down! The characters were filled with emotional depth. An impressive debut!"
—Elizabeth Blackwell, author of *In the Shadow of Lakecrest*

BY THE TIME YOU READ THIS

BRIANNA LABUSKES

This is a work of fiction. Names, characters, organizations, places, events, and incidents are either products of the author's imagination or are used fictitiously. Otherwise, any resemblance to actual persons, living or dead, is purely coincidental.

Text copyright © 2025 by Brianna Labuskes

All rights reserved.

No part of this book may be reproduced, or stored in a retrieval system, or transmitted in any form or by any means, electronic, mechanical, photocopying, recording, or otherwise, without express written permission of the publisher.

Published by Thomas & Mercer, Seattle

www.apub.com

Amazon, the Amazon logo, and Thomas & Mercer are trademarks of Amazon.com, Inc., or its affiliates.

EU product safety contact:
Amazon Media EU S. à r.l.
38, avenue John F. Kennedy, L-1855 Luxembourg
amazonpublishing-gpsr@amazon.com

ISBN-13: 9781662527555 (paperback)
ISBN-13: 9781662527548 (digital)

Cover design by Damon Freeman
Cover image: © Melanie Wintersdorff / ArcAngel; © kozhedub_nc / Shutterstock

Printed in the United States of America

To Grammy Judy,
a woman who loves her family above all else

CHAPTER ONE

Raisa

Day One

FBI forensic linguist Raisa Susanto wanted to go home.

It was a novel feeling, considering she hadn't lived anywhere that had felt like *home* in nearly two decades. But six months ago, she'd finally given up her attachment to off-white walls and gray linoleum and moved into a 1930s-era bungalow with wood floors that had more personality than her past six apartments combined.

Putting down roots.

The concept scared her more than she wanted to admit, but on nights like these, driving back to her house exhausted after hunting down a killer, she was glad she'd put on her big-girl panties and applied for that mortgage.

She still had to find time to make it actually feel like *hers*—including decorating literally any room—but she no longer hated the place she lived.

Baby steps, as her quasi-partner, forensic psychologist Callum Kilkenny, would say. For him, anything that made her a slightly more open, vulnerable human and slightly less of a gremlin with concrete walls around her was a victory.

Even if those walls were well earned.

As Raisa pulled to a stop at a light, her fingers found the place where a bullet had torn through ligament and muscle two years earlier. The ache wasn't real—she had completely healed from the injury. But it pulsed sometimes, a ghost, reminding her of how far she'd come over the past two years.

How far she still had to go.

Just the thought of it had her checking her rearview mirror, as if Isabel, her psychopathic serial killer sister, were following her through the outskirts of suburban Tacoma well after midnight.

There were plenty of reasons why that idea was ridiculous, but the primary one was that Isabel—on that night she'd put a bullet into Raisa—had finally been arrested after a prolific and violent twenty-five years of an ever-escalating victim count.

When Raisa turned onto her street, her fingers relaxed against the steering wheel, the anxiety that came with thinking about Isabel blessedly releasing her from its grip. Her sister was safely behind bars at a high-security women's correctional facility serving multiple life sentences. And Raisa? Raisa was home.

It was past midnight and all the houses around hers were dark, everything soft, quiet, and cozy. Tucked in. The silence when she walked into her bungalow welcomed her rather than putting her on edge.

The moonlight shifted and Raisa caught sight of a white envelope that someone had clearly slipped under the door. Her name was written across the front, but that was the only thing on it—there was no postage or return address. Raisa's heartbeat ticked up a notch, but just as soon as it did, she remembered Alicia from down the street had mentioned sending her a flyer about a block party later that month.

Considering Raisa had been gone for almost two weeks, Alicia'd probably gotten tired of knocking.

Raisa picked the envelope up and dropped it on the side table, along with her keys and purse. She would deal with everything in the morning. What she wanted now, more than anything, was sleep.

She barely managed to drag her clothes off before collapsing into bed.

But she didn't fall asleep.

Instead, she stared at the ceiling, something itching at her brain. The sensation was similar to wondering if she'd turned off the oven before leaving on vacation.

It was the envelope. It was seeing it right after thinking about Isabel and that night two years ago.

Raisa sat up and grabbed a sweatshirt on her way out of bed. The thing was oversize and worn-in and offered a comfort she shouldn't be craving right now. She also thought about getting her gun—which would offer a different sort of comfort—but that was probably overkill. Especially if she opened the envelope and found an invitation to a block party.

A few strides later, and she was standing in front of her entryway side table.

She had read plenty of letters in her life as a forensic linguist for the FBI. Bomb threats, kidnapping demands, manifestos, terrorist plots, suicide notes—the list went on. She'd seen the worst humans could write to each other, the words somehow more damning when put down in ink rather than just spoken.

Raisa was never nervous to read any of them. They were problems that needed to be solved, peeks into the darkest souls that satisfied a curiosity in her that she'd had since she was young.

Her heart never raced like this when simply looking at any of them.

Once again, her fingers found the spot where a pink, puckered scar lived.

She was being paranoid, she knew.

But sometimes paranoia was justified.

The first time Isabel had ruined her life, Raisa had been only three years old. Isabel had killed their parents—Tim and Becks Parker—in their bed, too many stab wounds between them to count. She'd maneuvered their brother, Alex, into the claw-foot tub in their parents' bathroom, slit his wrists, and then left a suicide note "written by him" that confessed to the murders.

Isabel had been fifteen years old.

The second time, Isabel had wanted to see how Raisa, who'd been adopted by kind and loving parents, was growing up. That had kicked off a series of events in which Raisa's adoptive parents died in a car crash. Raisa had survived a series of progressively worsening foster homes until she'd pretty much landed on the streets, raising herself.

The last time Isabel had tried to ruin Raisa's life . . . well. Raisa had ended up with a scar and the memory of pulling a trigger with the intent of killing her own sister.

There was no reason to think the letter came from Isabel.

And yet, somehow, Raisa knew it did.

The darkness no longer seemed welcoming, but sinister, her home—her haven—now tainted with the presence of a monster.

Raisa fought the urge to call the correctional facility to have them go check to make sure Isabel hadn't escaped from her cell. Of course she hadn't. This wasn't a movie. However this letter had gotten to Raisa, it wasn't because Isabel was crouching in the bushes outside her bungalow.

The image was enough to break the spell her paranoia had cast. Raisa laughed at the thought of Isabel—who wanted nothing more than to be thought of as brilliant, cool, and mysterious—trying to peek into her window.

Raisa picked up the envelope because it wasn't a bomb.

Not one that would explode in her hands at that moment, at least.

Whatever was inside might explode her life, but that would be something she would have to deal with whether she stared at it until the morning or ripped off the Band-Aid now.

She glanced at the pane of glass in her door, caught only her reflection, and then dropped to the floor. Anyone outside could see her. Safety procedures were still smart, no matter what the actual threat level was.

Raisa took a deep breath and finally opened the envelope.

There was a single piece of paper inside.

By the time you read this, I'll be dead.

Beneath that was an address on the Olympic Peninsula, one Raisa didn't recognize at a glance.

The paper trembled in her hands, surprise overtaking any other emotion.

There was no doubt in her mind that it was from Isabel.

It could be a lie, but what would that accomplish?

It would get Raisa to visit.

She hadn't seen her sister in more than a year. In fact, Raisa had tried to completely forget that Isabel even existed. She'd blocked her name on all the social media apps, she'd made sure to stay away from the suggested listens on any podcast platform, she even squinted at the home screens of all the streaming services because now was about the time that docuseries were coming out about Isabel's long and violent killing career.

Maybe Raisa had done too good a job. Maybe there was a reason Isabel was trying to summon her and, having grown frustrated with any previous attempts to do so, went for the shock value.

But Isabel hated looking foolish about as much as she hated being wrong. She would never have sent this note if it weren't true.

Raisa's breathing had gone ragged, and she only realized it when black started creeping in from the sides of her eyes.

She didn't *care* if Isabel was dead, not like she probably should at losing one of her two remaining family members. Nothing in Raisa's life would really change at all. And yet the idea of it sent shock waves through her body.

Losing something that was evil was still losing something.

After that night when she and Isabel had aimed guns at each other and both pulled the trigger, Raisa had wondered if her family was simply *bad*. After all, there had been a moment during the standoff where Raisa had been sure that Delaney Moore, their third sister, would help Isabel get away with killing her.

She had grappled with that idea for a long time—for if Raisa had been born to a family of monsters, what did that make her?

It had really only been after she and Kilkenny had gone to Texas to look into the decade-old death of his wife, Shay, that Raisa had come to realize that she wasn't defined by her blood. She was defined by the family she *chose*, not the one she was born into.

Isabel had served as a stark reminder of what Raisa could have become. It had reminded her whenever she wanted to make the lazy choice, the selfish choice, the choice that was unjust, that the road to hell could be paved with those missteps.

The sky lightened, and still Raisa sat on the floor staring at perhaps the last words she'd ever get from Isabel.

There would be plenty of time to dissect them later. Right now, she couldn't think of much beyond the confusing miasma of relief, joy, grief, anger, fear.

Raisa's cell phone rang, vibrating on the floor next to her foot. She grabbed for it and checked the screen.

Kilkenny.

She let it go to voicemail, though she offered him a silent apology as she did.

Most of her life had been spent as a loner—beyond the little band of foster kids who'd grown up on the streets alongside her. As one of two forensic linguists employed full-time by the Bureau, she was shipped around the country more often than she was in Tacoma. She became friendly enough with some agents—the ones who didn't see her as an irritating paper pusher—but she never stayed long enough to transition to actual allies.

That had been before Kilkenny, though. As a forensic psychologist, he was also loaned out to investigations all over the country. Prior to getting to know him, she'd thought him too aloof to care about the fact that they both had lonely jobs. Now that she'd spent the past year being able to call him a friend, she realized they'd both been craving a partner in a way their positions would never allow them to have.

She didn't want to ignore his call, but she also couldn't bring herself to answer it. She knew what he was going to tell her.

For just a little longer, she wanted to live in this Schrödinger's moment where Isabel was both alive and dead. The minute was ruined by a text from Kilkenny anyway.

Turn on the news.

Raisa fumbled for her remote, half-glad and half-irritated that she'd sprung for basic cable when she moved into the bungalow. She knew what she would find, but needed it confirmed.

Needed to see the cat actually dead.

Across the bottom of the TV screen, the chyron read:

Serial Killer Isabel Parker Found Dead in Cell

CHAPTER TWO

Delaney

Day Four

Someone was watching Delaney Moore.

Even though she was usually the one on the other side of the feeling, she recognized when there were eyes on the back of her neck as easily as any prey animal would.

Her basement apartment had a tiny window that let in light on only the sunniest days in Seattle—and those were few and far between. Delaney stared at the bushes beyond the glass for a long while, but of course, there was no one there.

Still, she had survived to nearly forty years of age because she listened to her gut.

Her eyes flicked to a piece of paper that she kept pinned to the corkboard above her computer.

You're as guilty as I am.

At the time she'd received it, she'd wanted to litigate the accusation she'd known was from Isabel. It was unfair, even though both of Delaney's sisters seemed to think it was accurate. But Isabel had been a prolific serial killer; Delaney's only crime was not being able to stop her.

It was true that Delaney hadn't wanted Isabel to end up dead, which she'd thought was the likely outcome of going to the FBI about her suspicions. So she'd never given any law enforcement agencies information about how to find her sister—or even told anyone her sister was likely killing people.

Perhaps that *did* make her at least half as guilty as Isabel.

She was certain philosophy and ethics classes could have a field day with the Parker sisters.

None of that mattered right now, though.

Isabel was dead.

And someone was watching Delaney.

Possibly.

Perhaps it was someone who felt the way Raisa and Isabel did, that Delaney was to blame for a loved one's death. Perhaps the person had a monster to feed, one created by grief, one that wouldn't be satiated with just Isabel's passing. It would want to feast on Delaney's bones as well, because creatures like that, ones born of sorrow, were never satisfied.

Maybe she was being paranoid right now.

Or maybe she was right and someone was about to kick through her door.

Maybe was enough for her.

She shoved aside stacks of journals and scrap paper until she found an empty thumb drive. She jammed it into the port on her computer and then transferred everything over to the little device. While that loaded, she crossed the studio to her closet and pulled down a bag she kept ready and waiting on the top shelf.

The one nice thing about poking around on the dark web since she'd been fifteen was that she knew exactly how to get everything she needed in order to disappear in under twenty-four hours.

The lurking habit had begun as a way to search for Isabel, and in the process, Delaney had learned more than any teenager should. She'd learned the language used by predators, the way they signaled their interest to other participants in any given forum, the breadcrumbs they left to other, even darker sites. Delaney had started tipping off the police whenever she came across something that could lead to an arrest.

When she'd needed a full-time job to fund her search for Isabel, it had been an easy transition to become a moderator for one of the video-based social media sites. Anything she hadn't learned as an amateur lurker had been filled in by watching thousands of videos a day that were flagged for inappropriate content.

It probably hadn't done anything good for her mental health, but it would help her now.

She had three different passports, two social security cards and driver's licenses, a stash of burner phones, and enough prepaid credit cards to last her a year on the run.

The computer dinged, but she ignored it for now. Instead, she went to the bathroom and grabbed the kit that would allow her to cut and dye her hair if needed. She wasn't even sure yet if leaving was necessary, but the best way to be successful in a crisis was to be prepared.

With everything packed, Delaney paid three months' worth of rent to her landlord—she didn't want to get rid of this place as an option yet—and then wiped her computer.

Even the best hacker wouldn't be able to get anything off it, and she didn't think any law enforcement outside of the CIA employed the best hackers anyway.

She kept her phone on her for now. She wanted anyone tracking it to think she was leaving Seattle.

Delaney made a few calls on her walk to the ferry station downtown so there would be a used clunker of a car waiting for her in Bainbridge.

The terminal was busy when she arrived right alongside the morning commuters. She'd made the trip a few times in preparation should she ever need to leave in a hurry, so she easily navigated her way into the right line. The next boat would leave in twenty minutes.

Delaney hadn't felt the eyes on her since a few blocks away from her apartment. That might be because she'd taken a route designed to shake a tail, or it might be because she'd fully descended into paranoia.

Maybe Isabel's death had sent her reeling far more than she'd realized.

She wiggled at the knowledge that her sister was dead as someone would the gaping hole left behind by a missing tooth. She found pain and a weird sort of pleasure.

Delaney had never been good at untangling complex emotions, and hers toward Isabel were as complex as they could be.

There was love and devotion and guilt and hatred. Isabel had always equaled protection for her—but then Delaney had realized Isabel had probably exaggerated all those dangers in their childhood. Their brother, Alex, had been a predator, but Isabel had made it seem like he would kill them and baby Larissa at the drop of a hat.

She'd fostered a dependence on herself through scare tactics, and even with distance and maturity, Delaney still *felt* like Isabel was her guardian angel.

"Miss, can you spare any change?"

Delaney looked up to find a man standing over her. She'd seen him with two others hanging out in the doorway of the furniture store across the street. None of them had looked her way when she'd passed. Delaney stood and dug in her purse for a twenty.

He stepped closer to take it. "Thank you."

Delaney nodded, watching him as he went to talk to another passenger, who shook his head and looked away. Delaney kept watching the man, but once he'd stopped by each person in the terminal, he left. Her shoulders relaxed.

A soothing digital voice came over the speakers, informing those waiting that they could board. Delaney clocked everyone else nearby, letting them go first. Then she stood up at the last minute so she would be able to tell if anyone got on right behind her.

It wasn't a foolproof method of losing a tail, but it was a good one in a pinch. Whoever was following her might have been in a car, or might have simply trusted that this was the ferry she was going to take.

Still, when the gates shut, she exhaled some of the tension she'd been carrying over the past hour.

When they reached the halfway point, Delaney dropped her phone into the sound without bothering to reset it. There was nothing interesting on there anyway. She'd learned long ago not to keep that kind of stuff on a device that could be lifted out of your pocket at Pike Place by someone no more skilled than a toddler.

If someone was tracking her movements, though, it would be a clear sign that she'd clued in on the fact she was being followed.

You're as guilty as I am.

And in that moment, despite the fact that her sister was dead, she hated Isabel more than she ever had before.

Because the truth was, now, because of Isabel, Delaney actually was.

EXCERPT FROM ISABEL PARKER'S JOURNAL

Everyone always wants me to start from the beginning.

But where is the beginning?

The first time I felt the urge to kill? Or the first time I acted upon it?

The first time I laid hands on a vulnerable creature and wondered not how I could protect it but how I could best destroy it?

The first time my parents said "no" and I envisioned swinging a lamp at mother's head before using the shards to slice father's throat? That had been when I was eight, for those keeping track.

The first time I heard the voice in my head, whispering that all these things were right and good and were my destiny?

Or is the beginning simply when my DNA mutated wrong, all the way back in the womb, giving me that voice in my head, giving me those ideas to swing the lamp and kill the bird, giving me this black hole where everyone else said a conscience should live?

They say there's no psychopath gene, but I think that's bullshit. My parents weren't what anyone would call stellar, but they weren't abusive either.

There was no terrible childhood section on my Wikipedia page, not like the ones that fill the rest of the big-name serial killers.

Alex, our golden boy older brother, was a shithead with some kind of personality disorder who deserved a slower death than I gave him, but he wasn't terrible enough to change the trajectory of my life.

That voice had started long before Alex even knew what his dick could be used for. So maybe the beginning was when our parents met, both of them secretly harboring genes that would cause their oldest children to develop into things that society deems monsters.

Lana and Larissa had escaped those genes, as would be expected when breaking down the statistics and probability of dominant versus recessive traits.

I watched them all their lives for signs that they were like me.

I wanted them to be like me.

Was that the beginning? When Lana—she goes by Delaney now, but I refuse to use that—was born and I thought mine.

By the time Larissa—Raisa, you correct me and I suppose you are not wrong—came the voice had grown so loud I was shocked others couldn't hear it.

When I held that baby, it was no longer a whisper, that thought.

It was a roar.

Mine.

I never understood why people wanted to protect the toys that belonged to them when all I ever wanted to do was to destroy them. Because I could. Because it felt better to see a doll in pieces than the boring version of it that was whole and healthy.

I wanted to make them the same as me.

Broken.

Lana and Larissa aren't broken.

But wouldn't it be more fun if they were?

CHAPTER THREE

Raisa

Day One

Raisa sat back on her heels and laughed, though there was nothing funny about the news that Isabel was dead.

The shiny-toothed broadcaster on her TV had adopted a very serious expression as he informed the audience that police didn't believe any foul play was involved.

Isabel had been found unresponsive in her bunk at morning roll call. There had been no one else in the cell with her, and there were no signs of a fight. The medical examiner would proceed with the autopsy, but Raisa, and probably everyone listening, knew it would go to the bottom of the priority list. In another state her death would have been mandated by a jury of her peers. There were few out there who would look at this as anything other than justice served by Mother Nature.

When the broadcaster began detailing Isabel's crimes, Raisa muted the TV. She was quite familiar with her sister's body of work.

Raisa crossed to her desk and carefully laid the letter down, before picking up her notebook.

No foul play, the broadcaster had reported.

And Isabel's note said *dead*, not *murdered*. But if the COD had been natural causes, how would Isabel have known to write to Raisa? How would she have known the exact night she was going to die?

Raisa read the note again.

By the time you read this, I'll be dead.

The forensic linguist in her noted the use of *read* instead of *get*.

Raisa had been working in law enforcement long enough to know that most criminals weren't the masterminds that TV portrayed them as. They usually stumbled backward into their success if they ever had any. In the case she'd just come from working, a woman's boyfriend had taken her phone after he'd murdered her and had spent the night texting the woman's friends to disrupt the timeline.

But he hadn't tried to sound like the woman over the texts—even using Spanish slang despite the fact that his girlfriend hadn't spoken the language at all. He'd been arrested ten days after Raisa arrived.

That wasn't Isabel.

She was the rare exception: a criminal who actually was brilliant. That's what happened when your parents were two world-famous mathematicians—which seemed to have translated into an extreme proficiency with language patterns in their children.

The difference between *read* and *get* was a small thing, but Raisa's cases were built on small things.

Isabel had help, Raisa wrote in the notebook. That much was obvious just from the method of delivery, but the person who had helped her knew the time she'd be dead by. That was interesting, considering it had been the middle of the night.

Below that note, she scribbled, *Suicide?*

She almost crossed it right back out again. Isabel was nothing if not dramatic. If she'd died by suicide, the whole world would know.

Raisa bit her lip before writing, *Homicide.*

No question mark.

Isabel had made plenty of enemies in her life, both outside and—Raisa presumed—inside prison. They'd identified more than a dozen of her victims from her twenty-five-year killing career, and Raisa knew there were ones who had never been found, who would never *be* found.

A list comprising the families and loved ones of those victims could fill a book.

And this was one of the many things Raisa hated about Isabel. Because if she'd known enough to know the date she was going to die, wouldn't she have come up with an idea for the motive? Or even the killer themselves?

Why not just send that to Raisa—or better yet, the police?

The worst thing was that Raisa knew the answer to her own question.

Isabel's main priority wasn't that her murder would be solved; it was that she once again could make Raisa dance to her tune. There was no way for Raisa to ignore this note, and she was almost certain there would be more coming.

Raisa's palm connected with a lamp she'd bought at Goodwill that first night in her new place when she realized she didn't have any overhead lights. Her fingers curled around the neck, and she ripped the cord from the wall as she threw the thing against the fireplace.

Shards of glass sank into carpet that should have been replaced two decades ago.

Breathing hard, she stared at the aftermath of her uncharacteristic rage and flushed hot with shame.

Raisa wasn't a person who threw lamps. She wasn't that person—except when it came to Isabel. Her sister had always managed to bring out the worst in her.

To get herself back under control, she returned her attention to the letter on the desk.

A quick Google Map search of the address showed that it was a residence in some harbor town on the peninsula, looking like a dime a dozen in that stretch of the state.

Maybe it was some complicated code instead of straightforward coordinates, but Raisa didn't think so. She would need to know the key to break any cipher Isabel had sent, and this wasn't set up like one.

Isabel wasn't the type for a parlor trick like invisible ink, either. She had wanted to be thought of as clever, using wordplay and manipulation, not through doing something ten-year-olds experimented with in kits bought at Target.

What it might be was the piece of a larger puzzle, the first of many messages Raisa would get over the next several days.

Or maybe . . .

Delaney.

The middle sister, as the press had dubbed her.

Whereas Raisa hadn't known until recently that she was the survivor of a family massacre when she was a baby, Delaney—who had been twelve at the time—always had. Delaney had spent most of the twenty-five years that followed the killings searching for Isabel, all the while knowing that she was out there racking up more victims.

Delaney had sworn that she'd been on a mission to stop Isabel, but she had not once contacted the police about their sister's long killing career.

It didn't matter how Raisa viewed the situation anyway. It mattered what Isabel thought. And Isabel had loved Delaney most, whatever her version of love was.

If Raisa had received a letter, surely Delaney had as well?

As Raisa reached for her phone, a part of her rebelled.

She was doing exactly what Isabel wanted, she was sure of it. Why else send such a cryptic message?

But wasn't that the genius of her sister?

Even if you knew you were caught in a riptide, there was nothing to do about it but swim toward the ocean.

Delaney didn't answer her phone.

Raisa tried twice and then sent a text.

She wasn't surprised that her sister hadn't picked up. She didn't even know where Delaney lived. She could be in Bali, actually enjoying the freedom she'd so dubiously preserved, and Raisa wasn't sure she'd blame her. For that, at least.

When the knock on her door came a second after she gave up on contacting Delaney, Raisa knew it was Kilkenny without even having to look.

He stood on the little stoop, dressed as casually as he would ever get in pressed, tailored jeans and a cashmere sweater. His salt-and-pepper hair was styled perfectly, pushed back away from his face so that his eyes and cheekbones got the spotlight they deserved. Other people would certainly deem him handsome; Raisa just found his face utterly dear at the moment.

They weren't big on hugging—that wasn't their relationship. But when he held out his arms, she fell into them gladly, letting him take her weight for a moment.

"You didn't have to come," she muttered into his shoulder.

He pinched her arm. "Right. Like you didn't have to go to Texas for me."

Raisa hadn't thought twice about going to Houston the year before when his late wife's murder case had been unexpectedly reopened. Even if Isabel hadn't had her fingerprints all over it, Raisa would have done whatever she had to in order to be there for Kilkenny.

It was funny how things could change so drastically in unexpected ways. Two years ago, he'd been just a distant colleague whom she'd thought of as stuffy and judgmental. She'd been intimidated by his quiet confidence, while also being grateful for the respect he'd always shown her, unlike some of his peers. But she would never have thought they'd get to this point, where they had become a little team against the world.

"How are you?" he asked, holding her at arm's length to get a better look. His eyes flicked to the broken lamp she still hadn't cleaned up yet, and then back to her face, which she knew was a little rough.

The past ten days had taken their toll, as any intense investigation always did. Her brain was sluggish and her body tired despite the fact that she hadn't worked in the field at all. Normally, she would take a day or two to recharge before even thinking about homicides and linguistics and maybe even words in general.

"I'm . . . ," Raisa started, and then trailed off, pulling away from Kilkenny. She headed toward the kitchen, knowing he would take that nonanswer without pushing her too hard. "Is black okay? I've been out of town, so I don't have any mix-ins."

"You got your guy," Kilkenny guessed. It was a thing with them now, the way he was always so sure she'd had a successful trip whenever she was sent out on an investigation. The confidence from him was a welcome change from her career up until then. Agents who were in the field every day didn't particularly like being told what to do by a linguist—and a female one at that. Through years of head pats and shrug-offs, she'd been conditioned into defensiveness when talking about her cases.

Not with Kilkenny, though.

"I got my guy," she confirmed, though he hadn't needed it. He leaned against the counter while she got the coffee started.

"So . . . natural causes?" he asked. "For Isabel?"

"Maybe," Raisa said, turning back to him. "She sent me a letter."

His brows shot up. "Saying what?"

"'By the time you read this, I'll be dead.'"

"A suicide letter?" he asked.

That had been her initial thought, too.

"I don't mean to be the vibes girl," she said, "but that doesn't seem like it would be up Isabel's alley."

"She would have made a bigger splash," he agreed. "If it was suicide, why not make sure everyone knew it?"

"That was my thinking," Raisa said, pleased he'd gotten there as well. If Isabel had ever killed herself, there would have been a lot of blood and theatrics involved. "And how could she have predicted her own death from some kind of rare medical condition? It wasn't as if she was old or sick."

"So, she just wanted to screw with you one last time?" Kilkenny asked. "Maybe if that's the case, she simply paid someone off to watch for news of her death and then slip you this letter."

"Oh, I'm a hundred percent sure she's messing with me, either way," Raisa said, closing her eyes for a moment to enjoy the scent of coffee as it saturated the air. "But this was waiting for me when I got home last night. Way before it hit the media."

"Still, they might have had an inside source," Kilkenny said. "A guard who could text them when the body was found."

Raisa made a noncommittal sound and then straightened. "Actually, speaking of sources, I never did check my Ring footage."

"Shockingly irresponsible behavior," he drawled. "It's almost like you had something else on your mind."

She threw him a self-deprecating look as she opened the app, though she wasn't expecting much. Anyone hired by Isabel would have to be smart—and they proved that.

Raisa had been ignoring the chimes for the past ten days—as they'd been mostly the mailman. But there it was. The ping must have come when she was dealing with her luggage.

A person had been on her front porch yesterday.

She held the video out to Kilkenny. It showed a hand sticking duct tape over the camera. There had been enough of a humanlike figure caught on tape—or her alarm wouldn't have dinged—but they were wearing a black hat, a black hoodie, and they'd kept their face down for the few seconds the video footage hadn't been obscured. Raisa couldn't even tell the gender of the person doing it.

"Not their first rodeo," Kilkenny commented, handing her phone back. "I wonder if it's someone she paid off to deliver it for her, or if they're doing it for free."

Raisa made a face. "How is Isabel the one person who can create loyal servants while in prison?"

"Not the one person," Kilkenny pointed out.

"I was employing hyperbole," Raisa said, rolling her eyes. "But, man, if she has minions on the outside . . ."

"I'm surprised she didn't have them running more errands before this," Kilkenny said.

"I guess she was saving them for the grand finale."

Kilkenny made a sound of amusement. "So, what are you thinking?"

Raisa sighed and said what she'd been thinking since she'd opened the envelope. "She wants me to find her killer."

"Classic Isabel," Kilkenny murmured and Raisa huffed.

"I'm just surprised she didn't add any more *incentives*," Raisa said. She wouldn't have put it past her sister to frame Raisa just to make sure she actually tried to solve the murder. "I guess we should add the caveat: if there is a killer."

"I'm inclined to agree with you," Kilkenny said. "But it would have had to be something that looked like natural causes."

"Right." Isabel had been young and relatively healthy as far as Raisa knew. There were only a few ways to kill someone like that and not raise suspicions. "Didn't the Bureau just send out a memo about an increase in insulin-related homicides?"

Kilkenny nodded. He was as much a teacher's pet as she was, and read all those updates, no matter how tedious. "Hard to trace and yet one of the easier substances to get in prison. Someone could have paid off a guard to do the actual injecting—it wouldn't take much or very long."

"And if the person who wanted the killing done had paid in cash, there won't even be a trace," Raisa said. "But we should tell the facility to look for close, possibly incidental, contact in the hours before roll call."

The coffeepot beeped, interrupting them, and Raisa poured two hefty doses in her overlarge mismatched mugs. Once she handed Kilkenny his, she waved him into the living room, where she showed him the letter.

He studied it carefully for several quiet moments. "The address?"

"Residential, from what I can tell from a quick search," Raisa said.

He nodded and then lifted his eyes to hers. She saw the question there, but she made him ask it.

"Have you tried Delaney?" His tone was neutral, but she knew if she said no, he would gently chastise her. The topic of Delaney was the main source of conflict in their friendship.

Kilkenny saw Delaney as a victim of Isabel's manipulative personality. And he'd worked with her for years before realizing she was Raisa's biological sister, so he had a past with her that, strangely, was deeper than Raisa's.

He also liked to remind Raisa that Delaney had helped on the investigation into Shay's death, and, in his eyes, that had earned her a fair amount of grace.

"No answer." When he made a considering sound, she asked, "What?"

"You're not concerned?"

"That she hasn't responded in the past half hour? No," Raisa said slowly. "She might not even have my number saved."

"She does," he said, sounding more sure than he should be able to. "You might not like that she's your sister, but she definitely sees herself that way and would act accordingly."

"Well . . ." Raisa trailed off, not sure what else there was to say. "I'm sure she'll respond eventually."

"Hmmm."

A tiny voice she didn't want to listen to whispered that if Isabel had been a target, Delaney could be one as well. Someone out there seeking vengeance might have taken the same stance Raisa had—that Delaney should have paid more for her role in Isabel's killing career.

"Do you know where she lives?" she asked, a bit resentful that she was being dragged into caring.

"Seattle, but that's the extent of it," Kilkenny said, and Raisa didn't know why she was surprised. Delaney, a tech wizard and all around odd-girl would fit in perfectly in the city. Maybe because she'd thought Delaney would try to put as much space between herself and their hometown as possible. "I can try to send out some feelers."

"Thanks."

"So, what do we do next?" Kilkenny asked.

She hid her smile with another gulp of coffee. She liked that she finally had someone on her team, no questions asked.

"The correctional center first," she said when she reemerged from her mug. "But then that address."

"Doing what Isabel wants," Kilkenny said, neutrally again.

"You have a better idea?"

"No, I just want to make sure. Do you want to do this?" he asked quietly. Seriously. "We don't have to say anything to anyone. We can just pretend you never got this letter. No one else has to know."

The thought hadn't even occurred to her, but she knew the answer immediately. After Raisa had found out who her biological family was, had found out what kind of darkness ran in their blood, she had been thrown off balance for a while, worried that perhaps her moral compass wasn't infallible, either. But she'd also realized how much power that gave her—to wake up every day and make a choice that she would uphold justice, she would do what was right when she could, and she would never become complacent about her own choices.

If someone had killed Isabel—or paid to have her killed, really— they deserved to be held accountable for their crime, whether Isabel technically deserved justice or not. When you started making exceptions to who was protected under the law, you got into slippery areas that never seemed to end well.

Maybe in a perfect world, Raisa wouldn't have to be the one to solve the crime. In a perfect world, she'd hand over her information to the local detectives and wish them luck.

This wasn't the perfect world, it was just theirs, and Raisa would do what she had to do to make sure Isabel didn't ruin that from the grave.

"I need to find whoever did this," Raisa finally said and Kilkenny didn't look even a little bit surprised.

"I wanted to make sure you realized you had the choice."

Raisa laughed at that, and he shook his head, still earnest.

"Hey," he said, waiting until she met his eyes. "You have a choice. No matter what Isabel wanted, no matter what tricks she set in motion before she died. You can just walk away."

"And go do what? Take a vacation where shirtless men serve me pretty drinks and I sit by the pool all day?" Raisa asked, and let herself imagine it.

"Would that be so terrible?" Kilkenny asked. "Our demons feel inevitable until we simply turn our backs on them."

Raisa swallowed her first—sarcastic—reply, the one that came from the girl who'd survived her teenage years in a shitty foster care system and emerged as one of the country's top forensic linguistic experts.

It might have come out something like, *How much do you charge for that insightful advice, doc?* And that wasn't fair to Kilkenny.

Instead, she went with honesty, making herself vulnerable to one of the few people she trusted not to make her pay for that. "Don't you see? The fact that I have a choice is why it's so important that I do it."

TRANSCRIPT FROM *ISABEL PARKER: THE GIRL NEXT DOOR* PODCAST

MELODY STEVENS: Hey, hey, murder-fiends! I think you're going to adore this episode—it has everything you guys love, love, love. Abuse, triple homicide, a family torn apart. Secrets. An FBI agent and her hunky partner. Yes, yes, yes, you heard that right. So buckle up while I take you back to the teeny, tiny town of Everly, Washington.

The year is 1998. It was a hot summer day when the three Parker sisters came home to their parents, Tim and Rebecca "Becks" Parker, murdered in their bed. Let's just say the scene was . . . *not* pretty. We're talking over forty stab wounds here.

The culprit?

Alex Parker, the only boy of the four siblings and the oldest at that. He was found dead in the parents' bathtub—claw-foot, I checked—with a note beside him confessing to the murder-suicide.

Easy-peasy for the local cops, huh?

Hold. The. Phone.

The real story is even messier than that.

But first, let me introduce you to the girls at the heart of this narrative. The three sisters.

Larissa Parker is our baby. She was only three years old when her parents were killed. She'll play a bigger role later, so remember her.

Next is Lana Parker. The middle child, age twelve at the time of the deaths. She was smart, so smart, and also a bit of an odd duckling, bless her. That wasn't anything notable in a family of math geniuses—I'm not using that word as hyperbole, either, folks. The parents were world-renowned.

And then there was Isabel Parker. The oldest at fifteen.

She viewed herself as the other girls' protector, their big sister. She was the shield between them and Alex Parker, who reportedly had signs of his father's schizophrenia and a vicious temper peeking through.

From all accounts Tim and Becks Parker were neglectful parents, not so much hateful or abusive, but too wrapped up in each other and their careers to ever have time for their children.

After the alleged murder-suicide, the three girls were given new names to protect them from the media circus surrounding the scandalous incident. Then they were put into three different foster homes. And again, that could be the end of the story.

But ladies, gents, and nonbinary folks? It's not.

We're just getting to the juicy parts. But first, a word from our sponsors, Bountiful Bras for that blessed beauty in your life!

STEVENS: And we're back! We just have to fast-forward here twenty-five years. No, I did not stutter. Twenty. Five. Years. Remember baby Larissa? Well, she grew up to become FBI forensic linguist Raisa Susanto. Now this lady is a badass. She worked her way off the streets to finish her doctorate in linguistics in record time. She could have played it safe and gone the academic route, but, no, our girl wanted to go into law enforcement even though she didn't know anything about her own history. It does make you wonder, you know? Like *The Body Keeps the Score* says. Trauma lives in our bones.

Now, Lana, the quintessential middle child, became Delaney Moore, vastly underperforming in life, given her potential. She was working the overnight shift as a content moderator at Flik. Imagine the kinds of things that poor girl saw day in and day out. I swear.

Well, Miss Lana herself flags a video to the FBI that shows two people dead on a bed, posed just like Tim and Becks were all those years ago.

And where did this video originate, you ask?

By the Time You Read This

Everly, Washington.

The next thing you know Raisa, Delaney, and—here we go, I know y'all were waiting for this one—our hunky FBI forensic psychologist Callum Kilkenny, ride into Everly thinking there's a copycat on the loose.

See the thing is, everyone still thinks it was Alex Parker who killed his parents and then himself.

But, my babies, my fiends, that was not how it went down at all.

Find out what happens next by slamming that "Subscribe" button.

CHAPTER FOUR

Delaney

Three months before Isabel's death

The first time Delaney saw Lindsey Cousins, the girl had been coming off a boat—the sea in her hair, the sun on her face, moving with the quiet confidence everyone who could sail seemed to carry.

She was young and pretty, with an athletic build and wavy brown hair she wore tied up on top of her head. She had a heavy sprinkling of freckles that were probably teased out by the sun, and an easy smile that guaranteed she'd get more tips than the other boy working the tourist sailing trip.

This was a small-group charter, so Delaney was slotted with two couples who had come as a group and two other women who had gleefully reported that they'd been friends for fifty years—longer than either of their marriages had lasted.

As she worked, Lindsey bantered with all of them, her eyes drifting toward Delaney every once in a while as if trying to figure her out.

Delaney had been so careful all her life. She'd never left a digital footprint, and there were no photos of her to be dug up except for—apparently—in the old local newspaper in their tiny town. And even those had perished in a timely fire not long after the night of the confrontation between Isabel, Raisa, and Delaney.

She had made sure not to be captured in any pictures at Isabel's trial nor during the media shitstorm that had followed.

There was no way for Lindsey Cousins to know that the single woman on her charter on this random Tuesday was Isabel Parker's sister.

How would she react?

With glee?

With horror?

Delaney couldn't guess. She would never understand someone who glorified her sister's killings.

Raisa probably thought Delaney had done so. Delaney would never be able to convince her otherwise, and frankly she had no interest in attempting to anymore.

Lindsey hadn't approached Delaney until they were out on the open water. "You having a good time over here?"

"Of course," Delaney replied. She wasn't good at this in-person sleuthing. Show her a chatroom of two dozen incels and she could narrow in on the actual dangerous one within an hour.

This, though? This involved interacting with actual people, and that had never been her strong suit.

"Oh, good." Lindsey gave her a crooked smile that came across as a little self-deprecating—as if she realized how naturally beautiful she was and had to atone for it. She was very good at this, which was probably why she had a job in tourism. "Can we tempt you into partaking in a glass of bubbly?"

Lindsey's shipmate stood behind her, his mouth in a flat line, like he'd never heard of the concept of a tip in his life. In his hand he had two champagne flutes, both of which were going flat.

"Sure," Delaney said, trying to match Lindsey's smile. She was certain it had come out a grimace, from Lindsey's reaction.

But Lindsey was a pro. She whirled around for Delaney's glass and then shooed the dude away. "So what brings you to our neck of the woods? You a *Twilight* fan? I was always Team Jacob. I know, I know. But it's my one pop culture hot take."

It was a valiant effort. Delaney probably looked like someone who might visit the town of Forks, which had turned into a somewhat creepy shrine to the novels and movies. But Lindsey, who had to be nineteen if she were a day, was trying to use millennial in-group speak as she did it, which made it grate against Delaney's practiced ears.

"I want to see the woods," Delaney said, and watched the gears shift in Lindsey's brain right before she launched into recommendations on some of the area's best trails. Delaney had the sense that if she'd said she wanted to fly airplanes or roller-skate across the peninsula, Lindsey would have nodded, all bright-eyed and eager to offer suggestions.

She was one of the most socially adjusted sociopaths Delaney had ever encountered.

"I'm really into true crime," Delaney said, not very gracefully, to be sure, but she was done waiting for the right moment to cut off Lindsey's clearly well-rehearsed spiel on Olympic National Park.

Lindsey stuttered to a stop, but like the good little practiced sociopath that she was, she simply grinned and prompted, "Oh yeah?"

"I heard Isabel Parker ended up in jail around here," Delaney said, watching the sunshine facade crack slightly under this unexpected pressure.

"Who?" Lindsey asked, taking the route Delaney would have recommended.

"I think she killed a bunch of teenagers up in the Cascades," Delaney said, dumbing down her voice, injecting it with just enough innocent curiosity to make it believable.

Lindsey looked like she'd sucked on a lemon. It must have been torture not to correct Delaney. "Oh, I hadn't heard about that one. I don't really have time for podcasts. Well, I better check on the gals." Lindsey gestured to the older ladies, who had commandeered their own entire bottle of champagne. Lindsey winked, back in control of her face. "You just let me know if you need anything, you hear?"

And with that Delaney did what she'd thought would be impossible—she'd chased Lindsey off. The girl avoided her the rest of the pleasure sail, to the point where the man at the rudder started throwing Delaney looks just to make sure she was okay.

Delaney tipped Lindsey generously, knowing that it wouldn't make her feel bad about avoiding Delaney all night. Sociopaths didn't feel bad about things.

But it would make her wonder.

Lindsey took the wad of cash with the same self-deprecating, natural smile she'd welcomed them all with. A persona so perfected she could deploy it even when rattled. "Thanks, hon."

Delaney almost laughed at that. She had to be twenty years Lindsey's senior.

"I think it's smart," Delaney said. At Lindsey's confused expression, she continued, "That you don't listen to true crime podcasts."

Lindsey hummed.

Delaney shook her head. "Nothing good ever comes from those."

CHAPTER FIVE

Raisa

Day One

Gig Harbor itself was a quaint touristy town nestled into a cove, watched over by Mount Rainier. The women's correctional center—about as nice a place as you could expect—sat just north of it.

There was a crowd outside, blocking some of the street.

"I wonder what that's about," Raisa said, and Kilkenny grimaced.

She wanted to smack herself, and she blamed exhaustion for being slow on the uptake. Sometimes she forgot Isabel wasn't just her black sheep of a sister, but also a nationally infamous serial killer. "They're here because of Isabel, aren't they?"

"Yup," Kilkenny confirmed a bit grimly.

Raisa studied the crowd more closely.

It was split into two distinct groups.

On one side, women dressed all in black carried flowers as they hugged each other, wiping at tear-streaked cheeks and even wailing from the ground.

"What . . . ?" she murmured as she realized they were . . . they were in *mourning*. The other side, the one with revelers drinking out of champagne glasses while holding signs declaring the witch dead, made far more sense than whatever the first group was doing.

"Isabel has gained a bit of notoriety in the past two years," Kilkenny said, as he crept toward the gate. It couldn't have been more than five or six hours since Isabel's death had been announced, but there were plenty of people here already. "There's even a hashtag-FreeBell movement that's picked up speed in the last couple months."

"She never went by Bell," Raisa said, bereft of anything sensical to say. Maybe Isabel *had* gone by Bell—she had barely known the woman, after all.

"They don't care, it wasn't really about her. They were just projecting an image onto someone," Kilkenny said, ever the psychologist. "They call themselves fans."

"Yuck."

"Yeah," Kilkenny agreed. "You see all sorts of similarities to cults in these kinds of groups."

"Yeah," Raisa parroted. Her eyes slid to the ladies who were celebrating. She didn't blame them, but she did wonder who would make the trip. "And the other side?"

"There's a fairly vocal 'anti-FreeBell' response. They were worried she was going to get her trial thrown out because of her popularity with true crime podcasts," Kilkenny said, and Raisa was amazed she hadn't heard of either side. "The group is led by a woman named Essi Halla."

"Finnish?" Raisa guessed. While she didn't specialize in foreign languages, she could usually at least get the country.

"Her family, maybe," Kilkenny said with a shrug. "She's from California."

"And she kick-started this we-hate-Isabel movement?"

"Or at least she's become the most vocal member," Kilkenny said. "She's positioned herself as something of an advocate for victims' families, though she focuses heavily on things that put her in the spotlight and not so much on the things that actually help people."

The scene all of a sudden made a whole lot more sense. There were always going to be people who flocked to national spectacles. Attention and the money that went with it were powerful drugs. "How is she even involved?"

"She claims her father was one of Isabel's unaccounted-for victims," he said. "Mikko Halla."

Raisa shook her head. She'd memorized all the confirmed kills, along with a good number of probable ones they weren't able to use in court. "Is he?"

"Honestly, who knows," Kilkenny said with a shrug. "But it's not impossible, so . . ."

"Hucksters gonna huck," Raisa murmured, and then waited for Kilkenny to flash his badge to the security guard at the gate. "Were they seriously worried she was going to be freed? She was serving multiple life sentences for crimes with strong evidence against her. It was the most slam dunk a trial could be."

"Not so much that she would be freed, realistically. This was an *anti*-movement," Kilkenny said. "Those only arise in repudiation of something else. They didn't think a court of law would overturn her sentencing—they were worried the FreeBell would have success in redeeming Isabel's name."

She stared at him. "How was that even a legitimate fear?"

"Well, the reason she had fans was because of the erroneous belief that she had only ever killed bad guys," Kilkenny said, before quickly climbing out of the SUV as if he didn't want to see her face after the pronouncement.

Raisa hurried after him. "How on *earth* did they reach that conclusion?"

Kilkenny tilted his head back and forth. "There are a good number of examples where she *did* kill bad guys. Like Delaney's professor."

As a teenager, Delaney had been so advanced, she'd been able to take college classes when she was still in high school. One of her professors had tried to corner her in his office to pressure her into an affair. Not long after, he'd purposefully overdosed and been found in a pool of his own vomit beside a suicide letter.

"Those tended to get more attention than the ones where she just didn't like the look of the victim's face," Kilkenny said. After a thoughtful pause, he added, "I hate this, but I also think it has to do with the fact that she's a woman. The vigilante angle is a more compelling and believable sell when it comes to women serial killers."

That much was true. Society saw women a certain way—and that didn't mesh well with the fact that some of them were simply sadistic psychopaths who liked torturing people. "I suppose the fact that only a few of her murders were graphic also lends itself to that story."

"The most personal ones were," Kilkenny observed. "But yes. The fact that a lot of her victims died in 'accidents' seems to have added to the mythology that she's simply ridding the world of rapists and pedophiles."

"Yikes," Raisa said, glancing back toward the mourners. Did they imagine they'd lost some kind of superhero today? "Even if that were the case, she shouldn't have just been let out on the streets to continue murdering 'bad guys.' We're not Dodge City circa the late 1800s."

He laughed at that. "Does it sound incredibly stuffy to blame movies and popular culture for glorifying vigilantes?"

"Yes, you sound like you're lecturing us from six feet down in your own grave," Raisa said, skipping to catch up with him. "But you're not wrong."

When they stopped in at the front desk, they found out that Raisa had been listed as Isabel's emergency contact. Isabel had apparently given the facility the wrong number, which was why Raisa hadn't heard from them yet.

The man at the desk suggested it was a typo on Isabel's part, but Raisa didn't think so. Isabel had wanted Raisa to find out about her death in the scripted manner she'd intended, not by a phone call from an administration official.

They flashed their badges, which got them a meeting with the facility's superintendent really quickly.

Aileen Baker was a no-nonsense woman with a face that carried a lifetime of experience in facilities such as the one they were in. She'd relaxed noticeably after Raisa had assured her she wasn't there to file a lawsuit over Isabel's death.

"I'm not sure there's much I can tell you beyond what we already did," Aileen said, looking between them.

"There was no way for anyone to get access to her cell last night?" Raisa asked.

Aileen had started shaking her head before the question was even out. "No, we've done a thorough review of the security footage. No one but the guard went near her cell, and even then he didn't get close enough to do anything to her."

"And the guard who found her . . ." Raisa let the question hang as delicately as possible. Superintendents usually got defensive in the face of criticism against their staff.

"She had been dead for hours," Aileen said. "We'll have to wait for more from the coroner's report, obviously, but you didn't need to be a medical examiner to tell Ms. Parker probably passed away not long after roll call."

"Do we know what guard last saw her alive?" Raisa asked.

"Yes, and the police talked to him this morning. I haven't heard anything, so I'm guessing they were satisfied with his answers," Aileen said. Her expression turned considering. "You don't think this was natural causes."

"We're just exploring all options," Kilkenny cut in diplomatically. "Did anything out of the ordinary happen in the days preceding her death?"

"No. Don't get me wrong, she wasn't the model inmate." She glanced at Raisa with an apologetic expression, but Raisa just shook her head. She didn't care if Aileen spoke ill of this particular dead person. "She liked to insert herself into the middle of all the power struggles going on around here. But she didn't really cause all that much trouble. The last incident that occurred involving Ms. Parker happened over six weeks ago."

"Incident?"

"She got into a fight with another inmate," Aileen said, her mouth tugging down. "Her hand was slashed, badly enough that she had to visit the infirmary."

"Her hand was slashed?" Kilkenny asked. "With what?"

"A shiv, Agent Kilkenny," Aileen said, her tone adding in *you idiot*. "I would have thought you'd be familiar with them."

Kilkenny gave her a tight smile. "I'm not wondering why an inmate had a knife, that's your job. I wanted to know if the weapon was big enough to cause actual damage beyond a cut hand."

Aileen seemed to finally understand Kilkenny's train of thought. "I would have to check the reports again. But I do remember thinking it could have been used to cause some serious injuries and Ms. Parker got lucky."

So it was possible that had been the original attempt to kill Isabel. What a clean way to take her out: make it look like she took a shiv to an important organ during a yard brawl. Raisa wouldn't have doubted that kind of death for a second, whereas a heretofore unknown medical condition raised at least a few—admittedly weak—alarm bells.

"Who was the inmate?" Raisa asked. She didn't think Aileen would tell her, not without a warrant, but she had to try.

"I'm sorry," Aileen said, the brick wall coming down as expected. "Unless this is part of an official investigation, I don't feel comfortable giving you that information."

They were always going to have to bring in the locals. This just made Raisa wonder if they should have made that their first step. "You do see how we might be suspicious about an attack six weeks before Isabel died under mysterious circumstances—"

"They weren't mysterious," Aileen cut in, any softness completely gone from her voice. "Now, I am sorry for your loss, Ms. Susanto."

"Agent," Raisa corrected, and Aileen's mouth pinched in. They weren't exactly doing a great job of making friends here.

"Well, you're not one right now. Right now, you're here as the next of kin," Aileen said, and stood. "The autopsy will provide all of us with more information to move forward with, but until then, I'm afraid I have other appointments."

Raisa and Kilkenny stood as well. "Would we be able to review the tapes in the hours preceding—"

"We'll be conducting the investigation," Aileen said. "Along with the local police. I'm sure they'll keep you informed."

She'd had to try. "Okay. Well, then, I'd like to collect Isabel's possessions. Are they still in her cell?"

"No, we boxed them up already," Aileen said, moving toward the door. "I'll have my secretary help you retrieve whatever was left."

They were closely watched the rest of the time in the facility, quickly handed a box, and then shown the door.

Raisa couldn't be too upset with the haul, though.

There were the clothes and accessories Isabel had come in with—a dress, Doc Martens, a watch, her wallet. There was also a small landscape painting that, with its soft colors, looked like it had been done in a therapy class. But the two most intriguing things were a leather-bound journal and a stack of letters.

A quick glance at the latter revealed that many of them were signed "Your Biggest Fan."

"I think we should check out the address Isabel included before we circle back to the locals," Raisa said, holding the box on her lap as they drove out of the correctional facility.

Kilkenny gestured toward the SUV's GPS system, where he'd already punched in the location.

The pleasant British voice informed them that the drive would take forty-five minutes, so Raisa settled back to skim the letters.

She would need to run her full analysis on them, which involved her laptop, linguistic software, and several Excel spreadsheets. But usually she could get a feel for a voice anyway. She'd been doing this long enough to pick up tics and quirks and habits—enough to build the bones of a profile in her mind. These letters were strange, though, stripped down—as if whoever had been writing them had known Raisa would, in the future, read them, and they wanted to hide their voice.

That in itself made Raisa feel itchy. Like she'd been dropped into a world that spoke in a language she didn't even recognize, let alone know.

"Maybe we can get a warrant for the name of the inmate involved in the shiv incident and any bank account information they might have," Kilkenny said, once she re-stashed the envelopes in the box. He'd been quiet as she did her thing.

Raisa nodded. "You think they were paid to do it."

It was what she was thinking, too, but there was a slim possibility that Isabel had simply made an enemy in prison, one who'd tried shanking her and then switched to a different method when that had failed.

"Yeah, because of the shifting MO," Kilkenny said. "If this was just one inmate who wanted Isabel dead, we likely would have seen another violent altercation. Not some devious plan to make it look like natural causes."

"Well, paying someone to kill Isabel is certainly one way to get revenge while avoiding getting your own hands too dirty," she said. Plenty of people imagined they'd go all *Batman* if a loved one was killed, but most people weren't murderers.

Kilkenny hummed in agreement. "*Aggrieved family member who wanted the death penalty* is quickly rising to the top of my list of suspects."

"Yeah," Raisa said. "I wonder why they waited six weeks to try again."

"Give it time for the incident to fade from memories?" Kilkenny guessed. "And if so, they were successful. The superintendent didn't seem to think it was connected to Isabel's death."

"She doesn't want to entertain the idea that there might have been a homicide in her facility," Raisa said. She didn't add that the superintendent might also believe Isabel had gotten her just deserts, but she thought it.

Raisa was a cynic most of the time. But she'd joined the Bureau when she could have done something else. She truly believed that it mattered how the government treated its "worst" citizens, because it maintained the integrity of the system overall. Everyone deserved a lawyer, everyone should be treated humanely.

If they didn't fight for the rights of the most dangerous offenders, then those rights couldn't be considered innate.

They were conditional.

And human rights should never be conditional.

Both things could be true, though. The world was better off with Isabel dead. And they should put in the best effort possible to figure out who killed her.

If this was indeed homicide.

"Revenge as the motive doesn't really narrow anything down for us," Raisa said. "I can think of at least a hundred people who wanted her dead. And I'm sure there are hundreds more."

"Maybe we should ask Essi Halla. She's a lawyer by day, but in her spare time runs the anti-FreeBell group," Kilkenny said. "She might be helpful at least in directing us to the right people, the ones who are angriest at Isabel."

"Maybe it *was* Essi Halla," Raisa offered, but Kilkenny tilted his head back and forward.

"I'm not sure she would have drawn so much spotlight to herself if she was plotting to kill Isabel," Kilkenny said.

"Or she's using it to blind everyone to her real motive," Raisa pointed out.

"Ah, true," Kilkenny said.

"But you're probably right," Raisa conceded. "I'm actually surprised the confirmed victims' relatives let her take the lead."

Even within grief support groups, there were hierarchies to conform to.

"Yeah, I thought that, too," he said, as they headed north, out of Gig Harbor. "But then I watched a few of her interviews."

"Let me guess, both charismatic and pretty," Raisa said.

"Very," Kilkenny said, and then he actually blushed. "I meant about the charisma."

"Rizz, I think the kids are calling it these days," Raisa said, amused. It actually was part of her job to keep up with current slang, and she enjoyed it. Kilkenny always got a little stuffy about language—far more than she did, despite the fact that people probably would have guessed she was the pedantic one out of the two of them.

As predicted, his nose wrinkled. "That's the worst possible bastardization of that very beautiful word."

"*Very* beautiful, like Essi Halla?" Raisa teased.

He grunted. "I'm not living that one down, am I?"

"Never." She paused, then glanced over at him, considering. "Why have you been following along with all that? The pro- and anti-Isabel stuff?"

Kilkenny had been traumatized by Isabel as well. Raisa had thought they'd both blocked any news or updates about her after she'd been sentenced.

Here he was, though, in the know about Isabel's—for lack of a better word—fandom.

He stared at her as if the answer were obvious, and when he said it, of course, it was.

"So you didn't have to."

EXCERPT FROM *CULT OF CELEBRITY MEETS TRUE CRIME: OUR WORST INSTINCTS COLLIDE*
By Sadie Richardson

Isabel Parker is underwhelming in person. Fan art of the prolific serial killer proliferates social media sites, and if it were to be believed, you would expect to meet a cross between Wonder Woman, Xena, and Tony Stark. If they'd all met a box of neon pink hair dye they couldn't pass up. Here, at the women's correctional facility in Gig Harbor where Isabel Parker is serving multiple life sentences, the fluorescent lights have turned her gray, the faded pink only remains at the very tips of her otherwise mousy hair, and her teeth are yellowed from incessant chain-smoking.

And yet, it's still easy to understand why so many people are intrigued with her—so much so that she's inspired a fandom of online supporters who want nothing more than to see her unleashed back into society. Well, they'd also like her to hook up with and/or marry various male and female celebrities of their choosing. But it's mostly the first one they talk about.

"There's a rush," Isabel purrs now, blowing a perfect ring of smoke from cracked lips, "in taking down the predator. Everyone wishes they could do it. I actually did."

She's referring to the lore that's grown around her ever since her trial revealed that several of her victims were what some would call deserving of the capital punishment that she doled out. It's why many of those fan artists draw her into a superhero costume.

When I asked about Janelle Stevens, a widowed mother of two who worked the register at a gas station in Wichita, Isabel sneered.

"She was a little cunt."

Parker's fans don't see this side of her—the petty psychopath who didn't look at killing as a moral calling but rather as a way to rid herself of irritants.

So how did this woman inspire thousands to create a FreeBell hashtag? How did she inspire over a hundred works of fan fiction and fan art? The concept isn't new. Hybristophilia is the diagnosis given to women who are sexually attracted to people who commit crimes. It's why serial killers have always received marriage proposals in the mail by the dozens.

But these fans' obsession with Isabel Parker seems more complex than that. "Our DNA primes us to fall victim to the cult of celebrity," said Dr. Rohan Anand, of the Mount Sinai School of Medicine in New York City. "We're social creatures, and they are at the apex of our social hierarchy."

Isabel Parker is a unique sort of celebrity, though. She's the infamous kind. In ten years' time, her name might be as well-known as Ted Bundy's.

"Attention is attention," Anand says to that. "And we've incorporated brutal psychopaths into our everyday routines. We listen to podcasts about them as we do laundry, we unwind with a glass of wine at the end of the day and turn on our favorite docuseries. They're in our lives, they're in our hierarchies."

When I asked Isabel what she thought of her fans, she grinned. "They would be fun to kill."

CHAPTER SIX

Raisa

Day One

The address Isabel had included on the letter to Raisa was in a small fishing town on the coast of the peninsula, one like so many others dotted along the stretch of land.

The cute red wooden house stood on the edge of a rise overlooking the water, the blue of the sky stretching out for days beyond it. Raisa tried to imagine more picturesque scenery and failed.

Kilkenny pulled to a stop in front of it, looking as hesitant as Raisa felt. Out of all the places Isabel could have sent them, this seemed strange.

There was nothing else to do but go forward, though, so Raisa hopped out of the SUV.

A woman in her late fifties, early sixties, opened the door wearing loose working jeans and a cable sweater despite the heat of the day. Her thick white hair was braided back away from a face weathered from a lifetime spent outdoors near the water.

"What do you want?" she asked.

They both flashed their badges. "We were wondering if we could ask you a few questions."

The woman squinted at them. "What's this about?"

"Could we go inside?" Raisa pressed.

"You tell me, is this . . ." The woman was getting worked up enough that words seemed to fail her. "Is this about my girl?"

Raisa's chest tightened. "Can we come inside, ma'am?"

"Helen," the woman offered, pulling a tissue out of her sleeve, and waved them in. "Yes, come, come."

The house was dark despite the fact that it was midday, the shutters all closed tight, the air stale with the grim neglect universally recognized as a sign of a recent loss.

Is this about my girl?

Raisa didn't know what she'd expected to find, but a victim hadn't been on her mind.

Helen led them to a small sitting room that probably normally had a beautiful view of the water.

The furniture was worn in a comfy way that fit the rest of the house, but that was the only thing normal about the room. Every inch of space was covered by photographs of a pretty young woman—alone, with friends, on a boat, with big groups at special occasions. But always the same girl in all of them.

Raisa touched one of them, and Helen whimpered, a soft, distraught sound that punched Raisa in the gut.

"Is this your girl?"

"Lindsey," Helen said, her eyes locked on the picture Raisa had chosen. It was a selfie of the young woman, alone on a boat, her smile wide enough to crinkle her eyes into oblivion. "She died two months ago."

Her attention shifted back to Raisa's face, everything about her sharpening. "Isn't that why you're here?"

Probably, Raisa thought.

"We have some questions regarding another investigation," Raisa said as gently as possible. "Can you tell us what happened to Lindsey?"

"What other investigation?" Helen asked.

"We can't disclose that," Raisa said.

"No one believes me." Helen sank down onto her couch, her eyes still locked on the photo as she brought a tissue up to swipe at the escaping tears. "Everyone keeps saying it was a tragic accident."

That sounded all too familiar to how Isabel liked to kill. Plenty of other family members had been told they were crazy for suspecting foul play. "What happened to Lindsey, Helen?"

"She drowned," Helen said, her lip wobbling. "They say she drowned."

There were so many pictures of Lindsey on a boat all around the room. It would certainly be an easy way to kill her without anyone—except her mother, apparently—thinking it was anything but what it looked like.

"What do you think happened?" Kilkenny asked.

Helen looked up at him, distraught. It was as if she'd just heard the news that morning instead of two months earlier. Maybe her grief had been frozen in time until someone listened to, and believed, her suspicions.

"There was a storm coming in, and Lindsey . . . she was so smart, she never went out when a storm was brewing," Helen said. "Everyone says she didn't know it was coming, but she knew it was coming. We'd talked just that morning."

"Did she mention going out on the boat?" Kilkenny asked.

"That's exactly what happened. And I said, *'Check the weather, girlie.'* It had changed overnight," Helen said. "And Lindsey said she'd better wait until the next day she had off."

"Where did she work?" Raisa asked.

"She was a crew member on one of those tourist sailboats," Helen said. "They always only took out a handful of people. But on her off days, she borrowed her friend's boat and took it out whenever she could."

"So she was an expert sailor," Kilkenny commented, even though that was obvious from the pictures.

"A natural—she spent more of her life on the water than she did on land," Helen said, her mouth trembling once more. She made a valiant effort to hold back her tears, but was only half-successful. "She wanted to sail around the world solo one day."

Raisa chewed on her lower lip, debating the right way to ask what she needed to know. Sometimes she marveled at the fact that she was considered an expert at language, but could be clumsy when it came to spoken words. She retreated to the safety of Kilkenny's previous open-ended question. "What do you think happened to Lindsey?"

Helen sniffed. "I think she was murdered."

"Why do you believe that?" Raisa pressed.

"She wasn't wearing a life vest," Helen said.

Raisa waited for more, but it didn't come. "And she usually wore a life vest?"

"Always," Helen corrected. She waved to the photographs. "Just look."

Now that Raisa knew what to search for, she saw it. In every single picture taken on a boat, Lindsey wore some kind of flotation device.

"My husband, her father, he drowned," Helen said, and Raisa's eyes flew to her. Helen had gone to sit by the window. What must that be like, to have lost both a husband and daughter to the water? And yet still live so close to it. "She was with him."

"Oh," Raisa murmured softly. How horrifying that must have been. "How old was she?"

"Ten," Helen said, the grief clearly faded, less jagged. But how could this not all bring everything back up? "They were swimming off the boat, some kind of current must have grabbed them. He used his last bit of effort to shove her on board. The coast guard found her hours later, just sitting in the boat by herself."

"My god," Kilkenny said. "Yet she wasn't scared of the water after that?"

Helen glanced over her shoulder, looking thoughtful. "No. Not for a minute."

Kilkenny's mouth did something interesting, obviously hiding a reaction he didn't want to reveal.

"But she always wore a life vest from then on. Religiously," Helen continued, oblivious. "Why wouldn't she have been wearing her life jacket?"

There were all kinds of reasons, ones that Helen wouldn't want to hear. Maybe a bird pooped on it; maybe she always made sure to wear one when Helen could see her, not for herself but for her mother. Maybe, maybe, maybe.

A lack of a life vest and a knowledgeable sailor did not a murder case make.

But they were here for a reason. Isabel's bread and butter had been accidental deaths, made to look so real no one questioned them.

Isabel obviously hadn't killed Lindsey, since she'd been in prison two months ago.

But she could have had a hand in it.

Or maybe she had seen news of this drowning and simply wanted to mess with Raisa.

"This might sound like an odd question," Raisa said. "But have you ever heard the name Isabel Parker?"

Helen squinted at her, thoughtful, but then shook her head. "Doesn't ring a bell. Why? Does she have something to do with all this?"

Maybe, maybe not. This could be the first clue Isabel gave them to help solve her murder. Or sending them out here could serve a purpose Raisa didn't yet understand. Helen didn't need to hear all that, though.

So, instead, Raisa asked, "Did anything odd happen? In the weeks leading up to her death? Did she act strangely at all?"

"No. Well . . ." Helen cut off her knee-jerk denial and stared off into space. "A few weeks before she died, she came home from her job . . . rattled. Angry, almost, but also a little scared."

"Rattled?" Kilkenny asked.

"Yes, and she never let the tourists bother her, so it was strange," Helen said. "But that can't be anything, can it?"

Raisa and Kilkenny exchanged glances.

Again, Raisa decided not to answer. "Would we be able to look around her room?"

Helen hesitated, but then nodded. "I don't see why not, if you think it could help."

Neither Raisa nor Kilkenny reassured her, but Helen didn't seem to need it. She just led them down a hallway that ended in a bathroom. On either side was a tiny room, one of which was clearly Helen's. The other was presumably Lindsey's, but the door was closed.

"I can't," Helen said, waving toward it. "You all just let me know if you need anything."

And then she was gone.

It was quite the strike of good fortune to be given free rein like this, but Helen didn't seem to have anything to lose. The two of them must have seemed like a last gasp of hope for someone shouting into the void.

The doorknob gave way easily beneath Raisa's hand, and she walked into exactly what she'd expected to walk into—a bedroom caught in time. Eventually, Helen might convert it into a shrine, much like she had the living room. But for now, she probably hadn't even been in here more than once or twice.

There wasn't much there. A narrow twin bed was pushed up against the window, this one overlooking the road that led into town. Oh, how Lindsey must have longed to rotate the house so she could see the ocean.

"What were you thinking?" Raisa asked without turning around. "When Helen said Lindsey wasn't scared to go back in the water."

A beat of silence passed, long enough to get Raisa to look over at him. Kilkenny was standing at the bookshelf, his finger paused where it had been dragging along the novels' spines.

"I've seen people who have lost parents in plane crashes," Kilkenny said finally. "And they worked for years to conquer that fear and become pilots themselves. I read about a case where a man's father died of a bee sting, and just the sight of one sent him into near paralytic fear. Then he decided to make honey as a hobby to face that terror head-on."

"Okay, so not so strange that Lindsey became an avid sailor," Raisa said.

"*Became* being the key word there," Kilkenny pointed out. "Every other instance I've heard of like that, it took years for the person to work through their trauma. From how Helen made it seem, Lindsey was back out there the next day."

Raisa turned fully. "Huh. What does that mean?"

"I don't know," Kilkenny said, looking a little cagey right before he shifted so his back was to her.

"What are you theorizing, then?" Raisa pressed.

"Oh," Kilkenny murmured softly as he pulled something from the shelf. Raisa would have guessed it was a delay tactic except he seemed genuinely interested in the book. He held it out to her. It was one of the more recent, popular true crime novels making the rounds. Kilkenny pulled out another and then another and then another.

"Safe to say she's a fan," Raisa said.

"It's a loose connection, but how many podcasts have come out about Isabel?" Kilkenny asked.

Raisa was about to answer when she caught sight of something that had been behind the books Kilkenny had removed.

Journals.

Three of them that she could see, maybe more beyond.

Raisa reached for one and flipped it open.

The first few pages looked like nothing in particular—a dry diary entry about breakfast calories and drinking plans for the night.

Then Raisa got to a sketch. It was a graphic drawing of a man being tortured, bodiless hands peeling the skin from his bones.

How long would you live without your largest organ?

Carefully, Raisa skimmed through the rest, most of which were sadistic diatribes and lists of people's names with what looked like possible "accidents" next to them.

Raisa exhaled a soft curse and realized Kilkenny had come to look over her shoulder. He didn't seem surprised at the contents.

"A classic marker of an antisocial personality disorder is a lack of fear," Kilkenny said, his voice grim. "It would have been noticeable even as a child."

She thought of those letters that Isabel had kept. They had been signed "Your Biggest Fan."

If they were looking for the author of those, a psychopath in training might be the exact place they should start.

But if that were the case, if Lindsey Cousins had been Isabel's Biggest Fan, then that made two psychopaths who had died under mysterious circumstances.

Maybe . . . maybe they weren't hunting psychopaths at all.

Maybe they were hunting someone who killed them.

CHAPTER SEVEN

Delaney

Day Four

Disappearing was the easy part.

Delaney had never struggled with that. Leaving her tiny apartment in Seattle behind had hurt more than putting other places in the rearview, but she was still good at it.

What she needed to do now was regroup and figure out a way to beat Isabel at her own game.

Hopefully, she had left whoever was tracking her behind in Seattle. They might find her again. But she'd bought herself some time.

Let's play a game . . .

It had been those words that kick-started this whole thing six months earlier. Isabel loved her games, and she loved pulling Delaney's puppet strings. She must have been so bored in prison.

Delaney decided to circle back toward Seattle, after her ferry ride to Bainbridge. That was probably the last thing anyone following her would think she would do. Most of the time, they would have been right. She would have bought a ticket to someplace in Latin America and lost herself for a few years to the anonymity of a different country.

She couldn't live with another death on her conscience, though.

They were already starting to stack up.

Delaney didn't go all the way to Seattle. Hotels were expensive, even the ones that rented rooms by the hour. Instead, she drove through Gig Harbor, past the correctional center where Isabel had spent the last year and a half of her life, and continued on down to Tacoma.

Her two sisters, so close to each other.

Delaney stopped at a Best Buy in Tacoma and bought a new laptop with cash. She kept her head tilted down, letting her hair cover her profile to deny any security cameras clean footage.

Then she found a hole-in-the-wall and ordered a Coke before waving off the bartender's Wi-Fi offer. He shrugged and went back to reading a battered copy of *The Fountainhead*.

It was 3:00 p.m. on a Tuesday and there was no one else in the place.

Delaney jammed her thumb drive into the brand-new laptop, and pulled up one of the file folders. It contained pictures of all the notes Isabel had sent her in the weeks before her death.

The second note had been a list of names, in Isabel's own handwriting.

Delaney had immediately recognized two on there. The girl who had arranged it so Delaney was sexually assaulted at a college party and the professor who had tried to coerce her into having sex with him when she'd been only a teenager.

There were twenty-seven in total—including, Delaney had soon realized, their parents and brother.

Isabel's victims. All of them, even the ones the court hadn't known about.

There was a man who'd set up a revenge porn website on his girlfriend. The case had made the news after the girlfriend sued. Some sort of plausible-doubt bullshit had let the man walk.

He'd died seventeen days after the verdict, an overdose in a cheap motel with all the damning, illegal files pulled up on his computer, just waiting there for the police.

There was also a priest who had been bounced around congregations to hide bad behavior with choirboys, a foster mother whose wards were frequent fliers in emergency departments, and a man who had a bad habit of beating every one of his girlfriends to a pulp.

Delaney had long suspected that it wasn't the murder that scratched Isabel's itch, so to speak, but the getting away with it.

That rush—the knowledge that she was smarter than everyone else—was also a reason she picked the scum of society. No one would ever admit it, but people were going to care a lot less about the death of someone who hung around kids too much than they were if one of those kids went missing.

To Delaney, it was the one thing that explained all the weird ways Isabel didn't resemble your run-of-the-mill serial killer.

And yet her so-called fans just ignored it. They glorified the impulse as something noble instead of an ever-ravenous ego needing to constantly be fed.

The door to the bar swung open and a woman walked in. Delaney could make out only her silhouette because of the light flooding in behind her, but she could tell the woman was tall and casually dressed.

"Vodka tonic," the woman ordered, before she even got to the bar. Her husky voice fit perfectly with the dive bar's dark wood and sticky floors.

She didn't glance at Delaney once.

Delaney covertly studied her, but when the bartender abandoned his book to start chatting the woman up, she went back to her computer.

It would make sense that whoever had found Delaney in Seattle was connected to someone on this list. Why wouldn't they want to go after Delaney now that Isabel was dead? She was, of course, the next logical target. Although Delaney hadn't read the transcripts, she was fairly certain that the fact Raisa blamed her for not speaking up about Isabel sooner had made it into the official court testimony.

"You from around here?"

Delaney slammed her laptop's lid down, startled. The woman who had come into the bar was now practically right behind her, sliding onto one of the empty stools.

"No," Delaney said, though it bordered on a lie. Tacoma was close enough to Seattle that she could have claimed it had she wanted to.

"I just moved here," the woman said, and then laughed. Laughter was one of those social things Delaney disliked the most—or at least, she disliked it when it wasn't connected to anything obviously humorous.

She stared down at her laptop, making sure to keep her fingers wrapped around the edges. There were two types of chatty people in the world—those who could navigate the social waters with extreme competence so they never got obnoxious and those who were oblivious to how annoying their chattiness was.

This woman seemed like the former, so Delaney hoped she would pick up on the *not interested* signs.

But the woman pressed on. "You're just visiting?"

Delaney thought about the victim her sister had killed just for the crime of being irritating and felt a sudden and terrible kinship with her. "Yes."

"I'm hoping I get used to the smell."

At that, Delaney glanced up, somewhat amused. The woman wasn't wrong about the stench that burned through your nose cells the second you hit the city limits. "It's the paper plant."

The woman laughed again, and Delaney wondered if it was at her. She'd never been good at telling that, either.

"It is indeed," the woman agreed.

Then she jerked her chin toward Delaney's laptop. Reflexively, Delaney's fingers tightened, even though the woman probably wouldn't think anything of the notes if she saw them out of context.

Let's play a game...

"I'm sorry, I'm being terribly rude," the woman said, her eyes still locked on the computer. "Are you working?"

Delaney nodded in agreement, because the woman *was* being terribly rude. But then she shook her head, because that hadn't been the question. "No."

The woman waited for more—as so many people did when they talked to Delaney. They never seemed content with the straightforward answers to their questions, as if Delaney were somehow on the hook for half of a conversation she'd never RSVP'd to.

The woman's mouth quirked up on one side, and she held her hands up, palms out. "Got it."

Delaney tilted her head, curious. "What did you get?"

"You're not interested in chatting," the woman said, shifting off her barstool.

"Oh, then yes. You're right. I'm not," Delaney said with a nod. "You did get it."

The woman laughed, as she seemed prone to do, and then grabbed a bar napkin. She whistled to the bartender, and asked for a Sharpie.

Delaney watched, curious, as the woman scribbled something on the napkin and then dropped a twenty on the bar.

"If you ever *do* feel like chatting," the woman said, handing the napkin over with a wink.

Then she turned and walked out of the bar, as easily as she'd come.

Delaney looked down at the phone number, a string of digits with a Seattle area code.

Above it, the woman had scrawled her name.

Maeve.

CHAPTER EIGHT

Raisa

Day One

All things being equal, Raisa would never interview people of interest in a case. She'd much rather spend time with words on paper than try to parse through someone's lies. So, when they left Helen and her shrine to a—possible—psychopath behind, Raisa exhaled. Helen had let Raisa borrow the journals with the promise that she'd return them, and so now Raisa had two different writing samples to work on.

That always made her analysis easier. Instead of just creating a profile of an unknown subject, she could usually rule out if the two authors were one and the same.

Journals were different from letters—people tended to write with a slightly different voice when they didn't think anyone else would read the thing. But there were always markers to pull out and compare, even if someone was trying to mask their idiolect.

The first thing people tried to do was dumb down their writing, which most would guess was easy enough. Only, it wasn't. Authors who had a poor grasp of spelling and grammar tended to make mistakes in a way that was difficult for proficient writers to mimic. It became a dead giveaway—like when an author spelled *cops* with a *k* but then *cash* with a *c*.

It was hard to change writing tics, especially for anyone who wasn't trained on what they were and how to spot them.

Raisa did a rough job of comparing the letters and Lindsey's journals on the drive back from Helen's. There were almost no similarities. Though she had noted on the way out that the letters seemed to be someone trying to change their authorial voice, it had been done by someone proficient at miscommunication, not a nineteen-year-old psychopath who was a middling writer at best.

The differences were ones few would think to employ.

Notably, Lindsey used discourse markers—phrases to organize thoughts, such as *I mean, on the whole, although*—in about 60 percent of her sentences. The letter writer used them in about 5 percent. Lindsey also liked anaphora—using the same phrase at the beginning of subsequent sentences for emphasis.

One of the more famous examples of the linguistic device was from *A Tale of Two Cities*: *It was the best of times, it was the worst of times, it was the age of wisdom, it was the age of foolishness . . .* et cetera.

Lindsey's use of it was a bit more violent.

This knife that cuts this flesh like butter, this heart that's so easy to consume as this blood rinses out my mouth, this death. This death.

There was a bit of emo-poetry girl to it that didn't quite match with the pictures Helen had up, but that was the beauty of writing. It revealed things people wanted to keep hidden.

"Not her," Raisa announced. "For the letters. And obviously she couldn't have killed Isabel, since Lindsey was already dead."

"What gives it away?" Kilkenny asked. "In the letters, that is."

"Lindsey is addicted to amplifiers," Raisa said, throwing out just one of a dozen small things she'd noticed. "With a particularly notable preference for 'deeply.' She uses it sixteen times in the span of as many pages. Not a single amplifier within the letters themselves—to a strange extent, given that it's signed from Isabel's Biggest Fan."

When Kilkenny didn't say anything, Raisa's shoulders tensed. "I know that sounds like a stretch, but it's just one of the examples—"

Kilkenny cut her off. "No. I'm not doubting you. It just seems like magic to me. I like to appreciate it."

Raisa flushed at her own defensiveness. Sometimes she couldn't help it, even with Kilkenny. "I'll have to do a more thorough analysis."

Those involved graphs and statistics and equations that no one but the nerdiest linguists loved.

"But you have a sense," Kilkenny said. "It's okay to be so good at your job you don't have to go through every step to come up with a general conclusion."

"Watch me be wrong," Raisa said, because she was far more comfortable at self-deprecating remarks than she was with accepting compliments. "But yeah. With the voices and styles as different as these, I can pretty confidently say that they were written by two different people."

"So, what does Lindsey have to do with Isabel?" Kilkenny asked.

"It looks like she was taking inspiration from the way Isabel got away with her crimes, but not much else." There were a few mentions of Isabel throughout the journals, but it was often just a passing thought. Lindsey had listened to at least one of the podcasts that had detailed the murders that had been Isabel's ultimate downfall, but Lindsey had also listened to a lot of other popular true crime content.

"But Isabel knew about her," Kilkenny mused. "And now they're both dead."

"Two dead psychopaths," Raisa murmured.

"Possible," Kilkenny warned.

"Two dead possible psychopaths," Raisa amended. "Well, one dead psychopath, one possible. You get what I'm saying. And it's weird, right?"

"Very," he said, though neither of them had a chance to speculate further before Kilkenny pulled to a stop in front of the Gig Harbor police station.

They had to flash their badges a couple of times, but eventually they were directed to the lead detective in the department.

Maeve St. Ivany.

St. Ivany had a face that would send photographers into raptures—prominent cheekbones and wide-set eyes that probably looked fantastic in pictures but seemed a bit too much in person. She wore her strawberry-blonde hair in gentle waves, but that was the only soft thing about her. Her shoulders were those of a swimmer, and her mouth had been pressed into a serious, annoyed line for the ten minutes it had taken them to fill her in on everything that had happened since Raisa had opened that envelope.

"You have an unsigned letter," St. Ivany said, with the same tone she'd probably use on a bunch of flat-earthers if they'd barged into her office.

"Yes, but it's from Isabel," Raisa said, trying to keep her own patience.

"You don't know that for sure."

"No," Raisa said slowly. "But I got it when she died."

"Near the time she died," St. Ivany corrected, gazing at the wall behind them, her mind clearly working. "It could have been a cruel prank, no?"

"Someone who knew she had died in the middle of the night before the facility even found her body?" Raisa asked, and St. Ivany tipped her head, seeming to acknowledge that scenario was unlikely.

"She was an otherwise healthy woman in her early forties who had been involved in a violent confrontation not even two months earlier," Raisa continued. If a woman with Isabel's profile had shown up in a normal emergency room, the medical examiner would've been all over the death.

"You're right, that is suspicious," St. Ivany agreed, but something about the way she said it rankled.

They were FBI, so she probably didn't want to be outright dismissive, but she obviously wanted to get them out of here so she could hand this off to someone much lower in the pecking order.

"I realize this isn't the most appealing case to solve—"

St. Ivany held her hand up, looking genuinely insulted. "If this was actually homicide, I'd want it solved even if Hitler was the victim. We're a small town, though. And we're already dealing with a death that's stretching our resources thin."

"So call us in on this," Kilkenny offered, before Raisa could ask what the other death was.

The FBI had limited jurisdiction when it came to local cases, but anyone could ask for their help. It would let Raisa and Kilkenny navigate the investigation so much more easily if they were there as law enforcement instead of as a relative of the victim and her friend.

"A forensic linguist and a criminal profiler?" St. Ivany asked, brows raised. "How exactly do I justify that?"

Kilkenny tensed beside Raisa. Out of the two of them, he usually garnered the most respect. TV shows like *Criminal Minds* and *Mindhunter* had legitimized forensic psychology in a way Raisa could only dream about when it came to her career. But some doubt would always linger for people who wanted to discredit his existence.

St. Ivany placed her hands flat on her desk in a conciliatory gesture. "Look. I promise, I'll keep an open mind, once we get confirmation foul play was involved from our—very competent and brilliant—medical examiner. Now, I'm going to set you up with my partner, who will take your statement."

She stood and they had no choice but to follow suit.

"If it is homicide, that means there's a murderer on the loose in your town," Raisa said. "If you don't care about solving it for Isabel, you should care about the safety of your residents."

It was a low blow, but Raisa was desperate. They wouldn't get very far if both the prison and the local detectives were against them.

"I already have a murderer on the loose. So."

"What?" Raisa asked, not sure she understood.

"A homicide, a violent one." St. Ivany shook her head and then took a deep, composing breath. "I'm sorry. Like I said, we're not going to prioritize the death of a serial killer when we're dealing with another case. But believe me, if the ME finds anything suspicious, we'll give it all the attention we would any other investigation."

"Two deaths, so close together," Kilkenny murmured as they walked past a conference room toward the back of the station. They could see a whiteboard with pictures and papers hung up on it, the scrawled handwriting of multiple different people colliding together with theories and suspect names.

Had they been anyone else, St. Ivany probably would have led them a different way, but being in law enforcement bought you some degree of trust.

"We've had a couple a year since I moved here," St. Ivany said. "But there's usually an obvious suspect. A domestic, or a bar brawl gone incredibly wrong."

"That's not the case in this one?" Raisa guessed, squinting to try to make out the name written at the top of the board.

All St. Ivany offered was a terse "No."

Perhaps she was defensive or just proprietary.

Or maybe she just didn't like them.

Raisa tried to think of any news alerts from the past couple of weeks, but she'd been so wrapped up in the San Diego case that it wasn't hard to imagine missing even a violent homicide so near to her house.

The man waiting for them in the smaller conference room was dumpy and forgettable, and his clothes did nothing to address either problem. His trousers were too tight and his blazer too big, while he had a coffee stain on a wrinkled shirt. He smelled of menthol and lavender, making her wonder if he had some kind of joint ailment.

St. Ivany left them with a tight smile and light knuckle-rap on the doorjamb. Off to try to solve her much more important homicide.

The detective cleared his throat, looking perfectly pleased to have been entrusted with the task.

Raisa gave her statement, repeating much of what she'd just told St. Ivany. And then they were seen to the door.

"It's going to be at least a few days before that report comes back," Kilkenny said, as they lingered by the SUV.

"That's optimistic."

"You've done more than anyone could ask from you," Kilkenny said. "We could just go home."

We're not going to prioritize the death of a serial killer . . .

Raisa thought of Helen and Lindsey, and this other murder victim. Of Isabel.

There was something here to unravel. Raisa always got a few days off after every case to make up for the weekends she missed while on the investigation. She owed it to . . . *someone* to at least try to follow a few leads here.

Even if that someone was herself.

"No," Raisa said. "Let's camp out a couple days. If you have the time."

"I have the time."

It sounded like a promise.

"Hey," she said as she climbed into the SUV. "We should probably look up the name of that homicide victim."

REDDIT THREAD: R/NOSTUPIDQUESTIONS

JAKE4537: If someone is blackmailed into committing murder, are they charged the same as someone who is just a psycho?

TIREDGIRL: What you're talking about in terms of person B (the blackmailed person committing the crime) is **duress**. It's an argument that can be used by a prosecutor, similar to self-defense, but they need to prove that any reasonable person would have acted the same way. They also have to show that they couldn't do something like . . . go to the police (guys always go to the police pleaseeeee I know they're like problematic but in that situation, just go! to! the! police). AND—here's the important part—most states have found that duress does NOT cover murder (or sexual assault) because even if the person is threatened with death they should have died rather than kill someone else.

TIREDGIRL: now back to person A who is doing the threatening—they won't be charged with murder. But that doesn't mean they'll get away with it. Think Charles Manson. He was the reason that Sharon Tate and Co. were killed but he didn't actually murder anyone. So he got conspiracy to commit and a death sentence (that was later commuted to life sentences). The lingo for this is *proxy murder*.

JAKE4537: even if they threaten your kid or wife or something? You still can't use it as a defense?

TIREDGIRL: yeah that's correct. You might get a lighter sentence from a sympathetic judge/jury, but you'll still get charged. I'm too tired (ha!) to get into the philosophical question about the morality of it all, but I'm guessing, even knowing all that, a lot of people would take the jail time.

CHAPTER NINE

Delaney

Four months before Isabel's death

Peter Stamkos was an evil man.

Delaney usually tried to stay away from labels like that. Absolutes were only her style when it came to mathematics. But Delaney had "stumbled across" his daughter's hospital records. She was allowed to call him evil.

But that was not all he was.

He was meant to be proof of Isabel's power, even from behind bars.

Let's play a game . . .

Isabel had a talent of figuring out just how to kill someone. Anyone simply looking at her victim list might think she chose based on convenience. If they drove at night on country roads—car accident. If they were a gun owner—suicide.

But that underestimated her genius.

Convenience factored into whatever scheme she hatched, but it was believability that really landed the plane.

Someone afraid of needles wasn't going to inject too much heroin into their veins. Someone afraid of heights wasn't going to jump off a tall building.

Isabel enjoyed this part, learning all about her chosen victims so that she could make their deaths perfect.

So what should Peter's demise look like?

Delaney contemplated that now as she watched his house. She was parked on the opposite side of the street, not exactly being stealthy. She wasn't in the mood to find a better hiding spot, though. Maybe that would come to bite her in the ass later on. Probably it would come to bite her in the ass later on. And yet, she had no desire to figure out a better option.

Anyway, no one would think Peter Stamkos's death was anything other than . . .

Well, that she didn't know yet. But, however he went, it wouldn't look suspicious.

Just as she had the thought, Peter and the girl turned the corner onto the street. The girl looked so small, with her enormous book bag, while Peter loomed over her. The daughter flinched when he went to reach for her hand.

Then she very clearly forced herself to accept it.

Delaney wondered what went through Isabel's mind in moments like this. For Delaney, anger burned beneath her skin, making her itchy, making her want to reach for a gun.

But Isabel didn't *feel*, not like a normal person.

Once upon a time, Delaney had tried to do some research about it all. Isabel had mentioned voices in her head enough times and casually enough when they were growing up for Delaney to know there wasn't just one killing gene that had been turned on.

Yet Isabel wasn't at all erratic. There were only a handful of victims who she'd killed without meticulous planning—and she'd gotten away with those because she was so practiced and disciplined normally that it had become second nature to her.

She wouldn't have gotten mad at seeing Peter's daughter flinch away from him. She wouldn't have found him abhorrent as a human being. She would have coldly assessed that he would less likely be missed if his daughter couldn't even stand him; she would have coldly assessed that there would be a way to kill him that wouldn't look suspicious.

Isabel could fly into a rage, Delaney was pretty sure, but it came out different. And it was almost never directly related to her killing someone.

Delaney tried to put herself in Isabel's shoes while she watched Peter close the door behind him and his daughter.

Suicide was the obvious answer here—he would just need to have a reason to have been triggered into it. Perhaps a visit from CPS would be enough.

She eyed the neighboring houses. No sign of movement.

Just down the street, though, there was a little playground, clearly built for the children of this development. A woman sat on the bench watching a kid—presumably one she was responsible for—play.

Delaney got out of the car, adjusting her clothing. She was dressed in a gauzy, multicolor skirt, a flowy blouse, and a vest to tie it all together. On more than one occasion, she'd been likened to an older Phoebe Buffay. She enjoyed the comparison, because people who loved *Friends* in the '90s tended to have positive reactions to her without Delaney actually doing anything.

"Hi," Delaney said when she reached the bench.

The woman gave Delaney a smile, but pretty quickly went back to watching her daughter.

"I'm looking at houses in the neighborhood," Delaney explained—because she didn't have a kid she could just use as a prop in this situation. "Do you like it?"

"Oh." The woman brightened. The tax bracket required for this area wasn't astronomical, but it was something beyond *broke*. "Yes, we love it here. That's Kaitlyn, I'm Maya. We're the blue house over there."

She pointed to one two doors down from Peter.

"You must know Peter Stamkos then," Delaney said, and Maya's shoulders tensed. It was a necessary evil to get them to this part of the conversation. "I literally just met him and his daughter."

Maya relaxed. "Yeah, he, uh . . . he keeps to himself."

"Why does it sound like there's a story there?" Delaney asked, pitching her tone low, so she just seemed nosy.

Maya glanced at Kaitlyn. "His wife died about . . . six years ago? I don't know; he seems fine. He just doesn't really talk to any of us."

"Does his daughter play with Kaitlyn? They seem about the same age," Delaney said, pressing slightly, hoping it wasn't too much.

"No." Maya made a face. "He doesn't let her hang out with any of the neighborhood kids."

"Really?"

"Yeah, it's kind of weird." Maya glanced toward Peter's house, her brows knit. A seed planted.

Then she shook her head. "Anyway. It is a great neighborhood, I swear. Just some odd ducks."

"I've been called that myself," Delaney said with a laugh. "I really appreciate your time. I hope to see you around."

Delaney stood and waved before Maya could ask what nonexistent house Delaney was thinking of buying.

Then she went back to her car, moved it to a slightly less conspicuous location.

She watched as Maya paused on the sidewalk on the way home, staring at Peter's house for a beat too long to be considered normal.

There was an art to this.

And while she was no Isabel, Delaney had to admit she wasn't half-bad at it.

CHAPTER TEN

Raisa

Day One

Gig Harbor only had one hotel in its town limits. It was cute and boutique and right on the water, within walking distance of three coffee shops, two restaurants, and a bevy of tourist shops.

Raisa had simply stuck her luggage from her work trip in the back of Kilkenny's SUV—and he always carried a go-bag in his car. They would probably need some reinforcements in the name of cheap T-shirts if they stayed more than a couple of days, though.

Something Raisa wasn't planning on doing.

Kilkenny was on his phone as Raisa took care of the logistics of getting them adjoining rooms.

"Emily Logan," Kilkenny said. He'd dropped his bag on his bed and then come through the connecting door to her room. "St. Ivany's homicide victim. She was killed about two weeks ago after a late-night shift. Apparently, sometime during her walk home from the restaurant she waitressed at, she stopped responding to her boyfriend, who was out of town at the time."

"He called the cops?" Raisa asked.

"No, he called her mom the next day," Kilkenny said. "At six a.m. Apparently he'd been worried the whole night."

"Could be that he wanted her found while he had an alibi." That was the cynic in her talking, of course. But they'd both seen this movie before.

"Maybe." No one would guess it, but Kilkenny was the optimist out of the two of them. "The mother found her in bed. She'd been stabbed twenty-three times."

Raisa let out a low whistle. No wonder Maeve St. Ivany had been stressed. "That's quite the overkill. No suspects?"

"Looks like they brought someone in a week ago, but they were released without any charges."

"Must not have been anywhere close to solid." Usually, if the cops had someone in mind and just couldn't find the evidence, they'd focus their attention on producing said evidence. From the quick glimpse of the murder board in that conference room, Raisa didn't think they'd zeroed in on any one person.

"You think it has something to do with Isabel?" Kilkenny asked, sounding—reasonably—doubtful.

"No," Raisa said, mostly believing it. "I don't know. Even taking Lindsey Cousins's death out of the equation, that's still two homicides in a relatively short amount of time, in a small radius, without any obvious suspects."

"And adding Lindsey back into the equation makes three," Kilkenny said. "What ties them together?"

"It would be interesting to see if Emily Logan was a psychopath, too," Raisa said, and then held up her hand. "Possible psychopath."

"Someone's taking out psychopaths?" Kilkenny mused. "What if it's the loved one of one of Isabel's victims?"

"Oh," Raisa drawled out. "That's a hot tamale."

Kilkenny stared at her. "What?"

"I don't know." Raisa laughed, running her hands over her face. "It's an interesting idea. Like, what if our UNSUB—rightly—blames Isabel for the death of someone they loved? They pay to have her killed, but it doesn't actually make them feel better."

"Or it creates some kind of psychotic break," Kilkenny added.

"Wait, wait," Raisa said, shaking her head. "Sorry. Isabel died after the other two. So maybe it is a loved one, but they were radicalized against psychopaths? Now they're just killing them indiscriminately?"

"Radicalized against psychopaths," Kilkenny said, with a laugh. "Aren't we all radicalized against psychopaths?"

"Work with me," she all but yelled, though it came out amused.

"Okay, right. They hate psychopaths, which is clearly a rarity. They start hunting them down, and Isabel saw it coming," Kilkenny said, his lips still twitching. "That's why she sent us to Lindsey Cousins's house. No one would have figured out that connection otherwise."

"Or," Raisa said, "she's messing with us."

"Lindsey and Emily died and she wants to insert herself in the middle of it all?" Kilkenny asked. "How does that fit with her essentially tasking you to find her killer?"

"I don't know. I just like to always assume she's messing with me and go from there," Raisa said, cracking her neck. Isabel liked to pretend she had more sway over things than she actually did. Maybe she really had noticed a pattern in deaths, and figured she might be next. Or someone warned her. Or she just wanted Raisa caught up in the hunt for a psychopath-killer. Not to be confused with a psychopath who was also a killer.

She loved language sometimes.

Always, really.

"So, we don't really know what we're doing," Kilkenny summed up. "And the locals have no interest in helping us."

"Bingo," Raisa said. "The most likely scenario here seems like Lindsey's death was an accident; Emily Logan's boyfriend colluded with someone to murder her, or somehow faked his alibi; and Isabel was killed by someone seeking justice for a loved one."

"That would all make sense," Kilkenny said, neutrally.

"Which, of course, the way our lives go, means they're all actually connected," Raisa said, with a sigh. Kilkenny grimaced, but she could tell he agreed. "Okay, I think the best we can do right now is follow where Isabel's clues take us, while also remembering that we're not trying to figure out who killed Lindsey or Emily."

"So where are Isabel's clues taking us right now?"

"Well, she kept those letters for me to find," Raisa said. "The ones from her 'Biggest Fan.' I'm sure she received plenty of other mail and she didn't bother to save any of it. Just those letters."

Kilkenny nodded. "So we go talk to her fans."

Raisa made a considering sound, and followed him to his feet. "You know, while we're there, we also might want to talk to the people who hate her, too."

They got two names from the crowd of people gathered at the prison's gates.

A group of tearful mourners told them to talk to Gabriela Cruz. The three young women all had a pink streak dyed into their hair and wore outfits similar to the style Isabel had been adopting when she was caught.

On the other side, they were told to talk to Essi Halla, the woman Kilkenny had been telling Raisa about earlier. The ringleader of the anti-Isabel movement.

"Oh, you just missed her," a middle-aged woman named Mildred Evans told them, taking a rather large swig out of the champagne glass she held. "Drove up from California the moment she heard the news this morning. She rented a boat to stay on in the harbor, but she wanted to swing by here first to check on all of us."

Mildred swiped at her lips. "She's such a strong woman and a real inspiration to all of us. In fact, she got me through the past year. If not for her, I'm not sure I'd still be here."

"Oh, I'm sorry," Raisa said. "Did you . . . did you know someone who was killed by Isabel?"

"Oh, no. No. My dog, he died," Mildred said, and Raisa tried to nod sympathetically, but some of the confusion must have shown on her face. "It's a common misconception that all Essi does is talk about Isabel. She offers so much more than that. She really held my hand throughout the whole grieving process."

Raisa hummed, going for neutral, which she thought was the best she'd be able to give this woman. "Did Essi say what boat she's staying on?"

"Oh, yes," Mildred said, looking thrilled. "It's called *Big Deck Energy*."

Raisa couldn't help but laugh. Behind her, Kilkenny snorted, and even Mildred giggled through her tears.

Big Deck Energy proved easy to find.

A woman stood at the rail, taking a phone call.

"Is that her?" Raisa murmured and Kilkenny nodded.

Kilkenny had been right—she was very pretty. She had an athletic build with white-gold hair and the glow-y skin of someone who'd probably never burned a day in their life. Her plum-colored pantsuit was tailored to perfection to show off stilettos that must have cost just shy of a thousand dollars.

When she turned and caught sight of Raisa and Kilkenny, she glanced at the watch on her wrist and then waved them aboard.

Kilkenny hopped on the boat with an easy grace that Raisa admired but would never be able to emulate.

Essi navigated the deck with the same effortlessness, and in any other scenario, Raisa would be thinking how perfect they were for each other. Slick and polished and pressed.

"Larissa Parker, in the flesh," Essi said, grinning playfully. "The baby of the family."

Raisa snapped back to attention. "Raisa Susanto. FBI Agent Raisa Susanto."

"Right, of course," Essi said, waving aside the correction, the slim gold bangles on her wrist clacking together. "And you are the good Agent Callum Kilkenny."

"Yes. May we have a few moments of your time, Ms. Halla?" Kilkenny asked.

"Of course," Essi said, dropping onto one of the bench seats, still seeming very amused for no good reason. Raisa and Kilkenny took the one opposite of her. When she asked, "Should I have my lawyer?" it came out teasing.

"We're not here in an official capacity," Kilkenny said. "We just have a few questions for you."

"What can I help you with, then?" Essi asked, one leg crossed over the other, forearms resting on her thigh, her posture open.

Not defensive.

"Can you tell us about your dealings with Isabel Parker?" Raisa asked.

"My dealings," Essi repeated with a laugh. "Well, she killed my father."

"Mikko Halla," Raisa said, and Essi glanced at her sharply, seeming surprised. Raisa wouldn't mention that Kilkenny had been the one to give her that information.

"Yes," she said. "He wasn't a confirmed kill for her, though."

"So what makes you think Isabel was the one who was responsible?" Raisa asked.

"There was a cluster of deaths around us at the same time that have been connected to Isabel," Essi said. "And my father's suicide never made sense to me. The official story was that he killed himself in the garage, the ole carbon monoxide trick. But he didn't drive. Ever. And he was a gun enthusiast who had about fifty options in his safe downstairs."

"Did he have a history with suicidal ideation?" Raisa asked carefully.

Essi shook her head. "No. He was on trial at the time, so all the detectives thought I was an absolute idiot for suggesting there was foul play involved."

"On trial? For what?"

"White-collar crimes that sound way sexier than they are," Essi said, impish once more. "We were obscenely rich and, yes, okay, we were about to lose everything. But my father . . . he didn't really *do* shame."

"What do you mean?" Kilkenny asked, and Raisa could tell that assessment had genuinely piqued his interest.

"Mmmm. Like, you know those Enron guys? Or is that too old a reference?" She eyed Kilkenny's silver-flecked hair. "Okay, I'm guessing not too old. But you know the type. Business guys who have no conscience. He didn't care what other people thought of him. If the government took all his money"—she held up a hand as if to interrupt them—"ill-gotten, I know, but still his at the time. If they took it, he wouldn't kill himself in some what-will-the-neighbors-think move. He would just figure out a way to scam different people out of money. And if he got sent to jail, he would spend his life coming up with ways to become the kingpin there. There is no way he killed himself. It just wasn't in his DNA."

"Narcissistic personality disorder," Kilkenny murmured.

"Oh yeah, bingo," Essi said, pointing at Kilkenny. "That probably was exactly it."

"I don't mean to be rude, but you don't seem too torn up about it all," Raisa said. "Yet you've launched a crusade against Isabel."

"Oh, no, you're absolutely right. I'm not torn up about it at all," Essi said. "But do you think these shoes pay for themselves?"

She crossed and uncrossed her legs, kicking her feet out as she did so. "Did you hear the part where we were obscenely, disgustingly rich and then lost everything?"

"I think I'm missing a step," Raisa said. The most money she'd ever had was the 10 percent she'd just put down on her bungalow. When she'd been a teenager, she'd lived off budget-brand cereal without milk, and life hadn't really improved all that much while she'd gone to college and then pursued her PhD. Her paycheck from the FBI wasn't going to cover red-bottomed shoes, either.

"Grief pays," Essi said, shrugging again. "And outraged grief pays even better. Attention is our society's current currency, and I command it in spades."

Raisa tried to make sense of that as she thought about the middle-aged woman who'd lost her dog. "So you sell manufactured outrage and performative grief over the death of your father and you . . ."

She trailed off.

"I sleep very well at night, thank you," Essi said. "In my extremely expensive sheets."

"All right." Raisa wasn't there to judge anyone. She was there to find a suspect.

And . . . Isabel's death would be a blow to Essi's lifestyle. She could probably ride this particular wave for a little, but eventually she would become yesterday's news, and yesterday's news didn't command any attention. No attention, no subscribers, no followers, no money. It would be in her interest to keep Isabel's notoriety burning for as long as possible.

They had also come here looking for someone out for vengeance, and that clearly wasn't Essi, either. She was a bottom dweller and an opportunist, but she didn't come across as some madwoman on the hunt for revenge.

Kilkenny glanced at Raisa, and she could feel him reaching the same conclusion.

"Is there anyone who follows you who is a true believer?" he asked. "Someone who really had it out for Isabel."

"I mean, *I* have it out for Isabel," Essi said, looking between them. "Oh, you mean do I know anyone who actually wanted to kill her?" She paused, seeming to put it all together. "You think this was murder?"

She didn't wait for them to answer. "You think I might have killed her."

"We were hoping you could provide us with some insight into who in your circle might actually be dangerous," Kilkenny said.

"Hmm." Essi tapped one of those impossibly long, trendy nails against the boat. "There are some true believers, as you call them, but none who would have the balls to actually do anything about it."

"Would you provide a list of those names?" Raisa asked. People didn't realize what others were capable of until they actually snapped.

"Sure thing." Essi gave her a little salute. Then she accepted the notebook Raisa handed over along with a pen. It only took a minute or two before she gave them back, with six names written down. "This is a little outside the box, but have you looked at the other side? Those little cult members who worship her, I mean."

They were headed to Gabriela Cruz's apartment next. Apparently the girl was local, which meant she either moved there for Isabel or got interested in her because of the proximity. Raisa hoped it was the latter.

It was interesting, though, that Essi suggested it. "Why do you think we should?"

"Love and hate being two sides of a coin," Essi said, shrugging again. For some reason, it came off as less casual than the other times she'd done it. No longer careless. Maybe she was worried they would stay focused on her, or maybe Raisa was reading into things. "I might be obsessed with making money off Isabel, but they're obsessed *with* her. I wouldn't be surprised at all if one of them took that a little too far."

"Anyone in particular you encounter frequently?" Kilkenny asked.

These two groups would be like their own little neighboring ecosystems. Though each was incompatible with life from the other side, they would still know each other best.

"Gabriela Cruz," Essi said without hesitating. Again, interesting. "She's their ringleader if ever there was one. She's always in everyone's DMs. She's the one who came up with the FreeBell hashtag. She hosts a Discord channel and moderates the FreeBell Reddit thread. I don't know how she has time for anything else, if I'm being honest." Essi rolled her eyes. "Okay, right, I'm being hypocritical, but I found a way to make this my job. She doesn't get any money for anything she does."

Raisa wasn't sure she found Essi's way any more commendable, but she kept her mouth shut on that one.

"What will you do now?" Raisa couldn't help but ask. "Now that Isabel is dead."

Essi shrugged, once more looking casual and carefree. "I'll find another way to survive. I always do."

EXCERPT FROM THE UPCOMING *REMEMBER THEIR NAMES*
By Essi Halla

I'll never be able to eat casseroles again.

Don't get me wrong, I can't complain about the outpouring of generosity that followed news of my father's death.

Suicide. Homicide. Whatever it was, he was gone. And though he'd never cooked a day in his life—nor had my mother, mind you—our refrigerator was now constantly filled with casseroles that tasted of sawdust and sympathy.

I had never realized we'd had that many friends. My parents were wealthy beyond most people's imagination. The only reason anyone could even get casseroles to us was because our gated mansion had been seized by the police two months earlier and we were in a major downgrade of a rental in the suburbs of Phoenix. I think most of the ladies that brought them by mostly wanted to gawk at my mother and me.

We still had our fancy clothes back then.

My mother still had some money the feds hadn't found so we weren't living on the streets. We even had a maid, so for those few kind souls who were about to feel anything but disgust for us, you should go ahead and rethink that sentiment.

The maid ate the casseroles. Well, she ate some of them, and then took others god-knew-where, after cooking us salmon or lobster or steak.

Do you hate me yet?

Should it matter if you do?

I'm still a person who lost her father.

My mother wouldn't eat the salmon or lobster or steak. I'd never thought my parents' marriage was a love match, but the death along with the loss of her lifestyle hit my mother hard.

Three months after my father's death, my mother took a bottle of some kind of pills liberally prescribed to her by a doctor too greedy to say no, and then never woke up.
I had lots of casseroles then.
That time, I tried to eat them.
I fired the maid, which was probably not a smart thing to do considering I'd never learned to cook in my life. But I survived off those casseroles—and take-out, I'm not a martyr here.
I ate those casseroles and tried to believe that they were worth waking up for every day.
Spoiler alert, they weren't. They were terrible.
I thought about making an appointment with that doctor who would still have prescribed me a lethal dose of something even though my parents had both just killed themselves.
I had my phone in my hands, ready to do it.
And then came a knock, just like so many others in the days before it. I couldn't stomach one more casserole.
But I answered the door, because if I didn't one of the ladies who brought the casseroles would probably call the cops.
Everyone knew I was hanging on by a thread.
It wasn't one of my neighbors at my door, though.
Instead it was a girl. She asked, "Do you know who killed your father?"
And that's when I found something besides the casseroles to make each day worth waking up for.

CHAPTER ELEVEN

Raisa

Day One

Gabriela Cruz lived in a pretty, well-maintained duplex about a ten-minute drive from the harbor that was much nicer than anything Raisa had lived in at twenty-two. The address had been listed in a trespassing arrest against Gabriela, and Raisa did wonder for a minute if she'd given the police wrong information.

But Gabriela answered only a few seconds after they knocked.

Her eyes slid over them before narrowing into a glare. "I know my rights."

Then she slammed the door.

Raisa and Kilkenny exchanged amused glances. Some agents didn't like the fact that this new, more online generation did things like this, but Raisa appreciated that people were learning more about protections granted to them by law.

Still, that didn't mean she couldn't try to convince Gabriela to talk to them.

"We just have a few questions about Isabel Parker."

A beat passed, but then, slowly, the door opened. "Will you tell me what really happened to her?"

Gabriela was all eyes and lashes, as if her face had been created by a Disney animation artist.

Raisa couldn't help but notice that, like the girls at the prison, Gabriela had styled herself to look like Isabel just before she was caught.

"We don't know what happened to her," Raisa said, honestly. "But we're hoping you can help with that."

Another beat, and then Gabriela shifted back, letting the door swing open all the way.

After Raisa and Kilkenny stepped into the tidy, well-lit apartment, Gabriela curled herself up on a fancy computer chair. She didn't offer them seats, but Raisa took the sofa across from her, while Kilkenny leaned against the wall. It was his preferred spot—where he could watch the person's face without being the focus of their attention.

"I'm not crazy."

Raisa tried not to react. "Okay."

Gabriela shot her a look. "Everyone thinks it. Because I'm interested in serial killers, like half the country isn't as bad as me. As if Essi isn't as bad as me." Her mouth tightened. "Is she the one who gave you my name? She must have, she just doesn't like anyone encroaching on her spotlight. She's such an attention whore and then acts all holier-than-thou in front of—"

"You two know each other?" Raisa cut into the diatribe. The two of them seemed to be the leaders of two different, warring factions, and the dynamic was fascinating.

"She doesn't know me," Gabriela snapped, and then took a deep breath. "Sorry, she's a sore subject."

"Because you guys are on opposite sides of the Isabel argument?" Raisa asked.

"That, sort of," Gabriela said with a one-shoulder shrug. "It's more than that, though. If she just left me alone, or criticized our movement broadly, you know, whatever. But she's flattened me into some caricature. She mocks me, she sends her cronies to troll me online, she sends the freaking FBI to come interview me."

Gabriela waved at them at that, and Raisa couldn't deny the girl had a point.

"She doesn't know anything about me," Gabriela said again. "She doesn't know I had a boyfriend once. I was fifteen and he was twenty-six."

Raisa nodded. She could guess where this was going.

"She doesn't know that he put me in the hospital four different times," Gabriela continued. "She doesn't know that not one goddamn nurse made him leave my side when he came to visit."

She plucked at her bottom lip. "She doesn't know that I prayed every day that he would just die. That someone would kill him."

Gabriela looked up at them. "Essi thinks I'm crazy. But she won't ever admit that Isabel saved people. Not me. But people like me."

Raisa exhaled slowly. There would be no point in arguing with Gabriela. Fanatics were fanatics for a reason. They were blind to logic, and their mind would perform Olympic-level gymnastics to allow them to maintain their worldview and biases.

That didn't make it easier to hear.

"I know she's evil," Gabriela said, sounding like she didn't believe it. "But, god, I don't care. She's saved so many people, and I'm pretty sure her positive balance outweighs the negative."

If Isabel had *only* killed people who committed horrific crimes, Raisa might concede there was an argument there. Not one she agreed with, but one that could be made.

That wasn't reality, though.

"She killed my parents," Raisa said simply.

Gabriela looked away. Raisa caught a hint of shame behind her expression just before she did. It would take a lot more than that to rip out the roots of her obsession, though.

"She was young when she did that."

"Right," Raisa murmured. "Budding psychopaths have to start somewhere."

Kilkenny tensed behind her, not because she was wrong, but because comments like that were just going to have Gabriela throwing up walls they would have to knock down to get any answers. Raisa wasn't helping—in fact, she was actively hurting the investigation. This was why it wasn't smart to get involved in cases that you were personally involved with.

Gabriela might be a bit strange, but she certainly wasn't the first person in the history of the world to defend a vicious killer and believe she was in the right.

"Did you start the FreeBell movement?" Raisa asked, trying to get them back on track.

"That got co-opted," Gabriela said. "After Isabel's trial there were tons of people like Essi that came out of the woodwork."

Gabriela spit the other woman's name like it was a sour thing in her mouth.

"Claiming Isabel had killed all these people she couldn't have possibly killed," Gabriela continued. "Just glance at the timeline once, and she's absolved of most of the crimes people put on her résumé."

There were moments even in this brief conversation that Raisa thought Gabriela understood the weight of everything Isabel had done, but then those were overturned by Gabriela equating Isabel's victim list to a résumé.

She was young, she heard in Gabriela's voice, and realized it could so easily be applied to this girl. She *was* young. She'd been through something extremely traumatic. Raisa felt for her, she did. But Gabriela was old enough to know better than this.

"They just wanted their five minutes of attention," Gabriela continued on, blithely unaware of Raisa's judgment. "Or in Essi's case, two years of attention."

"Are you saying you didn't want to actually free Isabel?" Raisa asked.

"No, of course not—she killed people," Gabriela said, everything about her earnest as hell.

"What was your goal, then?"

"I wanted her record cleared, and you know, Free Britney was so popular, it just kind of morphed into that." Gabriela must have seen some confusion on Kilkenny's face, because she explained directly to him, "Britney Spears was being held in a conservatorship where she pretty much couldn't make any decisions on her own. Like, she had to ask her father to spend her own money, things like that. Her fans launched this movement to get her out of it, and it worked."

Before either of them could say anything, Gabriela rushed to add, "I know it's not the same thing. I know."

"Then why did you keep using it?" Raisa couldn't help but ask.

"Because it got attention?" Gabriela shrugged. "People had this view of Isabel that wasn't true. They thought she was a psychopath, but they just didn't understand her or the situation."

"She was a psychopath." This time it was Kilkenny who dropped the hammer. His voice, usually so neutral and diplomatic, had taken on a sharp edge. "One of her victims was a four-year-old girl whose head she smashed into a tree so that it looked like she died in an accident."

Gabriela flushed pink, but it wasn't with shame this time. "That's a fake story."

Raisa hated the way *fake* could be thrown around these days anytime someone was confronted with a fact they didn't like.

"It happened," Raisa said quietly. "There are pictures of the scene."

Everything about Gabriela shut down, closed off. "What can I help you with?"

Raisa only half regretted pushing her to that point. She'd been defensive coming in, wanting to argue with them. There had been no avoiding this, and Raisa wasn't going to lie just to more easily get answers out of an interview subject.

Not about this.

"Did you have any contact with Ms. Parker?" Kilkenny asked.

"I wrote to her a few times," Gabriela said, back to not looking at either of them.

Raisa stilled. "Did you sign the letters as 'Your Biggest Fan'?"

"Ew, no," Gabriela said, genuinely surprised and disgusted. "That's so cringey."

Right. "Okay, did you visit her?"

"Once," Gabriela admitted.

"When was that?" Raisa asked.

"Like, a couple months ago?" Gabriela said. "I don't know—time blends together. But it was kind of strange."

"What was?"

"She didn't . . . she didn't want to talk about anything, even though she was the one who'd invited me there," Gabriela said, sounding a little pissed at Isabel for the first time. Maybe the hero worship had some cracks in the armor. "She only said one thing and then waited for the guards to come get her."

"And that was?"

"She said, 'Tell her to look at the dates on the letters.'"

Raisa's pulse kicked up. "How long ago did you say this was?"

Gabriela squinted into the middle distance. "Maybe three months?"

Which meant . . . which meant Isabel had been planning some elaborate game for at least that long.

She met Kilkenny's eyes and could see the same question in his.

How could Isabel have known they would even end up here? Were there more letters out there, ready to direct them to Gabriela had they not ended up talking to her themselves? Was someone watching their every move with directions from Isabel at the ready?

Or was it just inevitable that all roads led back to this girl? She was the leader of the FreeBell movement, they'd been pointed in her direction by multiple people. It would be a logical assumption that if Raisa was investigating Isabel's murder, she would eventually find her way to Gabriela Cruz.

More likely, Isabel had simply planted a bunch of clues along the way, figuring they would stumble onto the right combination eventually. She was the queen of covering all her bases. If it wasn't Gabriela telling them to look at the letters, it might have been some other *fan* imploring them to do something else.

Isabel was good, but what she was mostly good at was making everyone *think* she was omnipresent simply by working her ass off.

Still, Raisa itched to get her hands on the Biggest Fan letters once more.

"Okay," Raisa said. "Do you know of anyone in your FreeBell movement who would want to do her harm?"

Gabriela's eyes flew to Raisa's. "Like kill her, you mean?"

"Yes." There was no reason to beat around that particular bush. And Raisa wanted the answer. "Like kill her."

"No, never. Why would any of us try to kill her?" Gabriela asked.

There were plenty of reasons to suspect an obsession had turned violent, but Gabriela continued before Raisa could say anything.

"I mean, if you should be looking at anyone, it's Essi."

Raisa nearly laughed at that. The feuding generals—clouded by hatred and distrust of each other. "We're just trying to get some information right now."

"Well, I wouldn't look at the FreeBell group," Gabriela said. "I'd go looking for whoever is copying her."

Raisa hoped she hadn't heard her right. "What do you mean, copying her?"

But Gabriela lit up.

"I can't say whoever it is isn't a lower-level person in our group, but none of my friends would *ever*," Gabriela said, and Raisa tried to make the words make sense. She glanced at Kilkenny, who shook his head, looking more baffled than she felt.

"What?"

Gabriela stood and crossed to the closet, pulling out a whiteboard a moment later. "There's someone out there pretending to be Isabel. Or taking notes from her and doing something similar."

Your Biggest Fan. Raisa's stomach clenched, making her painfully aware that the only thing she'd had since the night before was that cup of coffee hours ago.

"Can you walk us through this?" Kilkenny prompted, though he probably hadn't needed to. Gabriela was already setting everything up. A real true crime aficionado.

"So, from what I can tell, there's been three homicides that I can connect to this . . ." Gabriela trailed off, tilting her head back and forth. She had completely come out of her shell. "Protégé. Can I call them that?"

"Sure," Raisa said, weakly.

"They weren't all in Gig Harbor, which is probably why Detective St. Ivany missed them." Gabriela tossed her dry erase marker. Caught it. Tossed it.

"Have you gone to her with all this?"

"She was . . . not receptive to my ideas," Gabriela said by way of an answer. "But anyway, I like to track police reports and the like—it's not weird, a lot of real true crime junkies do it."

Raisa thought of Delaney, tracking their sister across the country through similar reports. "I know."

"So, there's Emily Logan, of course," Gabriela said, pointing to the girl's name, before looking back at them. "You've heard of her, right?"

"Hmmm." Of course she and Kilkenny had wondered about Emily's death being related to their case, but she had no interest in encouraging the delusions of an armchair sleuth.

"That was the most obvious one," Gabriela said, now a completely different person. Where before she had been curled in on herself and shy, almost, now she was eager and energetic. "Stabbed to death in bed, not unlike your parents."

"Well, sure," Raisa agreed dryly.

"There are two more deaths that I think fit Isabel's preferred killing style as well," Gabriela said, fully stepping away from her board so they could see her work.

The first one was Peter Stamkos, who had apparently been a single father raising an eleven-year-old girl. Washington State CPS had been called to investigate after an anonymous tip came in that the state took seriously. He killed himself the day after the visit and left behind a letter that was a full-on confession.

"Did you get a copy of the letter?" Raisa asked before she remembered that she was dealing with a hobbyist and not an actual detective. It still would have been nice to see. Isabel had a signature symbol that hadn't been widely publicized and had let them identify several "suicide" deaths as her work. If this really was a protégé—someone who might have been in contact with Isabel herself—they might have left something similar behind.

"I wish."

Raisa hummed and her eyes dropped to the next name.

Lindsey Cousins.

It wasn't shocking, but her stomach gave a strange jolt that Gabriela had so casually figured out the connection.

"Between the three of them, she's my biggest stretch," Gabriela said, chewing on her thumbnail while staring at the whiteboard.

That was . . . ironic. "What made you include her?"

Gabriela tapped a sentence written beneath Lindsey's name: *There's only about eight-hundred drowning fatalities annually in the U.S.; that number goes down by 85 percent if the person is wearing a life vest.*

"She wasn't wearing a life vest," Helen had said. Lindsey always wore a life vest.

"That sounds like a tragedy," Raisa said, as carefully as possible.

"As do a lot of Isabel's kills," Gabriela pointed out.

That was true. Isabel seemed to like getting away with the murders at least as much as she liked the actual killing. And she'd found the easiest way to do that was to make her kills look like accidents, overdoses, suicides, things of that nature.

The case that had brought Isabel crashing back into Raisa's life two years ago had been an outlier—a double homicide that had been brutal and bloody and staged to look just like their parents' deaths.

The murders had been so different from Isabel's previous "work" that they had confused everyone on the team. On one hand, the killer had clearly been practiced. And posting a video of the scene to social media afterward was a decision more arrogant than you'd expect from a novice serial killer. Yet the FBI had been unable to uncover any similar crimes that could be attributed to the UNSUB—beyond the very massacre it was paying homage to.

They'd come to realize that the only time Isabel wanted to really put on a show was when the kills were personal. Once the FBI knew what to look for, they were able to identify the string of *accidents, overdoses, and suicides* in Isabel's wake.

What Gabriela was describing did sound a lot like Isabel's longtime MO.

"How did you connect these three?" Kilkenny asked.

"Emily's obvious, right?" Gabriela said, tapping the girl's name. "The other two . . . I don't know. I just keep an eye out for strange deaths. Like, for example, there are plenty of people who die in car accidents, right?"

"Sure."

"But a lot of those have a reason, like they were on a highway or it was bad weather," Gabriela said. "I came up with a formula that kind of gives a value to each component of a crash or accident. Then I run any odd crime through there, and if it pops up with a low number, it means the death was statistically unlikely to have been caused by natural circumstances."

Raisa blinked at her. "You created this?"

A shy grin broke out over her face as she noticed how impressed they were. "I'm studying to go into law enforcement. It's really kind of like how actuaries work? For life insurance companies and stuff like that. But I don't want to be an actuary—I just was inspired by some of their concepts."

"So your formula spit out these three—or two, I guess. Peter and Lindsey," Kilkenny summed up.

"Yeah, I didn't need it for Emily, obvs," Gabriela said. "It did flag Isabel's death as suspicious, though. So I'm glad someone is taking it seriously."

Raisa rocked back on her heels. "Did it really?"

"Yeah, her age and environment, plus the fact that she has probably four billion enemies who want to kill her, did the trick," Gabriela said. "There's, like, a point-five percent chance she died of natural causes."

"Have you talked to anyone except Detective St. Ivany about this?" Raisa asked, and Gabriela went a little shifty eyed.

"I may have floated a theory or two to some close friends who follow the crime reports, too," Gabriela admitted. "But I didn't put it on main anywhere."

"On main," Kilkenny repeated, and Gabriela rolled her eyes.

"Like in the main Discord channel or on Reddit under our subthread," Gabriela said, in that very-young-person voice that came out whenever they had to explain new technology to the olds.

"Right," Kilkenny said. "Of course."

"Well . . . that's all I've got for you guys. So . . . ," Gabriela said, gesturing toward the door.

They stood and asked her to call them if she remembered anything important. Raisa also took a photo of the whiteboard, with Gabriela's permission. Because why not have it?

"Does Peter Stamkos's death undermine our theory that someone's out there targeting psychopaths?" Raisa asked when they got back to the SUV.

"Why would it?"

Raisa cut him a look. She knew they saw the worst of the worst in their jobs, but the world wasn't actually that bad. "You think there were three in such a small radius? Peter, Isabel, and Lindsey."

"The rate of psychopathy in the US is one percent or so," Kilkenny said. "Though some studies have estimated it's as high as four-point-five percent."

"So in a state of about eight million people," Raisa mused. "Holy shit. There's eighty thousand psychopaths in Washington State?"

"In theory."

"Huh," Raisa said. "So maybe he *was* a psychopath. He did get a visit from CPS."

"Before killing himself, in theory," Kilkenny said. "Psychopathy and suicide have an interesting relationship that I won't get into. But it's unlikely that a psychopath would kill himself over the shame of a CPS visit."

"I would have guessed they wouldn't kill themselves at all," Raisa mused.

"They do actually have suicidal ideation, but it's not tied to an emotion like shame," Kilkenny said. "You see it connected to their tendency for impulsivity."

"None of this matters if he didn't kill himself *or* he wasn't a psychopath," Raisa said. "Or we're wrong about someone targeting psychopaths." She paused. "Especially if they're *mimicking* Isabel, right? Why would they mimic her while taking out her brethren?"

"Her brethren," Kilkenny repeated, amused. "Maybe it's meant as the ultimate insult? Not necessarily as an homage to her, but as a middle finger?"

Raisa cracked her neck. "All we have right now is speculation."

"And Isabel's message to you."

"Check the dates of the letters," Raisa said, some of the tension leaving her body.

Every time in her life, not just her professional career, she had been able to seek solace in language, in the quirks that could only be found in someone's choice of words.

The answer didn't lie in these interviews with Essi or Helen or Gabriela, as helpful as they might be.

The answer, as always, lay in the writing.

CHAPTER TWELVE

Delaney

Day Four

Delaney didn't throw the napkin with Maeve's number away, though she wasn't sure why she didn't. Maybe because she knew someone was hunting her, and what better way than to pretend you're new to town and want to chat up a friendly face?

Or a not-so-friendly face, in Delaney's case.

Maybe Maeve had been exactly who she'd said she was. Delaney kept the phone number just in case.

Then she put the woman out of her mind. She found a motel on the road leading into Gig Harbor, the kind where the *o* and the *a* on the No Vacancy sign had burned out long ago and would never be replaced. The kidney-shaped pool was empty except for a dirty mattress at the bottom, and her room smelled of cigarettes and Fritos.

It was perfect.

Delaney tried to wash off the thin layer of sweat that had broken out on her skin hours ago, but the weak excuse of a shower failed her miserably.

She somehow felt worse when she got out, but she shoved her legs into black jeans that cut into her hip bones anyway. They weren't her style, but she'd picked them up at a Goodwill a while back for one purpose. She paired them with a slinky top that clung to her nipples and boots with enough of a heel to change her gait.

The one remaining piece was a neon-pink wig cut into a sharply angled bob. It reminded her of Isabel's preferred look—the one she'd used as Jenna, an overeager podcaster with an ambitious heart and the wardrobe of a much younger woman.

She stared in the mirror and didn't recognize herself.

Delaney Moore dressed in Earth Mother tones and styles and had long, mud-colored hair she wore in a braid.

This was Lana Parker, coming out to join the fun.

They were so easy to find, the girls.

Delaney looked at them and saw all the ways they yearned. For better men, for better lives, for a better-tasting drink.

They weren't recognizable as a mirror to herself, to Isabel or Raisa. None of them had been girls who yearned. They hunted and were hunted, they lived with the scraps they were given instead of asking for more.

But she had a fondness for the yearners nonetheless.

They were recognizable as at least human, unlike the monsters Delaney so often encountered spending most of her time on the dark web.

Let's play a game . . .

There was a bonfire on the ocean, and it drew Delaney, a moth to the proverbial flame. In the dark, she almost fit in.

Stand in your enemy's shadow.

Someone shifted out of the darkness beside her. A girl. She huffed out an annoyed breath. "No one has cigarettes anymore."

"They're the leading cause of preventable disease and death in the United States," Delaney said, because she could look the part, but she'd never been able to act it.

She wasn't Isabel. She wasn't even Lana. She was Delaney Moore, and she had never been cool a day in her life.

The girl who'd sidled up next to her, a red Solo cup in one hand and a vape pen in the other, laughed. She had a bright, pretty smile, even though one canine was crooked. Her eyes were wide pools in the moonlight.

And she was just who Delaney had been looking for.

Because if she was going to get chased to Gig Harbor, she might as well take advantage of it.

"I mean, the superbugs or the wildfires or the mass shootings are probably gonna get us before I have to worry about hardened arteries," the girl said. "But you make a good point."

When Delaney didn't say anything, the girl held out her hand. "Gabriela. But everyone calls me Gabbi."

They watched the crowd of people on the beach for a while, before Gabbi tried conversation one more time.

"Do I know you from Intro to Calculus?" Gabbi asked.

Delaney nearly barked out a laugh. She could have taught Intro to Calculus when she was eleven.

"No, you don't," Delaney said. "I don't go to the college. I'm . . . doing a favor for a friend."

"A favor," Gabbi repeated, tossing her vape pen in the air. "What kind of favor involves looking hot and partying with a bunch of twentysomethings?"

Delaney hadn't just wandered onto this beach, mysterious though she might want to think herself in her own head. She'd gotten herself invited into a social forum for the local community college, because she had been playing this game for six months and had already done tons of prep work. This event was open to anyone in the group, so she knew Gabbi wouldn't be suspicious that a stranger had wandered onto this stretch of beach.

"My friend's daughter is here," Delaney said, gesturing toward a gaggle of young women. If Gabbi knew them, Delaney would just say she'd been pointing elsewhere. "It's her first party, she's underage. I just want to keep an eye on her without it being a big deal."

Gabbi side-eyed her, probably justifiably so. It was a strange excuse, but it would soon launch the very conversation Delaney wanted to have.

"I can't tell if that's sweet or creepy," Gabbi said. Delaney found her honesty refreshing. Too many people would have smiled politely and edged away from Delaney posthaste.

Delaney shrugged one shoulder. "It's tough out there for girls these days."

A pause. "These days? Try at any point in history."

Gabbi wasn't wrong.

"It seems like a good group here," Delaney said, her eyes locked on a group of boys, one of whom had a girl tossed over his shoulder. Everyone, including the girl, was laughing.

Girls sometimes laughed because they didn't want to be killed.

But this one seemed to genuinely be enjoying herself.

"We all kind of watch out for each other," Gabbi said, and then showed Delaney her cup. "Just water. A group of us take turns, a designated driver without the driving part. To make sure everyone gets home okay."

And this was where Delaney had wanted to go. "Do you ever have problems?"

"Sometimes."

"Anyone I should keep my eye out for?" Delaney asked.

"Benny Thompson," Gabbi said without missing a beat. She jerked her chin toward a tall guy at the edge of the revelers, watching the party with a greedy expression. He slouched, in a way that was both unattractive and betrayed a lack of confidence. "And Brad."

This time Gabbi pointed to Benny's opposite, a handsome kid surrounded by admirers. His jaw would make the incels Delaney waded through on the daily weep with jealousy. A dimple winked to life every time he smiled, and the crowd around him jockeyed for space at his side.

As Delaney and Gabbi watched, Brad made eye contact with Benny.

They work together, Delaney thought, right before Gabbi said it.

"They work together."

"Smart," Delaney murmured.

Gabbi's startled silence was louder than anything she could have said.

That had been a slip on Delaney's part. A normal person wouldn't have said that.

A normal person would have asked if they should call the cops.

"I mean, why hasn't anyone done something about them?"

Brad No-Last-Name bent down to whisper in one of the girl's ears. She laughed up at him, swatting his bicep.

The two of them broke off from the larger group, heading toward the tree line.

Benny watched them.

Then he put his beer bottle down into the sand and followed.

"We have to do something," Delaney said, mostly to herself.

Gabbi blew a ring of smoke into the air, her head tipped back, her face bathed in starlight.

"You think I haven't tried?"

CHAPTER THIRTEEN

Raisa

Day One

On the way back from Gabriela's, Kilkenny pulled into a diner.

"The letters can wait twenty minutes for us to actually eat," was all he said, before jumping out.

Now Raisa stared out the window at the quiet port. The tiny town was so idyllic, yet so much darkness lurked beneath.

"I know there's a crazy murderer running loose out there, and yet I feel safer knowing Isabel's dead," Raisa murmured. "Is that odd?"

"Isabel's greatest trick was that she was able to make herself seem all-knowing, all-powerful, even when she wasn't," Kilkenny said. "Sending you that note . . ."

"It makes me feel like she can hurt me even beyond the grave," Raisa finished the thought, and Kilkenny nodded. "Because she recruited a protégé."

"Hmmm."

Raisa slid him a look. "Sounds like you don't agree with Gabriela's theory."

"Isabel wasn't the type to want her legacy carried on by anyone else," Kilkenny said. "My bet is if it *is* a protégé, Isabel wanted to use them for a different reason than just teaching them how to kill."

"Like maybe to send me a letter," Raisa said. "And take more drastic actions if I'd ignored it?"

Kilkenny lifted one shoulder. "If this person viciously stabbed Emily Logan to death, then . . . yeah. I think we can safely assume they're willing to go to extremes to follow Isabel's orders. And that one of those orders might be to take you out if you don't play Isabel's game."

"Well, isn't that a delightful thought," Raisa said. It worried her and it didn't. Logically, she knew Isabel's reach could extend beyond the grave; emotionally, it was hard to be too scared of a ghost.

They didn't speak as they finished off their meal and then headed back to the hotel.

When they got to their floor, Kilkenny paused outside her door.

"Do you need company?" he asked. There was no hint in his voice that he could tell she was spooked, but she was sure the offer was at least partly because of that.

Raisa truly thought about it, which was new. At any time in her past, she would have immediately declined the offer, preferring silence over any other choice.

"I want to study the letters," she said, so that she made it clear it wasn't his presence she didn't want.

He lifted his hand, and she wasn't sure whether he was going to give her a gentle nudge on the shoulder or wrap her up in a hug. Instead of either of those, he palmed the top of her head for one brief moment. Human touch, contact with someone who cared.

It made a difference.

She pressed into it, and for a moment time stood still.

He pulled back with a soft, fond smile. "Good night."

"We'll attack it in the morning," she said.

The moment she got inside, she stepped out of her shoes and changed into her comfy clothes, though they were no longer clean.

A chair and desk by the window overlooked the harbor.

The sun was just dipping below the horizon, the day long this deep into summer.

Boats rocked gently against the pier and Raisa thought of Essi Halla. *Sleek.*

That was the word that came to mind. She was a lawyer, she had measured every word she'd said to them, even if she had come across as casual during parts of the conversation.

Raisa would kill for a sample of Essi's writing.

She did a quick search and found that Essi had a book coming out in two weeks. When she did a broader search for an excerpt, though, she came up blank.

Maybe she would be able to ask Essi for an early copy.

For now, Raisa put her out of her mind and turned her attention to the Biggest Fan letters.

Look at the dates.

She did. She logged them all on a spreadsheet. Nothing jumped out at her, though.

Codes were fine and dandy, but if one person—Isabel—actually wanted to communicate to another—Raisa—she would have to give some guideposts that mattered.

Look at the dates.

Raisa shook her head, ignoring Isabel for now. Her sister had an agenda, always, and Raisa didn't need to follow it anymore.

Instead, she read through the letters, one by one, without trying to run any analysis. The messages were frustratingly dull, but Raisa got a feeling for the pattern of them.

An update on the weather, and then a mention of a hiking trail, every time. Raisa googled all the trails mentioned, but there were no common similarities among them. The author said they'd summited a mountain in New Zealand one day, and a week later they were in the Alps, and then in California, and so on.

Of course, they weren't just hiking trails. Isabel would never have kept these letters if there wasn't some kind of secret communication going on in them. And the killer thing was, she absolutely wanted Raisa to figure them out.

Isabel didn't do things by accident.

The letters always wrapped up with a signature from *Your Biggest Fan*.

Raisa slumped into the chair and rubbed at her eyes, tired from the day, tired from Isabel's games.

Tired of being the puppet at the end of a string that had outlasted the puppeteer.

She checked her phone again, but really didn't have to. Delaney hadn't responded. She wasn't going to respond. Still, because Kilkenny's sad face haunted her, Raisa tried one more time. The call went to voicemail.

Raisa shot off a quick text and then tossed the phone back on the desk, staring at papers spread out on the desk once more.

She wished she had Isabel's responses.

The journal.

Raisa let the legs of the chair fall back to the floor, hardly believing she hadn't thought of it before. She had Isabel's journal.

It didn't take long to find it and then match up the letters with the corresponding dates.

On the surface, the journal entries were tame by Isabel's standards. But Raisa thought about codes, thought about messages. Thought again that Isabel *wanted* to communicate something here.

To a linguist.

Or . . . *Tell her to look at the dates on the letters.*

Dates were numbers, and those were Delaney's purview.

What if the *her* hadn't been Raisa?

She straightened, and ripped a fresh piece of paper from her own journal. She wrote down the numbers that comprised each of the dates.

1-7-2-5

3-6-2-5

When she had all twelve lines written, she crossed out the years. Anything that was a common factor could either be used as an anchor—unlikely in a situation like this one—or could be discarded.

Then she went to the journal, to the first date. January 7. She looked at the first sentence, and then the first letter of the seventh word in that sentence.

Please.

P.

Raisa typed that into her computer and flipped to the March 6 entry. She found the sixth word in the third sentence.

Exist.

E.

She repeated the process for all the letters from Isabel's Biggest Fan. When she finished, she sat back and huffed out a breath.

P.E.T.E.R. S.T.A.M.K.O.S.

Peter Stamkos—the single father who had abused his daughter and then died by suicide after a CPS visit.

He had died months after the date on the first journal entry.

Raisa chewed on the inside of her cheek, trying to figure out what this all meant.

The only way Isabel could have made all that line up was if she'd written the journal out completely *after* she'd received the Biggest Fan letters. The journal wasn't meant to detail her life or be a record of the final months before her death; its sole purpose was meant to confirm that Isabel had known who Peter Stamkos was, he was linked to the Biggest Fan letters, and both were important to figuring out who had killed her.

"Fuck you, Isabel," Raisa said, and felt immediately better. If her sister was going to create an entire journal out of thin air just to play simple word and number games, she could have simply written: *these are the people who want me dead the most.*

Sick of it all, Raisa slammed the thing shut. If, as a person, she were slightly stronger or slightly weaker, she would've packed her bags right now and left at dawn.

Instead, she took a shower and fell into a deep, dreamless sleep.

In the morning, she looked up the number for the CPS office that had visited Peter Stamkos and left a message along with her badge number.

She was playing with fire, introducing herself as an FBI agent even when she wasn't working an official investigation, but she was mostly convinced she could get St. Ivany to invite them on to consult. Especially once the medical report came back that Isabel's death might've been a homicide, which it would.

After she got dressed, she collected Kilkenny, and they walked to the coffee shop a block away. Raisa filled him in on the dates and letters after they got their drinks.

"So Stamkos's death does have something to do with Isabel," Kilkenny mused. They were back outside, meandering along the walkway that had been built up next to the water. Raisa looked for Essi's boat, but a few more had come in overnight and it was blocked from view.

"Or, or, or, what if she saw his obituary and just decided to mess with me?" Raisa asked, and then let out a frustrated, though muted, yell. "I hate this second-guessing whenever it comes to Isabel. She's a mastermind until she's not. She's an opportunist and a genius and kind of a dumbass sometimes and I never know which side of her we're getting."

"As long as we keep in mind that she's trying to manipulate you, I already think we're ahead of the game," Kilkenny said. "Or at least better than we have been before when it comes to Isabel."

"I wondered . . ."

When she didn't finish, he nudged her. "Wondered what?"

"If the messages were meant for Delaney instead of me," Raisa said.

"You were the emergency contact," Kilkenny pointed out, and Raisa tipped her head in acknowledgment. "And you were the one she made sure knew she was murdered."

"Thinking about Delaney got me to the right answer, so maybe that's why she did it. She wanted me to think about Delaney and—oh my god, do you hear me right now? I'm acting like Isabel is playing 4D chess, and really she's probably only playing checkers," Raisa said, with a sigh. "And yet we have to act like she's a grand master because every once in a while she is. She gave Gabriela Cruz a clue to give to me *months ago*."

"Let's just forge ahead for now," Kilkenny said, with the calm air of someone used to high-strung horses. "One of the more interesting things to note is that if we do have a protégé on our hands . . . well."

"'Well' what?"

"They're killing at quite a clip," Kilkenny said. "Let's say they've killed four people in the last four months or so? Isabel averaged that many a year, in a busy year. That, to me, signals the protégé could be escalating at a startling rate."

Raisa grimaced. "Why?"

"They weren't built for killing?" Kilkenny offered. "They thought they could, but taking that first life—"

"Peter Stamkos," Raisa offered. "According to the timeline."

"Killing Stamkos broke them," Kilkenny continued, with a nod of thanks. "They're not going to be functioning well, they're probably holding it together by a thread at the moment. They're going to make a mistake sooner or later, or even turn themselves in. But there will be more deaths before that happens. If I had to guess."

"Yeah, your guesses tend to be pretty accurate," Raisa said. She very much enjoyed when they set up shop in his area of expertise. "What kind of killer do you see this person as?"

"Erratic, is what I'm getting mostly."

"Even though she's killing like Isabel?" Raisa asked.

"Isabel killed for twenty-five years without ever getting caught," Kilkenny pointed out. "Our person here? They were found out by a twenty-two-year-old with a homemade algorithm."

"Because they stayed local and their cooling-off period is nearly nonexistent," Raisa said. He made a, perhaps unconscious, move toward his holster. Raisa dropped her voice, even though there was no one following them. "You really think we're in danger?"

"Not us," Kilkenny said.

Raisa rolled her head, just enough to peek over her shoulder. "Me."

"Yeah," Kilkenny admitted. "Isabel wanted you in Gig Harbor. I think she sent you that note not just to get you to look into her death but because she has plans for you here."

A shiver slid along the length of Raisa's spine. The theory seemed to cut through all the maybes, the second-guessing, the what-ifs.

If Isabel had wanted Raisa to solve her murder, she would have given her more information.

If Isabel wanted Raisa in Gig Harbor, she would send the exact note she had.

"We'll just have to stay four or five steps ahead of her," Raisa said, though she wasn't convinced they could do that. Not with so many different paths they could go down.

"We should get the visitors' logs from the correctional facility," Kilkenny said. "Gabriela probably wasn't the only one to visit Isabel. Maybe we'll get lucky and her Biggest Fan will have put their real name down."

Raisa checked the time. They still had an hour to kill.

"They'll probably all just say 'Delaney' and 'Gabriela,'" Raisa said, though she didn't disagree that they should get them.

"You think Delaney visited her?"

She glanced at him, trying to read his expression. "You don't?"

"Delaney seemed like she'd come to her own realization about how dangerous it was to associate with Isabel," Kilkenny mused.

"Yeah, I don't know about that," Raisa said. "A nearly forty-year-old habit is hard to break."

"Have you heard from her?" Kilkenny asked.

Raisa checked her phone even though she didn't need to. "No."

When he didn't say anything, she glanced at him. "You're really worried, aren't you?"

"Just as much as I'm worried about you," Kilkenny said. It was reasonable, but Raisa didn't feel like being reasonable. Not when it came to either of her sisters.

And anyway, you could say a lot of things about Delaney, but one thing you couldn't was that she needed protection. Delaney Moore might look like a computer nerd, but she could handle her business. "Delaney always lands on her feet."

"Well, if we've got the motive wrong, if it's not a protégé, I think whoever killed Isabel is a pissed-off family member," Kilkenny said. "Which means they would likely target either you or Delaney next. And honestly, a civilian is a lot easier to go after than an FBI agent."

"You would like to think they'd go after the person who sat on the sidelines for twenty-five years, too," Raisa muttered. "She doesn't deserve to die, but it's not like her hands are clean, either."

"Raisa . . ."

"I don't know why you refuse to hold her accountable for her actions," she said, letting some of the long-held frustration seep into her voice.

"I do—"

"No, you don't," Raisa said, raw now. She hated this argument and she hated that Kilkenny had never budged on it. Every time Delaney was brought up, he acted like Raisa was in the wrong for icing her out. As if now that Isabel was in prison—dead, she was dead—it all shook out in the wash. "What? Is it because she's a woman? You don't think she knew what she was doing? Is it easier for you to make her into the victim?"

Kilkenny reeled back at that. "What?"

"I don't know," Raisa all but yelled. The morning was sleepy, only a few tourists wandering the streets now. Still, she realized she was making a scene, so she took a deep breath. "Why do you care what I think about her? She's not getting charged, and I have no power over what happens to her. Yet you can't just let it go."

Hurt flickered in and out of his expression, before he shut it down completely. He was such an expert at that.

"She's done a lot more good than bad," Kilkenny said after a moment of letting the silence sit between them, loaded with her anger. "You can blame maybe two of Isabel's victims on her, and you could say the same about yourself."

He held up a hand to cut off her indignant reply. "Which is to say, neither of you is responsible for Isabel's delusions and obsessions. And as our anonymous tipster, Delaney helped scrub the dark web clean of a lot of men who would have gone on to do very bad things. In my eyes, her ledger is balanced."

"I know that's what you think—"

Kilkenny interrupted her again. "But that's not why I care." He shook his head, staring at her so intently she had to look away underneath the scrutiny. "I care because . . . she's your sister, and you could actually let yourself enjoy that. Maybe it wouldn't be smooth sailing all the time. You're both prickly as hell. But you would have someone in your corner. Always."

"I have you in my corner," Raisa said, almost desperate for the validation.

"You need more than just me," Kilkenny said.

At some point in the aftermath of learning she was related to Isabel, Raisa had unearthed a letter from her adoptive parents, the ones she'd thought were her birth parents most of her life. Her mother, Pia, had wished that she would find her sisters once again and recognize them as *hers*. As family.

She supposed that was what Kilkenny wanted for her as well.

Raisa just didn't understand how he looked at Delaney's past and thought Raisa would want someone like that in her corner.

She'd rather be by herself, but the amazing thing was she no longer had to be.

What she didn't need was Kilkenny lecturing her about her life. Maybe he looked at it as sad, but he didn't exactly have a full stable of friends, either. As much as he liked to pretend he was in a better place than she was, they'd recognized the loneliness in *each other*.

"Right now, I need another coffee," she said even though she had barely touched her first cup. What she really needed was space. For the first time in a long time, that included from Kilkenny.

He sighed and reached for her, but she danced back a few steps.

A car started in the distance, and he turned. She used the opportunity to dash across the street.

When she looked back, his arm was still outstretched, his expression some complicated mix of anger and grief and irritation.

Join the club, she thought.

"Raisa," he said, stepping off the curb.

Out of the corner of her eye, she saw a blur, movement that shouldn't be there.

A second later, she could only watch as a dark SUV slammed into Kilkenny at full speed.

CHAPTER FOURTEEN

Raisa

Day Two

Blood. Sirens. The heavy, dead weight of a body in her arms.

Raisa couldn't breathe but it didn't matter. Nothing mattered right now beyond helping Kilkenny.

There was blood on her hands, warm and slick, his skin going slippery beneath her fingers. Frantic, she searched for the source of his worst injury, and found it at the back of his head.

A whimper escaped her lips, and she moved so she could cradle his skull in her lap.

Breathe. Think. Concentrate.

Raisa finally let herself glance at Kilkenny's face, only to find it ashen. Everything in the world stilled.

He was alive, he was. She could see his heart still pumping in the hollow of his neck.

It didn't matter what his face looked like right now.

She glanced down again at her hands, the cracks in her skin dyed red.

Someone gripped her arms and she curled over Kilkenny's body as if they were in a war zone.

"Ma'am, ma'am, let us get to him."

It was the paramedics.

"His head," Raisa said, as she kept it off the pavement, all while shifting back, away from him.

They needed to work on him.

They needed to save him.

The sunlight caught on their scissors, on the railings of the stretcher, on the pool of copper on the pavement.

Raisa shifted, retched, her body rejecting the images.

"Ma'am?"

The paramedics again.

Hands on her arms again.

"Do you want to ride in the ambulance?" It was a question, but it really wasn't. He was already helping her up the stairs, onto the seat next to the bed.

Kilkenny wasn't conscious.

She took his hand anyway. The other had wires and IVs and a Pulse Ox attached.

Beeping filled her skull, pinging off the bone inside.

It wasn't long before a paramedic gently shifted her out of the way. They were working on Kilkenny some more. She didn't know what they were doing.

There was a bag of blood swinging with each bump in the road, each turn.

Four seconds or four years later—she couldn't tell—they pulled to a stop.

The beauty of a small town, the hospital was right here.

Hands again, directing her out of the way.

Then Kilkenny was gone.

Raisa scrambled to keep up, but they were too fast, disappearing through a door, yelling stats to each other even as it slammed closed behind them.

She stopped, her body refusing to move.

She couldn't even imagine what she looked like, her skin smeared with Kilkenny's blood.

"Miss, are you okay?" someone asked. A nurse in pretty pastel scrubs.

Raisa shook her head. "No."

Nothing was okay.

A baby cried, his mother trying to soothe him across the waiting room. The woman sent Raisa an apologetic smile.

Raisa tried to force her face into something understanding, but it might have just come out a grimace. The woman seemed to understand anyway.

Kilkenny was in surgery, someone had finally come out to inform her. She might have claimed she was his partner, and they'd run with the assumption that she was his next of kin. He wouldn't care, and at least it meant that she was getting updates.

It had been three hours.

He'd sustained a skull fracture. That was bad.

His leg had been broken in two different spots. That was also bad.

There was other damage, the kind sustained when an SUV slammed into a vulnerable rib cage.

But that was all secondary.

They needed to save his life first. Then make sure he would wake up.

A pair of heels appeared in Raisa's line of sight. She wanted to ignore them, but she couldn't.

"Did you catch them?" Raisa asked, lifting her eyes to meet Maeve St. Ivany's gaze.

"No," St. Ivany said, taking a seat near Raisa, but leaving one in between them. "We have an APB out for the make and model of the SUV. A few bystanders caught a good enough look to give us that."

"But no license plate, am I right?" Raisa asked, going back to staring at her hands. Someone had helped her get cleaned up a while ago, and she was wearing the extra scrubs one of the nurses kept in her locker for emergencies. "Not even a letter or number to go off of?"

There was a beat. "No."

Raisa nodded. This hadn't been an accident. "They probably covered it with mud."

"Probably," St. Ivany agreed. "What are you thinking?"

"That it's a pretty inefficient way to kill someone," Raisa forced out, her lips numb.

St. Ivany didn't say anything, which Raisa appreciated. Of course St. Ivany agreed with that assessment—any law enforcement officer would. But if she had made some comment that hit just left of acceptable, Raisa would have burned the bridge as quickly as she could come up with something to say that would do it.

"I don't think it was an accident, either," Raisa said, and this time St. Ivany nodded.

"A scare tactic gone wrong, maybe," St. Ivany said.

Raisa glanced at her. That was . . . smart. They had talked to both Essi and Gabriela, along with a handful of women at the correctional facility gates. They'd also met with the very person in charge of making sure there weren't any homicides in her prison. They'd talked to multiple employees. Any one of those people could have gotten spooked and tried to chase them out of town. They might not have known they would catch Kilkenny just wrong.

Raisa didn't care what their intent was, though. She was going to find the person who had done it and make them pay.

"So you might be onto something with Isabel's death," St. Ivany said.

"Yeah, you think?" Raisa bit off.

"You're a linguist, not a field agent," St. Ivany said, which got Raisa to finally look at her. She held up a hand. "I'm not insulting you or insinuating anything. I just mean I can't simply request you join the investigation. I have superiors, too, believe it or not. And I'm guessing yours aren't going to be happy to have you on this case, no matter how much free rein you might have."

That wasn't untrue. She probably *shouldn't* be working it, if she were being honest with herself. The rules existed for a reason, and even Emily Logan's investigation brushed too closely to Isabel Parker for anyone to feel comfortable with Raisa's participation.

"I'll put in a request from our end," Raisa finally said, though she wasn't sure what the outcome of that would be. Normally, if she was contacted independently about an investigation and raised it to the level of her supervisor, he generally signed off on it. But this case couldn't get more personal.

"If it helps make your case, we do have Emily Logan's blog posts," St. Ivany said. "We didn't find anything useful in them, but they're printed out and ordered chronologically. You might be more successful."

Raisa nodded, though she had no desire to dig through the dead girl's blog at the moment. She wanted to find whoever had been at the wheel of the SUV. "I'll take a look at it."

St. Ivany seemed to understand Raisa wasn't exactly going to do an in-depth analysis on the thing immediately. "I've requested a warrant for the bank account of the woman who was involved in the shiv incident with Isabel six weeks ago."

Raisa straightened at that, finally curious enough to really engage with the detective. "Who was it?"

"A woman named Taylor Bultman," St. Ivany said. The hit-and-run seemed to have changed her entire demeanor, as if she realized there really was an active threat in her town and she might need FBI assistance. "She's in for multiple life sentences and had nothing to lose. But she has a kid on the outside who is currently applying to colleges. I'm curious if the money ended up going to him."

"It must have been a significant amount of money," Raisa said. "Might help us eliminate suspects when it comes time."

"Yup."

"But if the person is smart, that bank account will probably be untraceable," Raisa pointed out.

"Then we would know it was a hit, though," St. Ivany countered. "Or a possible one, at least. That would put pressure on the ME, not to mention the correctional facility. They don't want headlines about a murder in their system."

That was also not a terrible point. Raisa slid St. Ivany a look, assessing.

"Hey, I'm not actually the bad guy here," St. Ivany said. "You guys came to me out of nowhere, when I'm working a homicide."

"I didn't say anything."

St. Ivany nudged her. "I'm not an idiot, either."

It felt like an olive branch, albeit one covered in Kilkenny's blood.

"Here, give me your number, I'll keep you updated on the progress of the warrant," St. Ivany said, opening her phone. "I know you're not going to want to leave here for something less than a real lead."

"Did you bring Emily's blog posts?" Raisa asked after rattling off the digits.

"Yeah, the binder is in my car. I'll go grab it."

Raisa didn't have anything with her to actually analyze the writing. She usually worked off her laptop, which had software that allowed her to track her notes about the author's idiolect and stylistic quirks, along with breaking down each sentence so she didn't miss anything.

But sometimes reading a work without any of that hanging over her was effective in its own way.

When St. Ivany returned, she handed over a generic black binder you could buy for cheap at any dollar store. Raisa took it with the respect it deserved as the last remaining words of a woman taken from the world far too soon and in far too brutal a manner.

St. Ivany hovered over her. "Can I ask you something?"

"Depends on if it's a good question."

St. Ivany's lips twitched in the same way Kilkenny's did. Acknowledging the humor while not really giving in to it. "Why do you think the SUV was aiming for Agent Kilkenny and not you?"

Raisa thought about Kilkenny's warning. *Isabel wanted you in Gig Harbor.* If Kilkenny had taken a hit meant for her, she wasn't sure she would be able to live with herself.

Her mind supplied an alternative. "I think they just wanted to scare us, and they didn't care who was hurt."

St. Ivany nodded, but her expression remained clouded. "I'm going to post a uniform by the door. Just in case."

The fact that someone else had reached the conclusion that Raisa might have a target on her back made it seem all the more real. "You think someone's after me?"

"Or Kilkenny," St. Ivany said, neutrally. "But it won't hurt to have someone in place."

St. Ivany wasn't wrong. And there wasn't just the possibility of one threat out there. Whoever had been driving the SUV could have been Isabel's protégé working under her direction, but it also could have been a relative of one of Isabel's victims, operating independently of anything else.

"It's not just me who might be in danger," Raisa said slowly, finally, *finally*, shrugging off the anger that stopped her from acknowledging it. "It's also my sister Delaney."

St. Ivany's face flickered with an emotion gone too quick for Raisa to catch. "Well, there's only one of you I can protect."

CHAPTER FIFTEEN

Delaney

Day Four

The eyes on the back of Delaney's neck had returned.

When they had caught up with her—how they had caught up with her—she didn't know.

But they were there.

Delaney stripped out of the costume she'd worn down to the bonfire to meet Gabriela Cruz, and then she flipped the motel's shower on, watching it ramp up from a trickle to a stronger trickle.

At least the water was scalding. Usually in places like this she had to deal with both a weak flow and glacial temperatures.

It took a while, but eventually Lana Parker swirled all the way down the drain and she was back to being Delaney.

A comfy pair of sweats finished off the transformation.

Delaney made a cup of coffee that was more water and false promises than anything else, then grabbed her computer and went to sit on the edge of the kidney-shaped pool outside.

Her socked feet dangled over the chipped NO DIVING warning painted on one of the walls, and she stared at the one other room that was lit up against the night. She wondered who else was there with her.

She didn't think it was whoever was hunting her. They wouldn't announce their presence like that.

The air smelled of weed, even though there was no one around, and Delaney wished the pool were full. She wanted nothing more than to slip beneath the cool water and disappear, really disappear. There would be no eyes on the back of her neck, no sour scent clinging to the inside of her nostrils, no memory of Isabel, staring at her from across the table of the visitors' room at that correctional facility, a master plan brewing behind her eyes.

But there was no water and Isabel's face would forever be burned in her mind and there was definitely someone tracking her.

Maeve? Or maybe Maeve was just someone her hunter had hired. Someone sent in to get a lay of the land before the real predator struck.

Delaney sighed and woke her laptop up. She punched in Lindsey Cousins's name, as she always did. No new articles about the "drowning."

She was going to be forgotten as just a tragic statistic. That was probably for the best.

A headline at the bottom of the page caught her eye.

Police Mull Curfew as Search for Emily Logan's Killer Continues

Emily Logan. The girl who had died just like Isabel and Delaney's parents had. On a bed, stabbed too many times.

Psychologists had said that kind of homicide could only be driven by rage or a psychotic break. Yet with the Parkers, it had actually been Isabel's cold calculation.

She'd wanted to mimic rage. She'd never actually experienced it herself.

Let's play a game . . .

Delaney shook her head and left Emily in the past, bringing up Gabriela Cruz's Flik page. Delaney had been a content moderator for the video-based social media site for several years before Isabel made her triumphant return into her life via the app.

She knew it well.

Gabbi had established a following for herself in a particular corner of a very popular community. True crime girlies, she'd seen them called. Gabbi had also picked up a slice of the users who liked to advocate for better mental health treatment for women.

Delaney scrolled through her posts, searching for the start of the obsession.

Isabel Parker: Psychopath or Misunderstood Vigilante?

After that, there were a dozen or so other videos that focused on Isabel. Delaney made her way through them, coming to the conclusion that Gabbi idolized Isabel but didn't want to, and the cognitive dissonance of connecting to something positive in a monster had caused her to break with reality a bit.

Delaney had seen it frequently in fandoms across popular culture. Bad behavior was explained away by the person's fans; bad behavior was exaggerated by their haters. Being considered a "good" person who adhered to ever-narrowing and impossible social rules was the bare minimum expected for many celebrities these days.

The mental gymnastics that ensued if they stepped out of line would have been amusing to watch if Delaney didn't find it so confounding. So many people seemed hell-bent on creating a religion, where they would be assigned to live out their days in heaven or hell based on their social media posting and nothing else.

Delaney wasn't wired . . . normally. She knew that. So she had never really worried about being thought of as a good person. She was just trying to make it through having helped more people than she'd hurt.

She returned to the last video Gabbi had posted about Isabel.

This one was simply titled **Who Killed Emily Logan?**

It had half a million views.

"Mind if I join you?"

This time Delaney was interrupted by a male voice. This time she didn't flinch.

"Free country," she said, without looking up. Still, she could see him from the corner of her eye. This was the fourth person to approach her unsolicited on this day when she knew she was being followed.

If she let her wilder conspiracy theories take root, she'd start to think everyone was in on the hunt.

That couldn't be, though. This wasn't *The Truman Show*. Not every stranger was a threat.

Still, once was a coincidence and all that. So she killed the screen, holding the computer protectively on her lap as she stared at the night sky.

The man was thin, probably too thin, his face all sharp angles. His sandy hair was pulled back into a nub of a ponytail, and he wore beat-up leather sandals on surprisingly clean feet.

"Roan," he said, when he caught her looking.

"Like the mountains in North Carolina?" she asked, and he grinned, revealing teeth too white and straight to fit the rest of him.

"My mother was a glassworker in Asheville when I was conceived," Roan said, as confirmation.

That was certainly a thought-out fake name if it was indeed a fake name. Delaney closed her eyes, wondering if being paranoid was smart or dangerous.

The thing about being in fight-or-flight mode all the time was that it wore on the body; it wore on the mind. Her ability to make smart decisions was eroding because she saw every situation as full of threats.

But today, without initiating contact with any of them, she'd been approached by a homeless man, a beautiful woman, and then the very girl whom she'd gone to the bonfire to meet.

And now this, a man with a name too unique for it to work for undercover but also too strange and perfect for it to be real.

This was where she lived now, she supposed.

"What are you doing in Gig Harbor?" Delaney asked.

"Headed up to Olympic."

A hiker. That made sense. He had the vibe of one. Delaney's eyes slid to his feet again. No black toenails. No calluses.

Those weren't feet that had been in boots and wool socks for days on end.

Maybe he was a Seattle tech bro who fancied himself a bum. A weekend hiking warrior who stared at a computer the rest of his life.

"How about you?" he asked when she didn't say anything further.

Delaney donned her Lana Parker persona, even sans wig.

She was tired of her own brain, tired of the what-ifs, tired of the chess game she felt like she was playing against her dead sister. Roan probably was exactly who he said he was. And right now, she craved the relief that came with turning her brain off in this particular way more than she feared the consequences if she was wrong about that.

So she stood up, holding out her hand as she did.

"I'm playing a game," she said. "Do you want to join in?"

He followed her to her hotel room, because they always did.

EXCERPT FROM EMILY LOGAN'S BLOG POSTS

Three months before Isabel Parker's death

LC and I (separately but at the same time!) watched *Don't F**k with Cats* tonight and we could not have been more hooked! If y'all have been living under a rock, it's an old (2019!) documentary about a dude who killed two kittens by suffocating them in a plastic bag via a vacuum cleaner. (YEAH SICKO ALERT!) Some amateur sleuths launched an investigation and eventually figured out that he actually had also killed a girl (cue my surprise *end sarcasm).

I think the whole story shows how helpful it is to enlist as many people as possible to help solve cold cases, but LC isn't convinced. I don't *need* to convince her per se, but it would be cool if she could like throw me a bone or two. She's a cynic, though.

Professor OB (perv, but good teacher) will be happy with the paper, though. I'm like using real life examples to support my argument in favor of amateur sleuths and everything. Apparently that's important when it comes to psychology research.

I wrote four-thousand words last night after watching the documentary, way more than I need for the essay. But I don't think that's where I'm going to stop. This topic is *so cool*, and I have to keep working on it. Maybe it could even be a book one day, who knows!

LC made fun of me when I said that, but she has like a C+ in the class, so what does she know. (OK she knows a lot, and she has a C+ because Prof OB doesn't like that she's remote. But ANYWAY.)

I need to start making a list of family members to talk to—people who might hate my ideas in every single way.

Some people wouldn't have the balls to actually go talk to them, but I'm better than those people.

CHAPTER SIXTEEN

Raisa

Day Two

When Raisa finished reading Emily Logan's blog posts, she pulled up St. Ivany's contact and hit "Call."

The hospital's loudspeaker crackled to life just as the woman picked up, and Raisa waited until she could hear herself before asking, "What was this class?"

"What?"

"What was this class?" Raisa repeated with what she thought was profound patience. The waiting room was bright because of the fluorescent lights, but the night sky had gone dark outside. The doctor hadn't come out to give her any update on Kilkenny. She didn't want to think about whether that was a good or bad sign, because in what world was that a good sign? "The class that Emily Logan took with Professor OB, who is a perv but a good teacher."

"I don't know."

"Okay," Raisa said, and then hung up. She had no time for fools. Not now, especially, when she swore Kilkenny's blood was still caked beneath her fingernails.

She brought up the website for the local community college and ignored the incoming call from St. Ivany.

Raisa narrowed the available classes down to the psychology department—since that was the one specialty Emily had mentioned—and then scrolled until one jumped out at her.

Media Ethics: Fandoms and the Cult of Celebrity.

The phone rang again.

St. Ivany.

Raisa ignored it and found the name of the professor. Declan O'Brien.

The pervy professor.

The first death that Raisa accredited to Delaney—even if Isabel had done the killing—had been a professor. He'd targeted Delaney when she'd been a precocious high schooler taking college classes for credit.

She didn't know why that thought had popped into her head. But just like Delaney and Isabel, Raisa was good at spotting patterns, in writing and in life. That didn't always mean that they were important, but it was good to acknowledge they existed.

The swinging doors to the ICU opened, but the nurse who walked out was wearing a jacket and fiddling with her phone. She was off shift, clearly.

Raisa watched her, hoping against reason that the woman would turn around and tell her Kilkenny was going to be just fine.

Her stomach rolled as the nurse disappeared into the elevator and she went back to her phone.

A few minutes later, she found O'Brien's schedule. He had a night class that was set to end in forty minutes. If she was lucky, he would stop by his office after.

First, though, she had to bring herself to leave.

Raisa crossed to the nurses' desk. The man behind it glanced up, his expression sympathetic. "No news."

"Is he . . . ?" Raisa trailed off, not even knowing what to ask to try to shake loose *something* from these guard dogs, who had been tight-lipped all afternoon. They'd informed her at some point that he was out of surgery, but there had been no updates since then.

"Listen, why don't you go get some sleep," the nurse suggested, somehow both gentle and firm. "Your partner is going to need you in the morning."

Raisa swallowed and nodded, getting the message.

She wasn't about to go sleep, but she probably wasn't going to be let back there tonight. Unless anything catastrophic happened in the next hour or two, she wasn't about to miss an opportunity to go sit with Kilkenny.

"You have my—"

"Number," he said, with that same kind smile. "Yes, we'll make sure to call you right away with any updates."

A helpless anger flared in her chest at being interrupted. She knew there was no actual reason to be mad at this man; she knew this feeling stemmed from frustration and fear and was simply searching for an easy outlet. But if she didn't walk away in that moment, Raisa wasn't sure she could maintain the generally positive relationship she had with the guard dogs.

So, without saying anything, she turned and left.

Kilkenny's SUV was back at the hotel, so when she got outside, she called for a car.

While she waited for the ride, she did a simple search on O'Brien. He had several research papers published and even a few videos popped up—a sure sign of someone who was on the TED Talk circuit. The thumbnail picture of him revealed that he was young and handsome, with dark hair and blue eyes.

All his work concentrated on parasocial relationships between public figures and the worshipping masses, along with the ways that social media blurred the boundaries on what should and could be expected from each side.

In another situation, Raisa would have found the topic fascinating, but now, her eyes kept being drawn to the hospital lights.

Her biggest fear right now was that Kilkenny was going to die in there. Alone.

The thought was almost enough to drive her back into the building. But that would do nothing to help catch the person who had put Kilkenny in there. And maybe tracking down a professor in a class that may have a weak link to Isabel and one of the other victims wasn't doing much, either, to catch whoever had been driving the SUV, but it felt like forward movement.

Like when you pulled off a highway during a traffic jam and took a much longer route, but at least you were driving.

A white Tucson pulled to the curb a moment later, the license plate matching the information on the rideshare app.

The man behind the wheel was the quiet type, and Raisa continued her basic search for Declan O'Brien as they traveled through the darkened streets.

She pulled up a map of the small campus just on the outskirts of town, and when she got dropped at the main hall, she easily navigated her way to the psychology wing of the social sciences building. Then she simply wandered until she found O'Brien's office.

Her knees gave out then and she slid down the wall beside the door. At the hospital, she hadn't let herself close her eyes because all she could see in the darkness was Kilkenny's body, crumpled on the pavement.

He shouldn't have broken like he did. The car must have hit him just right. Or wrong.

Whatever.

She gulped in air, pressing the heels of her palms to her eyes so the tears gathering there wouldn't escape. She'd never once cried on the job and she wasn't about to start now.

"Hello?"

Raisa glanced up to find an extraordinarily handsome man hovering over her. Black hair, blue eyes. Emily Logan's professor.

The perv, if the girl was to be believed.

"Do you need help?" he asked, and she remembered just then that she was still wearing the borrowed scrubs.

She scrambled to her feet and held out her hand. "I'm Raisa Susanto. I'm an agent with the FBI."

He didn't flinch the way people who were guilty tended to when she introduced herself unexpectedly.

O'Brien slipped his palm into hers. "Dr. Declan O'Brien, though I assume you know that."

"I do," Raisa said with a nod. "Would you mind if I asked you a few questions?"

He glanced at his watch, and sighed. But then he stepped around her to open his office door. "This is about Emily Logan?"

"Yes," Raisa said, almost surprised he'd been able to guess, but she supposed she shouldn't have been. It was a small town, and no matter what Gabriela Cruz thought, homicides weren't exactly common in a place this size.

"I don't know how much I'll be able to help you, but I'll try," he said, waving at her to take a seat in one of the chairs across from his desk. The office was cozy in a way she hadn't been expecting, with warm artwork, more than a dozen plants, and a soft, colorful rug he'd obviously brought in himself. There was a messy air to the random stacks of books, loose paper piled up on the desk and personal photographs scattered throughout the room.

"Emily was in your class about the relationship between celebrities and their fans, correct?" Raisa asked.

"Yes," O'Brien confirmed. "It was a six-week summer class that has become quite popular in recent years."

"What was she like as a student?"

"Engaged and eager, though she didn't have the highest grades in the class," he said, considering. "She didn't seem to make any friends, but that's not unusual with older students like her."

"She was only twenty-three," Raisa pointed out.

"Which is five years older than your average freshman," O'Brien said. "I'm certainly not saying she was long in the tooth, only that I didn't find her behavior odd or off-putting."

But what about LC?

"Was there someone in the same class with the initials LC?" Raisa asked. "She was remote."

"Ah, yes, now that you mention it, they did pair up on a few projects," O'Brien said. "That would be Lindsey Cousins."

Raisa had suspected as much, but she hadn't wanted to leap to conclusions, seeing patterns where none existed. "Were you aware that she died two months ago?"

What looked like genuine surprise flashed into his expression, and he sat back in his chair. "Ah, that's a shame."

"Two girls who took your class are now dead," Raisa said, to make sure he picked up on exactly what she was saying.

His eyes narrowed, and she remembered then that they were in a mostly empty building and she hadn't brought a weapon.

"They were my students, yes, but I have hundreds of students a year," O'Brien said. "And Lindsey was virtual, which meant I pretty much checked to make sure she was attending. Beyond that, I didn't know much about either of them."

"Did you have any interactions with them outside of class?"

"No," O'Brien said, his brows collapsing into an insulted vee. "Should I have a lawyer?"

She stared at him. "It's your right to."

He sighed and ran a palm over his jaw. "I don't know what happened to either girl. They showed up for class, did assignments on time, and rarely talked to anyone else. That's about the extent of what I can tell you."

Raisa had a feeling that he was telling the truth, no matter how damning this connection was. "Okay. Can you tell me more about the class?"

O'Brien reached for one of his desk drawers, and a minute later she had a syllabus in her hands.

"That goes over everything," he said. "But broadly speaking we cover the A-listers in every part of the industry. And then we touch on more niche celebrities as well. The chefs, the reality TV show stars. And at the end we wrap up with the gray-area celebs."

"Gray-area?"

"The ones who only have a career because of their parasocial relationship with the audience," O'Brien said. Raisa thought about Essi at that, because what better way to sum up the woman? "So the social media influencers mainly, who pay their bills by making their followers think they're best friends. The Flik dancers who've monetized their accounts. People like that."

The words might have been harsh—*people like that*—but his tone wasn't. Raisa glanced down at the syllabus and tried to skim it quickly. She paused when she caught sight of the title of one of the sections, but she didn't want to lead him into an answer.

"Did Emily seem engaged in any one section more than others?"

O'Brien squinted in thought, his face serious. He probably could have run for office and been touted as a JFK look-alike. "She did write her final paper on the true crime boom, drilling down on the rise of armchair detectives and their relationships with law enforcement."

Raisa flexed her fingers to keep them from gripping the papers too tightly. "Do you remember what her thesis statement was in that paper?"

"Even better," he said. He stood and crossed to the bookshelves lining one whole side of the room. Then he pulled down an accordion file folder. "She never picked it up."

Raisa couldn't believe her luck. "What?"

"The day she turned it in was the last day she attended class," he said, handing the paper over.

PLAY-ALONG-AT-HOME SLEUTHS: DISTRACTIONS OR GODSENDS?

"She makes a fairly convincing argument that bringing in more people—hobbyists who don't need to be paid, at that—to help solve cold cases is a net positive for society," O'Brien said. "She even cites stats that show how successful *Unsolved Mysteries* was. Half the cases profiled on that show were eventually solved. Statistically, that's the average solve rate for detectives across the country."

"And the net negatives?"

"Revictimizing the families," O'Brien said. "A breakdown of the fourth wall, especially with podcasts. And then a muddling of timelines and evidence and suspects, of course."

"Did you ever listen to Jenna Shaw's podcasts for class?"

Jenna had been Isabel's cover for the time right before she'd been caught. She'd even established a podcast for "tinhatters" who wanted to listen to discussions about conspiracy theories.

His brows rose. "You mean Isabel Parker's podcast?"

"Yes."

"No, I didn't," he said. "Though plenty of my students have been interested in her, I didn't want to encourage anyone to get ideas about trying to visit her."

That was a pleasantly thoughtful take, which she probably shouldn't have been surprised at coming from a professor who taught about responsibly engaging in celebrities' lives.

"Okay, thank you," Raisa said, standing. "Can I ask where you were the night of the fifteenth?"

"The night Emily Logan was killed?" O'Brien asked, even though they both knew the importance of the date. "I was in Mexico, speaking at a conference. Feel free to email me for the details to verify them."

Raisa smiled, hoping to ease the sting of the question. "I had to ask."

"Yeah," O'Brien said, not looking too put out. "Can I ask *you* something?"

"Shoot."

"Do you think Emily got too close to Isabel Parker? Is that why she's dead?" He sounded worried, like his class had been what sent her careening headlong into danger.

"Honestly? I don't know." She knew why he was asking and felt reasonably sure she could offer him some comfort. "But I've read her blog posts. She was interested in the topic long before your class."

O'Brien nodded, though he didn't seem convinced. "Okay, thanks."

Her hand was on the door when he called out to her.

"Hey."

Raisa turned to find him studying her.

"Emily, she was intrigued the most about the families of the victims." He paused and licked his lips. "But also the families of the serial killers. I think she found that topic most fascinating of all—how it must be, to be associated with evil like that."

"So, everyone knows that I'm Isabel's sister."

"It's Gig Harbor, kid," O'Brien said, in a poor *Chinatown* impression. "Everyone knows everything about our most infamous resident."

CHAPTER SEVENTEEN

Delaney

Day Five

Roan, of the Carolina mountains, tried to linger, but Delaney shoved him on his way. He'd served his purpose—the few hours of mindless relief had been worth the risk. But she wasn't about to get sloppy now that dawn had broken.

Delaney sat cross-legged on the rumpled hotel bed and pulled her new laptop closer so she could plug in the USB with Isabel's notes on it.

Even though she had them memorized, she pulled up the first one she'd received, which had set this whole debacle into motion.

> Dear Delaney. Let's play a game. To get the rules, you must come see me.
> I know, I know, I know. You don't want to do that.
> But my dear sister, you will not like what happens if you don't.

She wondered, as she always did when she read these, if Raisa had received her own messages. What was the game Isabel wanted Raisa to play? How did the two of theirs interlock?

Because wasn't that the important part? It wasn't what Isabel *said* the game was—it was what she wanted her sisters to do, for reasons neither of them could know. Delaney had gone to talk to Isabel, had heard the parameters of the "game," had heard the consequences, and yet she still didn't know what part she was inadvertently playing on Isabel's chessboard.

"Find a killer," Isabel had said.

"Kill the killer," Isabel had said.

"Become as bad as me" had been silent, but relayed in the space between words.

Delaney still didn't understand the real *why*, though. And until she did, she wouldn't be able to beat Isabel.

The one thing she hadn't ever been able to do when her sister was alive.

The obvious choice was to simply not play.

But Delaney was pretty sure the consequence of such a decision was Raisa's life.

Not that her sister would be appreciative.

Normally, Delaney didn't care what people thought about her; she would have gone crazy a long time ago if she did. She wasn't particularly likable anyway. She said strange things at strange times—something Raisa had always called her out on. She cared more about numbers and patterns and logic than she did about someone else's emotions. She never got lonely. Though she had enjoyed the one long-term relationship she'd had, she'd had to break it off because he had been a detective who was too smart for his own good. Yet Delaney didn't *need* anyone, not like everyone else seemed to.

But she had built her life around Isabel. Not completely, not as much as Raisa probably thought. There were other people beyond even that one long-term relationship. There had been plenty of men like Roan, one-night stands to fill a need. She'd taken vacations and gone to the beach and swum in the water and walked in forests. When she looked back on her life, though, those were the moments that seemed *in between* the rest. Her thoughts had always returned to Isabel, how to find her, how to stop her.

There was a space there now, a void she kept returning to and hitting a brick wall when she did.

Isabel was dead.

And every time Delaney had that thought, she felt the tug from Raisa, off in her peripheral vision.

It scared her.

Not because Raisa scared her but because that tendency toward obsession was what had been so terrifying about Isabel. Delaney had the same compulsion—she couldn't even deny it. Her track record spoke for itself.

But if she couldn't channel it toward Isabel, why wouldn't it latch right onto Raisa?

With Isabel, at least, that obsession had been productive; it had let her at least get close to stopping a prolific serial killer.

It would not be productive with Raisa.

And with that thought, Delaney slammed the laptop closed. She slid it into a bag—she wasn't about to leave anything possibly incriminating behind while Roan knew what room she was staying in—and then dressed quickly.

There was still a game to be played.

———

"You never told me your name."

Delaney looked up, pleased to find Gabriela Cruz standing over her table. She was the reason Delaney had come to this coffee shop—the girl had posted stories to her Flik from here at least four times a week—and it had only taken two hours of loitering for Gabbi to do so.

"Kate," Delaney said, because it was easy and forgettable. Gabbi wouldn't be able to search it, either.

"Mind if I sit?" Gabbi asked, though she was already pulling out the chair.

Delaney laughed. "Seems like you don't need my permission."

Gabbi ripped off the top of the chocolate chip muffin she'd bought, and stuffed it joyfully in her mouth. It almost hurt to look at someone so impossibly young. Delaney had been a world-weary cynic by the time she'd been Gabbi's age.

"Did your friend's daughter make it home okay?"

"Yes," Delaney said. "Did you hear anything about what happened to the girl in the woods?"

"No, I asked around," Gabbi said, lifting one shoulder dismissively. But Delaney thought she might care more than she let on. She'd shared several date-rape infographics on her Flik page that morning. "No one seems to even know who the blonde was."

That surprised Delaney. "You didn't recognize her?"

"Nope," Gabbi said, popping another chunk of muffin into her mouth.

"What about the boys?" Delaney asked, pretending not to remember their names.

Benny Thompson.

Brad Something.

Benny didn't have social media, or at least if he did, it was under some other version of his name. Kids were smarter these days about their digital footprint, so she didn't find that unusual. She hadn't been able to find a Brad registered with the local college, but that didn't necessarily mean anything, either.

Delaney had been at that party, too, and she wasn't exactly a student.

"I don't know them that well, just friends of friends of friends," Gabbi said. "All I know is that Brad looks like he's going to do coke in the bathroom while he's clerking for a Supreme Court justice. And Benny seems to fit the mold for weirdo high school shooter."

She made a face. "Sorry, sometimes I use dark humor as a coping method to weather the shitstorm of terribleness in the world, and it doesn't always come out right."

A feeling Delaney knew well. "I don't disagree."

Gabbi's face lit up. But she just shrugged again. "Yeah, well."

Delaney needed to direct the conversation into a certain place, only she wasn't always very smooth at doing so in person.

"What have you tried?" Delaney asked, probably a little inelegantly, given the immediate confusion on Gabbi's face.

"What?"

"You said you've tried to do something, about Benny and Brad," Delaney said. "The other night. What have you tried?"

Gabbi's eyes narrowed as she studied Delaney's face. "Just stuff like I mentioned. We have DDs—not for driving, just for one of us to be clearheaded if we need to rescue someone."

"Nothing else?" Delaney asked.

"Like what?"

Delaney pressed a frustrated sound behind her lips. Gabbi wasn't going to come out and say anything damning to a stranger with just a few soft questions thrown her way. "Like going to the cops."

Gabbi full-on laughed in disbelief. "They don't even take on actual rape cases, let alone someone just saying that a couple of dudes make her uncomfortable."

That was true enough. Even when women showed up with bruises, at most they'd get a worthless piece of paper they could wave at their attacker right before they were killed.

"Sometimes I wish we lived in a comic book," Delaney said, and Gabbi leaned forward, arms on the table.

Intrigued.

"Why?"

"Vigilantes aren't actually cool in reality," Delaney said. "We have a justice system for a reason. But, god, wouldn't it feel nice just to have someone taking care of these assholes for us?"

"It would scare a bunch of other predators straight, too," Gabbi said, sitting back in her seat once more. "What kind of powers would you have? If this was a comic book."

For her, it was a no-brainer. It would be the power of invisibility. She'd wanted that from the time Isabel had them hiding in their childhood attic from Alex and his "attacks." She wouldn't do anything terrible or salacious with the power; she would simply be allowed to exist without having to constantly bend to someone else's wishes.

She thought of her apartment back in Seattle, the one where she'd begun to hang up posters and pictures and put books on the shelves. Then she thought about the eyes on the back of her neck when someone had found her hideaway.

Yeah. Invisibility would be nice.

But as *Kate?* Kate, who clearly had a background where she or a loved one had been a victim of sexual assault or some other unspeakable trauma? People like Kate didn't simply dream of disappearing.

"Laser eyes," Delaney said. "So I could burn the bad guys up and leave not a single trace behind."

Gabbi grinned and finished the last of her muffin. "Girl, you don't need superpowers for that."

EXCERPT OF TED TALK BY MALIK BAKIR: "TRUE CRIME OBSESSION AND ETHICAL BOUNDARIES"

Most people know the big serial killers—Ted Bundy, Jeffrey Dahmer, John Wayne Gacy.
The aficionados among us can even spout off some of their victims' names. Lisa Levy, Margaret Bowman. Steven Hicks, Anthony Sears. Kenneth Parker.
But violence isn't limited to the perpetrator and victim. Think of it instead as a rock dropped into a lake. The worst of the ripples, of course, are right around the point of impact, but then they flow out.
Those outside ripples? They're the secondary victims of violent crime. They're the loved ones, the family, the friends, the coworkers, even acquaintances who suffer the traumatic loss.
Depending on how big the stone—and considering we're talking about the victims of sadistic serial killers, that stone is pretty big—the impact can have devastating effects across the entirety of this metaphorical lake.
Our obsession with serial killers isn't new, or even all that disturbing. As highly social animals, it makes sense that we're intrigued by the abnormal. But in our current media environment, that obsession can turn into real harm.
The serial killer you're obsessed with is likely either dead or in jail. And it's too late to save their victims. But the loved ones? They're out there in the world, and you *do* have some responsibility to treat them with respect if you're engaging with their stories.

This isn't the junk food of culture, something to consume in a mindless haze.

I'm not here to tell you participating in true crime culture is bad or dangerous or wrong. All I'm asking is that you participate in it thoughtfully.

So, how do you do that?

Number One, ask yourself, whose stories are you listening to? Are they all some version of the Missing White Woman Syndrome? If so, is there a way you can branch out to listen to the stories of people from marginalized groups who have become victims, whose murders far fewer people are interested in solving?

Number Two, how much are the hosts commoditizing the murders? Are they selling merchandise? Do they have catchphrases? Are they constantly trying to get you to subscribe? Things of that nature are dehumanizing to the victim and their families.

Number Three, how are you participating in the culture? Are you becoming an armchair sleuth? Are you emailing the victims' families, or sending mobs after them because of your latest theory? Are you advocating for more awareness when people of color go missing, and not just young white girls?

What are the lines not to cross? I don't have the answers for you.

I'm not here to scold you, but rather present a reminder to myself as well.

Don't yourself become another rock dropped into that lake where people are trying not to drown.

CHAPTER EIGHTEEN

Raisa

Day Two

Raisa tried to make the puzzle pieces fit. She tried to make them fit as she called another car to come get her from campus, and she tried to make them fit on the ride back to the hotel. She tried to make them fit as she finally, finally, finally scrubbed herself completely clean of Kilkenny's blood.

And she couldn't.

So she finally returned Maeve St. Ivany's calls.

"Where do you live?" Raisa asked. "Send me the address."

St. Ivany hung up, but a second later, Raisa's phone vibrated with a text.

Raisa grabbed Kilkenny's keys from the adjoining room, slung her bag over her shoulder, and then headed for the door.

The house turned out to be one not unlike Raisa's own. It was small but cute and had a view of the harbor.

St. Ivany was waiting for her when she pulled up. "I am busy, you know."

Raisa glanced at the time. It was just after 11:00 p.m.

"Yeah, last time I got a full night's sleep was before Emily Logan was stabbed to death." St. Ivany turned, leading her back into the house. The living room was all bland beige walls and off-white furniture. There weren't any personal touches Raisa could see. It reminded Raisa of her apartment in Tacoma, the one she'd used as essentially a mailing address before she got her bungalow. Settling in had felt like too much work.

More notably, though, the room was messy. Papers were strewn everywhere, as were take-out containers and empty coffee mugs. A pile of clothes spilled off a chair and onto the floor, and the air was stale, smelling vaguely of sweat and artificial mango—the latter probably being St. Ivany's attempt to cover up the fact that she hadn't cleaned in at least two weeks.

"Yeah, it's not pretty," St. Ivany said. "Coffee or no?"

"Yeah, the strong stuff," Raisa said, as she lowered herself into the only clean chair. It was probably the one St. Ivany had been using, but Raisa didn't care.

Five minutes later, they both had their mugs and were eyeing each other, St. Ivany just as wary as Raisa was, clearly.

"I found a connection between Emily Logan and Lindsey Cousins," Raisa said, and then filled St. Ivany in on the last couple of hours.

"Declan O'Brien," St. Ivany murmured before leaning forward and typing his name into her computer. A minute later she shook her head. "No priors."

"He was in Mexico the night Emily Logan died," Raisa said. "Or at least says he was. Seems easy enough to check."

"I'll make sure someone gets the details in the morning," St. Ivany said, and Raisa nodded in thanks. It always sucked when she didn't have the full resources of the FBI behind her. "So, two girls in the same class, now dead."

"Both of them were involved in the true crime community," Raisa pointed out. "And the professor said everyone in town is interested in Isabel."

"Two deaths in the past two months," St. Ivany said, running a frustrated hand through her hair. "Goddamn."

"And Isabel," Raisa said. "And maybe a fourth."

St. Ivany squinted at her. "Get out of here."

"Gabriela Cruz flagged it with her formula," Raisa said.

"Gabriela," St. Ivany said on a sigh.

"What's your read on her?" Raisa asked.

"She's been working for or volunteering at the department for years now in various iterations of junior programs and internships," St. Ivany said. "I think she has the potential to be a great detective. I do worry about the way she latched on to Isabel, though."

"It will impede her career if she gets attached to every charismatic psychopath out there," Raisa agreed. "But I think she *was* right about Peter Stamkos's death being connected to all this. Isabel wrote his name in her journal—I'm guessing for me to find."

"Like I said, she'll make a good detective one day, if she can just get it together," St. Ivany said and then studied Raisa for a long moment. "What do you think Isabel was hoping to accomplish with that letter she sent you? The first one?"

Raisa thought again about what Kilkenny had said. *Isabel wanted you in Gig Harbor.*

"She wanted me to find her killer."

"Did she?" St. Ivany asked. "Because if she did, she would have said, 'This is the information I know, here is who I suspect is behind this, and this is why.'"

Raisa blinked at that. "Well. Yeah. But it's Isabel. She would never do something so straightforward."

"Even if she was trying to get whoever killed her locked up?"

"I never said that was the goal," Raisa parried before realizing what she was saying.

St. Ivany's expression turned smug. "Then what was the goal?"

To control me, Raisa thought, but didn't say. It felt too vulnerable. "To pretend she knew more than she did."

And that, finally, felt like the truth.

Isabel always wanted to be the mastermind in the room, and when she wasn't, she would try to fool everyone into thinking she was.

She had known she was being targeted—she was too smart and paranoid to write off that incident with the shiv as random.

But she hadn't known who it actually was, when it would happen, or how. Raisa guessed she'd simply paid someone to send Raisa that letter. She wasn't all knowing or all seeing.

She was dead.

"So you think we have a copycat on our hands," St. Ivany said with a sigh. "One who killed the person they were copycatting."

"There's still some logic to straighten out," Raisa admitted.

"A protégé who tried to run over Agent Kilkenny because you guys were getting too close to an answer?"

"That makes sense to me," Raisa said, not letting herself think of Kilkenny, fractured skull in her lap, face ashen. "And killed Emily Logan because she found something out, something damning. Or . . ."

"Or what?"

Raisa shrugged. "Someone wanted revenge on Isabel, couldn't get to her, so instead just started playing vigilante and killing psychopaths."

St. Ivany's brows shot up. "That would mean you think Lindsey, Emily, and Peter were all psychopaths."

"It could be what connects the victims," Raisa said. "We know Lindsey had signs of an antisocial personality disorder, and Peter abused his child. Isabel speaks for herself. So that leaves Emily."

"There's nothing that points to her being one," St. Ivany said carefully, but Raisa could tell she was intrigued.

"And nothing that doesn't."

"True," St. Ivany said, and then scrubbed her hands over her face. She was sitting on the floor in front of her coffee table, amid her stacks of file folders. And . . . she looked small, almost defeated. That lasted only for a second, before she stood, brushing off her pants. "I don't have the bandwidth to figure anything out tonight. I'm going to get some sleep, you can look through anything you want. Consider yourself officially invited onto the case."

And with that, St. Ivany left the room. Water started running a few seconds later.

Raisa stared out at the mounds of papers, most of which probably meant absolutely nothing, and instead went back to read through Emily Logan's final essay.

It was immediately clear off the hop how much Emily cared about this topic. She truly believed that the surge in true crime hobbyists was going to be a turning point in solving more cold investigations across the country. In fact, she seemed so passionate about it that Raisa searched for her name in the Bureau's unsolved cases, curious if Emily had a relative or loved one who had never received justice.

Nothing came up and Logan was too generic a last name to return anything helpful in a broader search. But Raisa noted to herself that Emily might have a personal stake in all this. That could always influence a person—radicalize a person, even. If the system had failed her, if a loved one's cold case was collecting dust somewhere, maybe that frustration had led her down the path to discovering something that had ultimately gotten her killed.

That's not the crime we're trying to solve, she heard in Kilkenny's voice. Raisa considered herself a competent agent and a fairly skilled linguist. But she wasn't perfect. She could get distracted when she got pulled in multiple directions. She knew her strengths and weaknesses—and a supervising agent she would never be.

She followed the rabbit down its hole too many times.

"What are we trying to solve?" Raisa asked the room, wishing she were asking Kilkenny himself.

Isabel's murder.

Raisa chewed on the inside of her cheek. Emily, Lindsey, and even Peter were all connected, and that path would lead back to Isabel, she was almost certain of that.

But the other path is clearer. Focus on Isabel first.

"No, it's not," she muttered, just to be annoying. Still, she dug in her bag for the Biggest Fan letters, the ones with the hiking trails mentioned in all of them. The ones that had been found in Isabel's cell, the ones that might be the key that Raisa was ignoring because she couldn't read her dead psychopath sister's mind.

There was something here that Isabel wanted Raisa to find; otherwise she would have left the letters and the rest of her possessions for Delaney.

The hiking trails, of course, stood out the most.

Whatever she was trying to communicate wasn't about the hiking trails themselves—a good thing, considering Raisa was a city girl through and through. All the letters that came in and out of the correctional facility had the chance of being read. It was even such common practice to infuse paper with drugs such as fentanyl that some prisons had moved toward scanning any incoming letters and sending them to the inmates as a digital copy.

Isabel and her Biggest Fan were using the hiking trail names to talk about something that would slip past all those guardrails.

It made Raisa think about how Delaney had communicated with Isabel when they were teenagers. She'd simply created a blog where she "talked into the void" about people who had grievously wronged her. Isabel had been there waiting to read it all and then act on it.

Not only had it been easy, but there was plausible deniability on Delaney's side of things. Enough that the DA hadn't even bothered to throw some conspiracy charges her way.

Of course, online blogs or forums like that would be a great way for someone to communicate with Isabel behind bars as well. Prisoners didn't have access to the internet beyond educational classes and monitored email—in theory. But Raisa had read enough memos from the Bureau to know there were plenty of creative ways to successfully smuggle cell phones into prisons. Once you had that as a tool, it was easy enough to find Wi-Fi somewhere. In one case, an inmate had even used the Wi-Fi set up for the nurse's printer.

Raisa didn't think Isabel would be able to run roughshod on the dark web, but it was believable that she would've been able to access someone's blog.

Or someone's . . .

Her eyes slipped to the hiking trail mentioned in the first letter.

"Holy shit." Raisa sat up, scrambling for her computer. She grabbed it from her bag and booted it up.

When she got to a blank internet page, she simply ran a search on the trail name. The very first response was from a website designed especially for hikers to track the summits they hit.

Raisa clicked into it. There was so much information, so many numbers that could have pulled her attention.

Instead of scouring any of that data, she scrolled down. There, at the bottom of the page, was a place for hikers to leave their reviews.

"Holy shit," Raisa breathed again. It really was as easy as that.

The trail wasn't a popular one. There were hikes in a sidebar that had 20,000-plus reviews, but the Muddy Waters Conservatory outside Macon, Georgia, had 126 total, and only 32 from the current year.

Raisa scrolled down until she found the posts near the time of the first Biggest Fan letter.

Her heartbeat ticked up and she laughed, incredulous.

Because there, posted the same day as the letter was dated, was a review from a user who went by *Becks P.* Their mother's name.

Terrible hike. This whole trail all I could think about was how much I wanted Isabel to stop going close to the edge. I wanted to remind her that if she fell, she would probably pull me down with her. Not that she cared. She would do what she wanted. One star.

There were a few comments underneath noting that maybe the user got confused about which hike they did, because there were no cliff edges on the trail. But no one had taken it down.

Raisa was almost stunned at the simplicity of it all.

She reread the message and then, slowly, she worked her way through all the letters. They didn't all have reviews—possibly a safeguard to anyone from the correctional facility deciding to randomly check this website. It became clear, though, that whoever was writing the "reviews" wanted Isabel to stop playing some kind of game. It had not worked out well for the letter writer before, and said author was nervous and resentful about the fact that she was going to get dragged back into whatever Isabel was doing.

The "Biggest Fan" was, it turned out, an ironic sign-off.

Raisa brought up her text thread with Delaney, and couldn't ignore the fact that her sister hadn't responded. She couldn't ignore the fact that this method was similar to how Delaney had communicated with Isabel before. Couldn't ignore the fact that she could easily see Delaney being dragged into a game even if she hadn't wanted to be.

She shook her head.

She might want Delaney to face consequences for the way she'd sat on the sidelines for so long, but she couldn't see her sister getting within a hundred miles of Isabel's bullshit again.

Delaney wouldn't.

Except . . .

She toggled back to that first review. Becks P. She couldn't ignore the fact that it was their mother's name the poster had used.

Raisa swallowed hard.

She found the last review and read through it again. It had been posted under the name *Magdaline*, which was the street Emily Logan had lived on.

Great hike, but I have to tell y'all, my daughter screamed the whole time. "I won't do it, I won't do it. You can't make me."

A few commenters commiserated beneath the post. And then there, in black and white, was a post from "Isabel."

My daughter's the same way. I always give her a choice. She can either do it or she'll pay the price for not doing it. She's never had to ask what the price is—she knows it will be devastatingly steep.

St. Ivany cleared her throat, and Raisa yelped, nearly throwing the computer. As calmly as she could, she closed the lid, not wanting to share what she'd just discovered. "You scared the crap out of me."

"You found something," St. Ivany said, in a soft voice. There was a strange expression on her face.

And this, this must have been how Delaney had felt all those years. Because Raisa knew exactly what she *should* do, which was tell the law enforcement agent standing in front of her exactly what she'd unearthed. What her gut was screaming at her to do, though, was to think on it for longer, make certain she was sure it really had been Delaney communicating with Isabel.

"No, just more nothing," Raisa said, her fingers clenching against the edges of the laptop.

St. Ivany cocked her head. "Oh yeah, is that right?"

How long had she been standing there? Raisa glanced toward the door, and only then realized she didn't have a clear line to it. Was it locked? She couldn't remember if St. Ivany had thrown a dead bolt.

"Yeah," Raisa said, standing. "I think I'm going to call it a night, too."

"You don't have to leave," St. Ivany said. She hadn't moved, but for some reason Raisa pulled the computer closer to her belly to protect it.

"I better . . ." Raisa gestured over her shoulder before bending to gather her stuff. She wasn't being as careful as she could with it, but all she could think was that she had to get out *now*.

"You're not telling me something," St. Ivany said, eyes narrowed. There was anger there . . . and something else Raisa couldn't read.

Raisa shook her head, backing away until she hit the door.

"You should lock this behind me," she called out, before stepping into the cool night air.

Maybe it was stupid to choose the dark and what waited there. In the light of day, she would probably find her own actions silly. After all, there was no reason to protect Delaney—if that was even what she was doing.

But, right now, she would take her chances with the shadows.

CHAPTER NINETEEN

Raisa

Day Three

When Raisa woke after a few hours of sleep following her flight from Maeve St. Ivany's house, she had three missed texts from the woman making sure she'd gotten home safe.

She sent back a quick reply and then called the hospital.

"He's stable, but still hasn't woken up yet," the nurse on duty informed her, and Raisa gritted out a "thank you."

She dropped back on the pillow and stared at a crack in the ceiling.

Had it been Delaney behind the wheel?

That was hard to imagine. Kilkenny had been the one to fight for her. He'd worked with her for years—maybe without ever knowing her name. But still, it had led to a loyalty that Raisa personally thought Delaney didn't deserve.

There had also been something meaningful that had happened between the two of them on that night Raisa had been shot. Kilkenny had glossed over their interaction when he'd found Delaney at the library, trying to destroy a picture of their family before Kilkenny could realize who she was.

But Raisa had always sensed there was more to it. A bond that had formed that couldn't be broken even by Delaney's bad behavior.

She wondered now how bad that behavior could get.

Before, Raisa tolerated Delaney because she'd never actually killed anyone.

Now she wondered if Isabel might have forced Delaney's hand.

I won't do it, I won't do it. You can't make me.

Raisa pressed her eyes shut.

She was leaping to conclusions again. Sometimes, though, that was a necessary part of an investigation. People who were able to see patterns often became agents or detectives. Just like with conspiracy theories, it could lead someone astray. But the skill itself wasn't a detriment.

So she let herself walk down that path.

Isabel wanted Delaney to *do* something. Kill someone? Maybe the protégé?

She'd threatened Delaney with a high price—death, perhaps. Of herself or Raisa. Or even Kilkenny.

Something that Delaney couldn't shrug off and give up like it was nothing.

That would be the ultimate power trip for Isabel, wouldn't it? Getting Delaney to kill for her?

Raisa's phone rang. She almost ignored it, but then realized who was calling.

"Agent Susanto here," she said, picking it up.

"Hi, this is Julia Davis, calling from Washington State Department of Children, Youth, and Families."

Raisa punched the air in victory. "Julia, thanks for getting back to me. I'm looking into a homicide that might have a connection with Peter Stamkos. Is there anything you could tell me about the case?"

"Oh, well, it was as clear-cut as day," Julia said. She had a warm, gossipy voice. "Between you and me, I'm glad he didn't take his daughter with him when he killed himself."

Julia went on to provide details Raisa could have gotten on a public request, which were helpful but not necessarily enlightening.

"Did anyone suspect it was anything but suicide?" Raisa asked.

"Oh no, honey, not for a minute," Julia said, and then seemed to catch up to the question. "*Was* it?"

"No, no, I'm just checking boxes," Raisa said.

"Well, the only strange thing to note was the woman," Julia said.

Raisa's heart stuttered against her rib cage. "What woman?"

"According to the very nosy neighbor, there was a woman who sat outside watching Peter's house for a few days before he shot himself," Julia said. "Should I have gotten more info about her? It seemed like a coincidence."

"Did they give any details?" Raisa asked, hardly daring to hope.

"Just that she was middle-aged and wore her hair in a braid," Julia said, sounding like she was reading off notes. "They called her a hippie. I always like to take some initial impressions down, but I didn't actually include any of that in the report."

"So helpful, thank you, Julia," Raisa said, glad she didn't have to control her expression in person.

"Of course, hon, good luck."

Raisa hung up and stared at that stupid crack in the ceiling.

"Delaney," Raisa murmured into the empty room. It was strange, this. Raisa had spent the past two years wanting Delaney to step over the line so she could arrest her. Now that she might have, Raisa wanted more than anything to find out that Delaney really was in Fiji, that she'd dropped her phone into the ocean, that she'd forgotten Raisa's number and name and the very state of Washington.

A hippie, a middle-aged woman with a braid. Sure, that could describe a lot of people, but it definitely described Delaney.

Still . . . her sister sitting outside Peter Stamkos's house didn't necessarily mean that Delaney had been the one to kill him in a fashion startlingly familiar to Isabel's preferred method.

What if Isabel had been using Delaney to extend her own reach outside that prison cell? Delaney had grayscale morals, and Isabel knew that already. Why not take advantage of it?

Raisa's stomach turned. Even if Isabel had been the one directing Delaney, Delaney was an adult. She could have warned Kilkenny or Raisa if Isabel had threatened either of their lives. At the very least, Kilkenny would have believed her.

It was never better to take a life—even if that life wasn't worth the oxygen it took to survive.

A sudden knock on the door had her eyeing the safe where she kept her gun.

She dismissed the instinct as paranoia and crossed the room.

The bored teenage girl who worked the boutique hotel's front desk stood there, holding an envelope by two of its diagonal corners so that it spun in an idle circle. "Mail."

Raisa took it with a "Thanks. Did you see who dropped it off?"

"Nope," she said. "It was waiting there when I came back from the bathroom."

The teenager held out a hand and Raisa nearly laughed at the chutzpah. Instead, she went to get a five-dollar bill before sending the girl on her way.

The envelope just had her name written across the front.

Raisa opened it.

Inside was a newspaper clipping.

It was from a few years ago, detailing a sad case of a dog having to be put down because it had bitten a young girl who'd been visiting the area with her family.

One quote in particular had been highlighted in bright yellow.

"He's got the taste of blood now. It's a tragedy, but you gotta do what you gotta do."

That insightful take on the situation had been from a school board member who clearly shouldn't have been asked about it, considering the blood thing was a myth.

There didn't seem to be any hidden codes here—this was a clear message. Someone had gotten the taste for killing and now needed to be stopped.

Raisa stood and quickly dressed, making sure to lock the article clipping in beside her gun.

Then she headed for the harbor.

The entire way there, she kept glancing over her shoulder, waiting for the rev of an engine. She even had to shove her shaking hands into the pockets of her blazer.

She thought of Kilkenny's warning. *Isabel wants you in Gig Harbor.*

She thought of St. Ivany's serious expression. *Why do you think the SUV was aiming for Agent Kilkenny and not you?*

And she let herself think about Isabel, what Isabel would want most, if Isabel had known she was marked for murder.

Raisa, Delaney, and Isabel all dead. Because how could Raisa and Delaney be permitted to live if it wasn't beneath the shadow of their older sister?

It was early, but Essi Halla stood at the rail of her boat, coffee in hand, watching the sun come up. The scene was so perfect it almost looked like it was a setup for a next possible book cover. The title could be *How to Use Your Father's Death as a Way to Grift the Real Victims of an Infamous Serial Killer.*

Perhaps a little wordy, but at least it would be accurate.

Essi turned when Raisa called out a greeting, breaking into a smile before she caught sight of Raisa's face.

"What's wrong?" Essi asked, and Raisa saw in that moment what so many of Essi's victims must have. Genuine concern—empathy, even. It was such a skill to be able to portray that.

"What do you mean?"

"Don't take this the wrong way, but you look like you've aged thirty years since I last saw you," Essi said. "And also like you're a Victorian child suffering from tuberculosis."

Raisa huffed out a breath. She couldn't even be insulted—she was sure that was exactly what she looked like. "My partner. He was involved in a hit-and-run. He's currently in the hospital."

"Oh." Essi had the controlled reactions of a practiced lawyer. Her mouth pursed into a distressed moue, her brows pinched together, her voice settled into something soft and gentle. "I'm so sorry. Will he . . . ?"

She shook her head, cutting herself off. "Well, what can I help you with? I'm sure you're not here right now to shoot the shit."

Raisa was thankful she didn't have to handle Essi's sympathy. That was one of the hardest things about grief and trauma. Everyone wanted you to make *them* feel better when all you wanted to do was curl up into a tight ball to protect yourself from feeling anything.

"Have you ever encountered a young woman named Emily Logan?" Raisa asked.

Essi considered it for a moment. "No, not that I can recall."

"She might have gone by another handle online," Raisa said. "She was a college student who was writing about the benefits of armchair detectives in relation to the rise of true crime podcasts and documentaries."

"Honestly, I get emails from people like that all the time," Essi said. She tapped a long neon-pink nail against her coffee mug. "Oh, here—let me search the folder I keep those in."

She disappeared into the cabin, only to emerge a minute later with a tablet. "Oh, shit. You were right."

Raisa's heartbeat ticked up as she took the device Essi held out.

An email from Emily Logan.

Interview Request, the subject line read.

The message was simple and professional, just laying out that Emily was looking to talk to people on the other side of the argument for a paper she was writing. She also acknowledged that she didn't expect to hear back from Essi but was trying to be thorough.

"Honestly, if I'd seen that one, I probably would have replied," Essi said with a shrug. "But my assistant manages my inbox for me. I went through a deluge in the beginning from those people. They all thought I could be convinced to their side. Some of them included death threats, so my assistant just filters them all into a folder we keep in case we have to show the police."

"Smart," Raisa murmured.

Essi shrugged and took a sip out of her giant mug, once again looking like a marketer's dream. It prompted Raisa to ask about something she'd been thinking about. "Hey, you have a book coming out soon?"

Essi grinned, proud. "I do."

"You don't have an early copy, do you?"

"No, I'm sorry, all out," Essi said, with a disappointed pout.

Raisa shook her head. "I'll just have to buy it like the rest of the commoners, I suppose."

Essi laughed again and Raisa studied her.

"Forgive me for saying it, but you don't seem the type to be bothered by harsh emails."

"Death by a thousand cuts," Essi said. "I have tough enough skin that it would take a while, but why put myself through that? As long as they're emailing me—which means I'm relevant to them—that's all that matters."

There were flashes of the mercenary side of Essi that Raisa had noticed last time, too, but that was more blatant than she'd been expecting. Raisa decided to nudge the impulse, just a little.

"What's easier, then? Getting the attention of the people who adore you or hate you?"

Essi's eyes narrowed, revealing a little glimpse beyond her bubbly facade. That warmth distracted from the fact that, beneath it, there was a thick slab of ice.

"You want honesty? I don't care. I want them looking at me," Essi said, holding her hands out to indicate herself. "I've never pretended to be a saint."

"You have, though," Raisa said, not sure where the brutal honesty was coming from. Still, she thought of Mildred in the parking lot, crying over her dog and the fact that Essi Halla had helped her move on from despair.

"To you," Essi corrected. "I've never pretended to be a saint to you."

For some reason, it seemed like, to Essi, that mattered.

Gabriela Cruz opened the door just as quickly as she had the last time Raisa had been on her stoop.

"I heard about Agent Kilkenny," Gabriela said, her eyes wide and curious. Without waiting to be asked, she stepped back, letting Raisa in. Gabriela curled up in her chair next to a whiteboard, which now had Kilkenny's name added to it. There was something so vulnerable about seeing *Callum* beside the rest of the victims that Raisa had to look away.

"I don't want to talk about him," Raisa said, firmly. Gabriela would try to get details out of Raisa—that was her personality. She needed to keep the girl focused. "Did you know Emily Logan?"

Gabriela licked her lips. Nervous, maybe.

"I mean, I knew her in passing. She waitressed at the Kraken's Favorite Fisherman." Gabriela looked up. "It's a popular tourist restaurant here."

"You ate at a tourist restaurant enough times to know one of their waitresses in passing?" Raisa asked. She began to wander the space, stopping by the bookshelf.

As Raisa would have guessed, it was stocked with psychological thrillers and cozy mysteries side by side with all the big nonfiction serial killer books of the last twenty years.

"My friend likes their fried calamari, and they have dollar-drink Wednesdays," Gabriela said. "Are you going to arrest me for taking advantage of a good deal?"

It was interesting that Gabriela had arrived at *arrest me* so quickly. "Did you know Emily through school, at all?"

"I saw her around," Gabriela said. "She wasn't super friendly when she wasn't waitressing. She mostly just kept to herself."

That was what the professor had said as well.

"Did you know Emily through the true crime community?" Raisa asked, hoping to catch her slightly off guard.

Gabriela scoffed and then turned it into a cough.

Raisa lifted her brows. "What?"

"Nothing."

"You knew her, didn't you?" Raisa pressed.

Gabriela shrugged. "She cared about true crime, not Isabel Parker in particular. So, yeah, we crossed paths in some online forums, but we didn't run in the same circles."

"It sounds like there's more to it."

"She was getting a reputation," Gabriela said slowly. "For being a nuisance, really breaking the fourth wall a lot. A lot, a lot."

"What does that mean?" Raisa asked, thinking she knew but wanting to hear it.

Gabriela looked at her like she was an idiot. "It's the boundary between any piece of work or performer and their audience."

Raisa shook her head. "I know what the fourth wall is as a term. What does it mean for your community?"

"Oh," Gabriela said, some of the teenager falling out of her posture. "Contacting police. Harassing family members of both victims and killers."

"She didn't contact me," Raisa said, though that wasn't where her mind had landed.

Gabriela shot her a look. "You're . . . off limits."

"What?"

"Don't you ever wonder why you haven't been bothered by . . ." Gabriela waved her hand in the air. "All this? There's, like, an unspoken agreement between everybody not to contact you. Even Emily followed it, apparently."

Raisa blinked at her. "Why?"

"You're FBI," Gabriela said, with a shrug. "You're bad for business, if you know what I mean."

"Is Delaney exempt from that mentality?" Raisa asked. When Gabriela stared at her blankly, she added, "My sister. Delaney Moore."

"Oh, right, duh." Gabriela shook her head. "No, but she's impossible to find."

"Really?" It didn't seem like anyone could hide in this day and age.

"Yeah, she's, like, a computer whiz," Gabriela said, the words coming out in a rush.

Delaney had spent plenty of time and energy making sure there were no pictures of her on the internet, too. She was a ghost.

Hopefully not an actual one.

Raisa pressed Gabriela for a few more minutes, but seemed to have tapped that particular well.

When she walked outside, it was to find Detective St. Ivany leaning against the SUV.

Raisa hesitated, but continued forward without too much of a hitch in her step.

"You good?" St. Ivany asked. "I was heading into work and I saw your SUV."

"Yeah," Raisa said, not sure if she believed this was a coincidence. In the light of day, her actions from the night before seemed weird. St. Ivany was checking up on her.

St. Ivany's eyes slid over Raisa's shoulder. "You were talking to Gabriela Cruz?"

"Yeah, I'm trying to get more information about Emily Logan, and how she fit into the FreeBell movement," Raisa said. "Turns out, she wasn't involved."

"Really?" St. Ivany asked, sounding surprised.

"Nope, just true crime in general," Raisa said, and then she realized she'd never asked St. Ivany a fairly important question. "Hey, who do you think killed Emily?"

"The boyfriend," St. Ivany said, without hesitation.

"He was out of town."

"Sort of. Just over in Seattle, and his alibi was that he was sleeping in a hotel room by himself," St. Ivany said. "And there was no reason for him to go—he just wanted to catch a Mariners game."

"Ah," Raisa said, because they'd all seen enough cases like that.

"He also works for the hospital, so he's used to cleaning up blood," St. Ivany said. "Which might explain why the crime scene was so clean."

"But you haven't brought him in?" Raisa asked.

St. Ivany made a frustrated sound before looking away. "I can't get him on anything. And the judge doesn't agree with my assessment of the kid's alibi."

"Did they have a fight? What's the motive?"

"Emily was apparently wildly jealous," St. Ivany said. "She posted his ex-girlfriend's nude photos on porn sites. He said he didn't know about it—which lines up with what several of her friends told us independently of each other."

"But he might have found out and flipped." It would explain the overkill. "Well, there's our obvious explanation if we believe in Occam's razor."

"Yeah," St. Ivany said dryly. "A little more believable than she somehow got caught up in a scheme involving a serial killer's protégé."

Raisa shrugged, even though she had just been the one to suggest they shouldn't be looking for zebras. Her life was full of unbelievable cases. It had started out with her parents being killed and her brother being framed for the murders, and had only gotten wilder from there. She did not struggle with suspending her disbelief.

"Didn't you bring someone else in?"

"Yeah, it was some guy she was spotted having coffee with a few days before she died," she said. "He said he was just an old friend passing through town, and we traced his whereabouts that night through a couple different security cameras. There was no way he could have been near Emily's place when she died."

St. Ivany paused and then laughed, though it wasn't with any kind of humor. "That's the first time you really asked about Emily Logan in a way an impartial detective would."

Raisa winced. "I'm sorry. You're right, we did come in with an agenda."

"Yeah, and I'm trying not to get swept up in it," St. Ivany said, running her fingers through her hair. "To me the boyfriend is still the most likely guy. And, honestly, it would be a dereliction of duty to proceed otherwise."

Raisa got it, she did. St. Ivany was likely dealing with one of her first homicide cases. But there was a huge elephant in the room she wasn't about to ignore.

"Then who do you think put Agent Kilkenny in the ICU?" Raisa asked. "And what exactly is your team doing to find that person?"

St. Ivany's cheeks went pink, though it could've been from any number of emotions. Anger. Embarrassment. Shame. Raisa wasn't about to presume she'd actually landed a blow.

"We're pulling red light cameras," St. Ivany said. "And I've got several guys out there looking for the SUV that hit him."

"That's going to be a fruitful search. One of the most popular versions of a black SUV," Raisa drawled. "Look, I don't know what's going on here any more than you do, but acting like there isn't a potential killer gallivanting about town with the balls to run down an FBI agent is dangerous."

"Thank you, Agent Susanto," St. Ivany said. "I don't know what our tiny backwater town would do without all your excellent advice."

"Right." Raisa reached for the door handle of her SUV so she wouldn't say what she wanted to, the movement forcing St. Ivany out of the way. "As fun as this has been . . ."

St. Ivany made a frustrated sound. "I'm trying my best, believe it or not, Agent Susanto."

"Oh, I believe it," Raisa said, before immediately regretting the barb. St. Ivany's face completely shut down. She turned and headed back to her cruiser.

Raisa felt Kilkenny's silent judgment all the way from the hospital, and she wondered when he'd become her Jiminy Cricket. "Hey."

St. Ivany stopped but only half turned.

"I'm fucking up left and right," Raisa admitted. "I can't tell my ass from my head in this case. I'm scared as hell that my best friend is going to die and our last conversation was a fight. And on top of all that, I'm worried that the sister I think should be locked up anyway is actually involved in all of this, because it means not only am I right that everyone in my family is a monster, but also . . . I wanted her to be better than that. I wanted her to be good."

At some point during that word vomit, St. Ivany had fully turned toward her. She'd even stepped closer.

Raisa exhaled and laughed at herself. "So. Yeah. I apologize for the sarcasm."

"Why do you think your sister is involved?" St. Ivany asked.

"That's what you got out of all that?" Raisa shot back.

"I mean, we can sing 'Kumbaya' and talk about your feelings if you prefer," St. Ivany said, with a tiny grin that seemed to mean Raisa's bloodletting had actually worked in repairing whatever had been fracturing here. "But I'm trying to solve a couple homicides and an attempted one along with it."

Raisa's lips twitched, before she sobered once more. "Delaney Moore, I mentioned her before."

"Right, you thought she might need protection," St. Ivany said. She tilted her head. "You're a bit of a worrier, aren't you?"

For my people, Raisa thought but then shook her head. Delaney wasn't her people.

"Maybe," she conceded. "But maybe ask Kilkenny if I worried enough."

"That wasn't your fault."

A blur of movement, pavement, blood. A cracked skull that was incompatible with life.

"Wasn't it?" Raisa asked, but then shook her head. She couldn't think about Kilkenny right now and she certainly couldn't think about the fact that he had been in the path of that SUV—that he'd been in Gig Harbor at all—because of her. "Anyway. It's just a feeling, about Delaney. I'm going to head to the correctional facility to check the visitors' logs. Kilkenny and I got derailed from doing that by the hit-and-run."

St. Ivany studied her for a moment. "Do you have an address for Delaney?"

Part of her wished she'd kept her mouth shut about it—but she knew that made her a hypocrite. "No. Just somewhere in Seattle. She's hard to find."

"Well, she's never had to hide from *me*," St. Ivany said, cocky.

"She's shaking in her boots, I'm sure," Raisa said, but it felt like banter rather than the insult from earlier. She climbed into the driver's seat. "I'll keep you updated."

"Sure you will," St. Ivany said. "I'll do the same."

Raisa rolled her eyes right before shutting the door. "Sure you will."

Still, she drove away from the curb thinking that she might have created an ally by letting her guard down. It was quite the concept.

Kilkenny would be proud.

DISCUSSION ON R/ISABELPARKERVICTIMS

MODERATOR: Hey guys, I've been thinking a lot lately about how many people are trying to claim Isabel Parker killed their family member. Like, I'm really sorry for them and everything, but you can't just pin every accident or suicide or whatever on Isabel. I think we have to figure out a way to get an accurate list of her victims so these fame-whores can't get their fifteen minutes of attention any more.

BELLYBELIEVER: I KNOW! It's actually soooooooo frustrating to have every conversation taken over by these "victims," it's like get a grip your dad OD'd because he was a deadbeat drug addict who didn't love you not because Isabel is some type of comic-book villain who can be all over the country in the blink of an eye

MOD: That's what gets me! *Most* of her victims were on the west coast—like she actually *did* have a pattern if you followed her even a little bit. Yet people in like Maine are crawling out of the woodwork and going on podcasts, it's so infuriating . . .

PARKTHATBUS: But what can we even do about it? It's not like she's going to just write a list out—she never has before, she won't even admit to the ones she was charged for.

MOD: I'm going to try to visit her. Maybe if she sees that there are people out there who want to make sure she's not pinned for every single death in the past twenty-five years, she'll share her real list. It's not like she can get *more* time on her sentence.

BELLYBELIEVER: oHHHHHHHHH!!!! So jealous!!! If you get to see her, tell her we love her and are rooting for her

MOD: I absolutely will

CHAPTER TWENTY

Delaney

Day Five

Roan, of the Carolina mountains, was waiting for Delaney by the empty pool.

"You drink?" Roan asked, holding out an open bottle of cab sav despite the fact that it couldn't be much past 1:00 p.m. It looked like a generic brand but Delaney wasn't about to be picky.

"Only on good days," she said, plopping down next to him and letting her legs dangle over the edge. She took the proffered bottle and swallowed a decent amount before passing it back.

"Today was a good day? It's not even over yet."

"Today was a not-bad day. Or, this morning was a not-bad morning," Delaney said, amused with herself. "So in my life that counts."

"Oh yeah?" Roan asked, with an easy smile, waggling the bottle to get her to take it once more. "Did someone nice share their wine with you?"

Delaney grinned. "Among other things."

"Do tell."

"No, I don't think I will," Delaney said, holding on to the bottle longer this time. "Tell me about your morning. Aren't you supposed to be gone?"

That last bit was a good reminder that not only did she not know this man, but she didn't know if he was secretly hunting her.

"Some kind of beauty caught my eye here," Roan said, nodding in her direction.

Delaney laughed because the implication was that she was beautiful and she wasn't. Once she started laughing she couldn't stop until she was flat on her back, looking up at the sky above, tears running down her cheeks from the corners of her eyes. "You don't need to use lines on me. Wine will do."

Roan lowered himself onto his forearm so that he was closer but still above her. "We don't need to watch sunsets but they sure make life better."

"You are something else," Delaney said. She wanted him to be who he said he was. She wanted this to be simple. "What did you do with your day so far?"

He looked away. "I thought about renting a boat. But I found a trail along the cliffs at the edge of town instead."

"Why not the boat?"

"Um, you know movies might have made you think every bum you run into is a prince in disguise, but I left my trust fund in another life," he said, eyes creased in amusement.

"I'll take you out," Delaney said.

It sounded like a dreamy promise, one that was meant to be broken even before it was made.

His brows shot up. "Are you a princess in disguise?"

Delaney laughed again. She wasn't wealthy—there was no trust fund—but she was comfortable enough. She was so good at investing that if she wanted to devote her life to it, she could probably do that as her sole job. As it was, she always had a cushion that made escape a little more doable.

She could rent a boat.

So she did.

It turned out Roan actually knew what he was doing, so Delaney took up a spot on the bow. As they sailed toward the horizon, Delaney thought about Isabel.

Not because she would have loved this day or this moment, but because she wouldn't. Delaney had rarely let softness into her life, had rarely seized happy moments.

But Isabel was dead now.

Delaney was allowed to enjoy this.

They found a spot to drop anchor and then broke out a basic late lunch of cheese and bread. They kissed and chatted and were free in a way Delaney hadn't been—save for the night before—in a long time.

She liked this, liked Roan. Liked who she was *with* him.

"When are you leaving?" Delaney asked, hardly knowing what she wanted him to answer. She shouldn't want him to stay, but . . .

"I don't know, a few days? You could come with me," Roan suggested in a rush. "We could go find some views to see and some oceans to sail." He paused. "Either off the peninsula or anywhere. I'm not picky."

"A rolling stone, huh?" Delaney teased. "I can't leave for a bit, though. Maybe on your way back."

"What's keeping you here?"

Delaney decided to be honest. Maybe she would regret it, but for once she didn't want to play a game.

"My sister died," Delaney said. "She lived here."

"Oh," Roan said. He pushed the sunglasses up into his hair. "Are you sad about it?"

That was a loaded question. "Yes."

"I'm sorry you're having to deal with that," Roan said. "Alone?"

"Yes," Delaney confirmed. She didn't want to think about Raisa right now, didn't want to bring her sister into this moment. But for one second, she imagined what it would have been like to experience this all with her. From the normal—making funeral arrangements.

To the abnormal that would only happen in their family—hunting down a killer.

"Do you need any help?" Roan asked.

Delaney thought about Isabel's notes, the games. "I don't know. Maybe."

"You just gotta ask, Delaney Moore," Roan said.

Delaney kept smiling through the realization that she'd never told him her last name.

CHAPTER TWENTY-ONE

Raisa

Day Three

Raisa's hotel door was cracked open.

She stuttered to a stop midstep and made quick work of her holster, the gun a welcome weight in her palm.

On the way up the stairs, she'd been lost in thought. All she'd meant to do was grab her laptop on her way to the prison to check the visitor logs, so she'd been moving on autopilot.

Now everything snapped into sharp focus.

Isabel wanted you in Gig Harbor.

Raisa positioned her body to the side, so she wouldn't be an easy target, and then she nudged the door fully open.

Raisa didn't announce herself, simply waited a beat and then stepped into the room.

No one rushed by her. No one shot at her.

No one stepped out from behind the door and tried to smash a lamp over her head.

Objectively, she took in the mess but didn't let herself linger on it.

Instead, she cleared the room, her eyes finding each corner as her heart beat a quick but steady pace against her rib cage.

The closets. The bed. The bathroom. The window, and the ground outside beneath it.

Only then did Raisa fully exhale and drop her gun to her thigh.

She finally let herself look at the damage.

The room was ransacked.

Her clothes were strewn everywhere, many of the shirts ripped apart. The furniture bore knife wounds, the guts spilling out. The curtains had been yanked down and were now pooled on the floor.

On the wall was one message in bloodred spray paint.

LEAVE

Raisa reholstered her gun and ran.

The young woman at the desk popped her bubble gum as Raisa stopped in front of her.

"Did anyone go up since you've been here?"

Joy—if her name tag was to be believed—rolled her eyes. "I don't know."

Raisa's nostrils flared as she tried to control her irritation. Instead of shaking the girl, she flashed her badge. "Did anyone go up to the second floor since you've been here?"

The fact that Raisa was FBI did little to impress Joy, who began toying with her gum, pulling it out of her mouth into a droopy string. "Um, some of the guests."

"Any strangers?"

"Not that I saw," Joy said with a shrug. "There's a back entrance, though."

Raisa closed her eyes, inhaled for patience, opened them. "Does anyone secure that?"

That got her a derisive look. "Uh, no? We're not Quantico."

"Thanks," Raisa gritted out. She took the time to do a sweep of the perimeter and then the hallways, but found nothing except a somewhat startled housekeeper.

She returned to the room. The door had been kicked open, she realized now, the flimsy wood hardly any challenge for someone's boot. She would have to speak to the owners at some point about the damage. But, for now, she just stood in the middle of the mess.

Isabel would never have done something like this.

She thought, *Erratic*, hearing it in Kilkenny's voice. He had theorized that killing Peter Stamkos had broken their UNSUB, and that all the moves since had been a product of their unraveling.

Raisa had looked at Emily Logan's death as different from Peter's and Lindsey's because it hadn't been staged as an accident or an overdose. She'd wondered if perhaps it had even been someone else who had killed Emily. But what if it had simply been the same killer who had lost control? Maybe that was why the girl's death had been so brutal.

Kilkenny was better at all that than Raisa, but she thought he might agree. She tried to look at the room now through his eyes.

It was performative, over the top.

That made her think of Essi Halla.

It was immature.

That made her think of Gabriela Cruz.

It was reactive, which made Raisa think of everyone she'd talked to in the past twenty-four hours. Beyond the nurses at the hospital, that boiled down to Gabriela and Essi.

And Maeve St. Ivany.

It could've been any of the three or none of them, but it was a stark reminder that Raisa was in a small town, without any backup, and her partner had already been put in the hospital with life-threatening injuries.

On her way out, she informed Joy of the damages, while assuring the girl she could stay in Kilkenny's room. Not that Joy had shown any signs of distress at the news either way.

Raisa then grabbed her laptop—thankfully unharmed, as she'd thought to lock it in the room's safe—and headed toward the prison.

The visitor logs were easy to access—they were technically public documents—but the front desk regretted to inform her that they couldn't filter the records by inmate.

So she was given a conference room and a thick stack of notebooks. She stared at them, wondering if it was a waste of time.

What else could she be doing, though?

Watching Kilkenny's heart monitor, rereading those letters from Isabel's "Biggest Fan," which Raisa was half-convinced was actually Delaney. Scouring Lindsey Cousins's journals to confirm that she was indeed a psychopath.

That wouldn't change anything besides maybe confirming a possible motive for her death.

It took Raisa an hour before she got to Isabel's first visitor. It had been a woman named Sadie Richardson, who'd made a documentary about Isabel. Raisa hadn't watched it, but she knew it had been the most-viewed movie for a month on one of the big streaming services.

It took her another forty-five minutes to get to Delaney.

"Crap." She'd known it was going to be there, but it still was upsetting to have proof.

Raisa let herself imagine it. Had Delaney come crawling back, or had Isabel threatened her? Either way, it had ended up in the same place—Isabel telling Delaney what to do. Delaney protesting, but likely doing it anyway.

Delaney had visited one more time, a few months before Isabel had died.

In all that time, Isabel had only received one other visitor.

The name . . . looked familiar.

She had never met the person, but she had seen the name somewhere recently. It was beautiful, unique, and that was why it had stubbornly stuck to her brain like a bur.

Raisa thought through all the material she'd parsed through over the past forty-eight hours or so. Emily's and Lindsey's journals; the Biggest Fan letters and the hiking reviews; Gabriela's murder board.

None of those were right, though.

She closed her eyes and pictured where she'd seen it. Long, pink nails. A blinking cursor. A swaying dock beneath her feet.

Essi.

When they'd first interviewed Essi Halla, they'd asked her to give them a list of "true believers"—family members who actually hated Isabel enough to do something as drastic as hiring someone to kill her. It had been the first motive Raisa had come up with when she'd been trying to figure out who would have done this. How simple it would be, if there was no protégé, there was no copycat, there was no need to parse the ethics of fandom and true crime.

This really might have been it all along, just a pissed-off family member.

Raisa quickly thumbed over to her notes app and then held the phone up next to the visitor log.

And there it was, matching Isabel's last visitor.

Roan Carmichael.

TRANSCRIPT OF EMILY LOGAN'S INTERVIEW WITH ROAN CARMICHAEL

EMILY LOGAN: Can you tell me your name and a little about yourself?

ROAN CARMICHAEL: Uh, Roan. Roan Carmichael. And, uh, I don't know what I should say? I work in the tech industry in Seattle. My brother was murdered ten years ago. That's . . . that's it.

LOGAN: That's great, that's all great. Now, from what I understand, you were a large part of the unsolved mysteries community online.

CARMICHAEL: I was, yeah. No one knew who killed my brother, and it drove my mom to, well, give up. On herself for years, really. She shut down, couldn't hold a job to save her life. I was paying her rent, I was getting her groceries delivered. She just . . . she wanted to know, you know. What happened to Mitch. I think if she'd just *known* she would have been okay to move on.

LOGAN: But you couldn't solve your brother's murder so you tried to solve others . . .

CARMICHAEL: Yeah, that's a good way to put it . . . yeah. *Tried* being the key word there. I didn't solve any. We all just talked, mostly. Bickered. There were power struggles. It felt like a community with a goal that we didn't really work toward at all. That sounds harsh, but I mean it in a good way. It was kind of just an online place for all of us to hang out and make friends. It was nice, especially for people not into sports or video games.

LOGAN: So you never contacted investigators or did your own digging?

CARMICHAEL: No.

LOGAN: Oh. Okay. So you said you *were* involved, does that mean you aren't anymore?

CARMICHAEL: About two years into being an active participant with the group, someone in the forum somehow found my mother's cell phone and landline. They called her incessantly, and then when she couldn't answer their questions to their satisfaction, they said terrible, nasty things to her. Blaming her for Mitch's death, stuff like that. And she had just started to get better, too. I had thought maybe she'd turned a corner.

LOGAN: Having to talk about the crime reopened her wounds?

CARMICHAEL: You could say that. She took a bottle of sleeping pills on top of a fifth of vodka a week later. She never woke up.

LOGAN: Oh. Oh. I'm so sorry.

CHAPTER TWENTY-TWO

Raisa

Day Three

Roan Carmichael agreed to meet Raisa at a nautical-themed pub a few streets down from the police station.

She had texted Essi to see if she had contact information for him, and had gotten his email. He'd responded almost immediately and confessed he'd come to town after he'd heard the news.

He wasn't the only person in the pub, but she spotted him easily, sitting in the back corner away from the family who had taken over two booths in the front and the couple at the bar itself.

Roan was tall and lean with messy hair he'd tied up in a topknot. He wore a poncho that looked like it was made out of alpaca hair and Birkenstocks with woolly socks despite the summer heat.

He shoved the chair out with his foot, inviting her to sit.

"Larissa Parker," he said, and Raisa narrowed her eyes.

She was tired of being addressed by a name that had never really been hers.

"FBI Agent Raisa Susanto," she corrected and he nodded.

"Of course, sorry." He seemed genuinely contrite, which she appreciated. "How can I help you, Agent Susanto?"

"I wanted to talk to you about your time with the anti-FreeBell movement," Raisa said.

"That's a popular topic these days," he muttered.

"Is it?"

"Yeah, even before Isabel died," he said, and then he winced. "Someone wanted to interview me about it."

"Emily Logan?" Raisa asked. It wasn't unusual that, in a niche group, so many members would know each other and interact, but she did find it notable that Emily had been quite the presence in a community Gabriela said she didn't have much interest in.

"Yeah," Roan said, his brows going up in surprise that she knew the name. "I feel like I should start earlier than that, though."

"How about the fact that there's no Carmichael on Isabel's victim list," Raisa suggested.

He smiled sheepishly. "That's as good a place as any. My brother actually is on the list of known victims, we just had different dads. Mitchell Johnston."

"Stabbing, outside a bar." Raisa hated that she had them all memorized, but she would have felt guilty had she not.

He laughed but there was little humor in it this time. "A full life reduced to a single sentence."

"I'm sorry," Raisa said, meaning it. She knew what that was like.

"No, I'm sorry. You're not responsible for your sister's crimes," Roan said, sounding like it was a line he'd practiced hoping he'd believe it. "He was far from the perfect victim. Everyone told me he was killed in some drug deal gone wrong or a gang initiation or something where he would have brought his death upon himself."

"Was he mixed up in those kinds of things?" Raisa asked.

"Yeah, a little bit," Roan said, lifting one shoulder in a careless shrug. "He'd sobered up three months earlier and cut most of his friends out of his life. But he was at a bar when he died, and that apparently was enough to convince a lot of folks he'd relapsed."

"Even if he had, it's not as if he deserved to get stabbed for it," Raisa said, annoyed on his behalf.

"Preaching to the choir," he said, holding his hands up. "We got lucky when Isabel was arrested. She'd apparently been active in the area, and there were some photographs in some old Facebook albums linking her and my brother together that night. But she probably picked him because she knew no one would care what happened to him."

"You cared," Raisa said.

"Right," Roan said. "Fat lot of good that did."

"So how did you get involved in the anti-Isabel group?" Raisa asked.

"I was fairly active in the cold-case community for a lot of the years after my brother was killed," he said. "I still lurked sometimes, and the group got a big surge with Isabel's arrest. Lots of people trying to connect their unsolved murders to her."

Raisa nodded—the thing about a prolific serial killer who'd taken her victims mainly via accidents and suicides was that anyone could latch on to her as the answer to the biggest question in their lives.

"Once you're in that space, it's kind of easy to find things like the FreeBell groups and then the antis, as we're called," Roan said, rolling his eyes. "As if not wanting a psychopath unleashed on the country warrants the 'anti' label."

The way he said *psychopath* rang an alarm bell in her mind. Because the second part of that pissed-off-family-member theory was that they'd redirected their rage toward anyone displaying psychopathic tendencies.

And this man had a connection to both Emily and Isabel.

"Have you ever heard of someone named Peter Stamkos?" Raisa asked, as neutrally as possible, so as not to put him on the defense.

He pursed his lips. "No. But people don't always use their real names online."

"How about Lindsey Cousins?"

Roan shook his head. "Nope. Doesn't sound familiar."

Raisa nodded, not sure she believed him. "Okay, so this 'anti' community. That's where you met Essi?"

He laughed. "Oh, Essi."

"What's the reaction mean?"

"Sorry, she's just. Funny," Roan said, shaking his head. "Her shtick is playing outrage queen and then you get her alone and it's all, *I don't care.*"

"You think she's performative?" Raisa asked.

"Yeah, but it's both ways," Roan said. "No one ever seems to realize that, and it's actually pretty fascinating."

Raisa tilted her head, curious. "What do you mean?"

"Everyone thinks that the blasé thing is her true form, right?" Roan said, truly engaged in the conversation now. This was a topic that he found interesting. "But they never stop to consider who they are as an audience might be playing into Essi's decision to put on that mask."

"Huh."

"Right," Roan said. "It's a trick to get you to think about her a certain way, just as all that faux outrage is a performance. I don't know what Essi actually believes but she'll tell you whatever it is she thinks you want to hear. Or see. Or experience. And the brilliance is that you think she's being honest because she's 'letting you in on a secret.'"

Raisa had to admit she had completely fallen into the trap, because who would want other people to think they were a money-hungry, callously ambitious bottom dweller instead of an actually outraged victim?

Essi had known the latter wouldn't play well for Raisa and Kilkenny. So she'd given them something that would make sense but would be nonthreatening. The second Raisa realized Essi just cared about Isabel because of the attention she brought, Raisa had dismissed her as a viable suspect.

She guessed the real question now was whether that meant anything.

If Essi could switch gears like that with such pinpoint precision, there was a solid chance she was a sociopath. While sociopaths didn't experience emotions in the same way neurotypical people did, one of their skills was being able to give an audience what it wanted.

What if she really did want revenge on Isabel, but she'd known the best way to convince them she didn't was to pretend to be in it for the money?

Kilkenny had said Essi wouldn't have drawn so much attention to herself if she'd been planning to kill Isabel, but maybe all that spotlight was blinding instead of illuminating. Maybe it helped her hide what she really wanted.

"So I take it you two aren't friends?" Raisa asked.

"Oh, we're friends—you just have to know what you're getting," Roan said. "And honestly, she's one of the best friends anyone could ask for. She always knows how to read your mood and give you what you want. I don't know what she gets out of that, but for other people, it's great."

Raisa would hate the idea of someone constantly performing for her. But she had a grand total of one friend, so she wasn't exactly an expert. "She gave us your name as a 'true believer.'"

"See, this is why, friend or no, she would never be the one I'd pick to help hide a body," Roan said, and then seemed to abruptly remember who he was talking to. "Just an expression, I swear. But, yeah, anyway, I am probably what you would call a true believer in that I truly believe Isabel should have gotten the death penalty for her crimes."

"You wanted to see her dead?" Raisa asked, pushing a little.

He wrinkled his nose. "I'm definitely not crying over the news. It was the universe righting itself, in my eyes. Sorry for your loss and everything."

As if Raisa didn't agree with everything he was saying. "The universe righting itself?"

"Yeah, who would have thought she'd have some mysterious disease that killed her in her early forties," Roan said. "It's all that karma catching up with her. And think about it. If you all hadn't stopped her two years ago, we might never have known she'd existed. So many families wouldn't have gotten closure. It's almost spooky, isn't it?"

Raisa studied him, trying to figure out if he was trying to pull one over on her, like Essi had. He seemed to genuinely think Isabel had died of natural causes, though. Where did that land him on her suspect list?

Especially since he had the strongest motive out of anyone she'd talked to yet.

When she didn't respond, his smile faded and his eyes narrowed. "Wait."

"Hmmm."

"You're asking me questions," Roan said slowly. "To find out if I really wanted her dead. There has to be a reason you're doing that."

"Hmmm."

"Oh, shit," Roan muttered. "You think it was murder. You think I murdered her? Jesus, why would I do that? No, *how* would I do that? I'm a tech dude, I don't know the first thing about prison rules outside of *Orange Is the New Black*."

"I'm just asking questions," Raisa said neutrally. "But there was a reason I wanted to meet with you, other than you being a 'true believer.'"

"Goddamn, Essi. You're right, she's a shit friend."

"Did I say that?" Raisa asked.

"No, but your face did," he said, and then sighed deeply. "Okay, how else did I make the suspect list?"

"Not the suspect list," she said, and he rolled his eyes, waving her to go on. "You were Isabel's last visitor."

His brows tugged together. "What?"

Raisa nodded. "She wasn't exactly Miss Popular, believe it or not."

"No, I mean, what?" Roan said, and she tried to make the words make sense.

"You were her last visitor," Raisa repeated. "I wanted to know what you two talked about."

Roan shook his head. "You must be mistaken."

"Nope, it's right there in the visitor logs," Raisa said. Even after she'd found Roan's name, she'd continued forward until she'd hit the date of Isabel's death. Roan Carmichael had been the last person not in the system to see her alive.

"No," Roan said. "You're not getting it."

"Not getting what?"

"I never visited Isabel Parker," Roan said. "Not a single time in my life."

LETTER FROM ISABEL PARKER TO DELANEY MOORE

Dearest Lana,

I know you wanted to stop me and never could.

I could feel you behind me, not every step of the way but most of them. Sometimes I went to hotter climates in the winter because I remembered how you didn't like the snow. Sometimes I took a break because I could feel you growing weary of the hunt. And then just when you thought I had hibernated—or god forbid, died—I would kill again, just for you. Just so you knew I was still there.

Waiting for you.

You never could catch me. The only reason you did was because I set a trap in the first place. Did you ever think about that?

Some people say all serial killers eventually want to be caught.

Maybe I did, not by the police, but by you.

You were never smart enough, though. Or skilled enough.

What if I gave you a do-over? Would you thank me or would you curse me? Or would you do both in the same breath—because you could be redeemed but your soul would be ripped asunder in the process.

(Can you hear Larissa rolling her eyes at my purple prose? What can I say? I have my vices.)

There is someone out there who reminds me of myself.

By the Time You Read This

Will you stop them in time?
I don't think you can.
But if you do, maybe you'll win a prize.
Your favorite sister,
Isabel

CHAPTER TWENTY-THREE

Delaney

Day Six

Delaney didn't let herself worry about Roan of the Carolina mountains. She tucked their afternoon on the boat away in her mind, something to reflect upon when she needed the fantasy.

She lived in reality, where kind men were actually just lying to you.

She did let herself wonder what he wanted from her. Was he a journalist in disguise? A cop? A family member of one of Isabel's victims? Delaney had done her best not to follow along with the trial—thinking that putting distance between herself and an airing of all Isabel's misdeeds would somehow help her move on.

Of course, it hadn't. Isabel wouldn't allow for that.

Let's play a game . . .

Delaney had made some excuse when they'd gotten back from their boat excursion. Roan lingered, but couldn't pressure her further without coming off like a cad.

Would he realize what he'd done? Later, when she disappeared from the motel and his life altogether, without even a goodbye?

He probably wouldn't—and she hoped that mystery haunted him.

Delaney could be petty, especially when she was being used.

You used him, too, some part of her whispered. But she'd used him in a way that had been honest. She'd wanted the relief of casual sex and had made no promises that she was looking for anything else.

He, on the other hand, had only wanted to get close to her because of who she was.

She hadn't seen him since they'd parted ways yesterday evening—he hadn't even tried to contact her. She now scrubbed the disappointment off her skin before dressing in all black for her plans.

When she left the motel, she couldn't help but stare for one extra-long moment at the light in Roan's window.

She should never have gone on that boat ride anyway.

There had just been something about enjoying the afternoon away from Isabel's mind games that she hadn't been able to resist.

A small slice of fantasy.

But that wasn't her life now.

As ever, her life was about death.

"Let's play a game, Lana," Isabel said. *Her hands were cuffed to the table, but she looked as in control as ever.*

Relaxed, amused. Pleased that Delaney had finally come to see her.

"Delaney."

"Look who's all grown up," Isabel purred. "*It only took you about forty years to grow a spine, my dear. Although it is nice that it finally came in.*"

"What do you want?" Delaney gritted out. *She had done her best to remove Isabel from her life, from her mind. She had hidden herself from all the vultures who wanted a piece of her because Isabel was infamous; she'd turned down book deals to write the Parker girls' story; she'd even let Raisa dictate their relationship, not for her sister's benefit but because looking at Raisa reminded Delaney that she, herself, was far more like Isabel than Raisa.*

"*You hate yourself, don't you?*" Isabel asked, flatly curious.

Delaney didn't say anything. How she felt about herself was . . . complicated. She understood why Raisa hated her, she understood why Isabel couldn't feel anything toward her. But she had survived by justifying her choices to herself—otherwise she probably would have drunk herself to death years ago.

Twenty-five years of that? Of telling herself that she'd done the right thing—for her family—had become fairly foundational to who she was as a person.

Did she hate that person? Maybe. She judged her, at the very least.

"What do you want?" Delaney spit out again.

"I want to give you a redemption arc," Isabel said. "Aren't those the very best stories? The villain becomes the hero we all deserve."

Delaney drove to Gabbi's place this time instead of the beach. She didn't have to wait very long for Gabbi to emerge.

The girl who had idolized her sister.

Who, if Delaney was right, had become her.

Or, a less successful version of Isabel.

That was a big *if*, though. So far, Gabbi had avoided incriminating herself. She'd made some leading comments about wanting to kill sexual predators, but they had all been couched in gauzy language, no matter how much Delaney had tried to draw her out into something more concrete.

The time for gentle probing was over, though.

Delaney needed to actually catch her in the act.

Something that would be harder to do with Roan Carmichael on her tail.

Had he been the one who'd found Delaney in Seattle? The one who'd sent her fleeing in the first place? Had he then followed her to that hotel, rented a room, slept with her, lied to her? All to . . . what?

Well, the answer to that was obvious. Kill her.

She tried to picture Roan with a knife at her throat. Or maybe a syringe of something so it would look like natural causes. Just like what must have happened with Isabel.

Delaney sucked in air. She could picture it because she could picture anyone a killer.

But then a memory nudged into the frame. Roan smiling at her on the boat, handing over his sunglasses.

He could have killed her so easily out there.

Not a single person in the whole world knew she was in Gig Harbor. It would have taken days, if not weeks, for her body to wash ashore somewhere.

Maybe he wanted to torture her instead of making her death quick and easy.

Get over it, she told herself, and then returned her attention to Gabbi.

The girl was nervous—her fingers curled tightly around the strap of her bag.

Delaney's own heart beat strongly at her pulse points. Maybe Gabbi was just going out for a drink with friends.

Maybe Delaney had gotten this all wrong.

But Delaney had been on this hunt now for six months. She wasn't often wrong for that long.

Although . . . she hadn't been sure. Gabbi had told Delaney about Lindsey Cousins in their private conversations.

They went to the same school, although Lindsey attended most of her classes online. She must have rubbed Gabbi the wrong way at some point, because Gabbi had confessed to Delaney—well, to Delaney's online persona—that she'd used her algorithm to figure out the likelihood that Lindsey's father had actually drowned. The results had come back that the chance he'd died of natural causes had been less than 10 percent, given weather and ocean patterns on the day of his demise.

Lindsey, Gabbi had posited almost gleefully, was a murderer, and had been since she'd been a young girl.

Find the killer.

Kill the killer.

Delaney had been intrigued by Lindsey. Not that Delaney was going to kowtow to anything Isabel said, but if there was someone out there killing people, Delaney wanted to know about it.

So she had set a trap.

A trap by the name of Peter Stamkos.

Isabel had wanted him dead. Delaney had offered him up on a silver platter to anyone who'd wanted to prove themselves to her sister. She'd taken all the steps Isabel would have, by making sure someone—someone other than her, because that could get messy—had called CPS as a concerned citizen. Peter's story was all set up for someone, the perfect suicide candidate.

Find the killer.

Kill the killer.

If only it were that easy. There was a reason Delaney had taken twenty-five years to stop Isabel—and even then it had been when Isabel herself had flown too close to the sun.

Delaney had been watching Peter's house. She'd set up cameras around the perimeter for anywhere she couldn't see.

And yet, whoever had killed him had avoided being spotted.

It made her wonder why she always tried so hard and came up short. Why couldn't her genius plans ever turn out like Isabel's did? Why was she so smart on some matters and yet constantly failing when it came to the important ones?

Delaney had been sure it was Lindsey Cousins, though. The girl was a psychopath. She was interested, at least tangentially, in true crime.

And then she'd died.

Delaney touched the hilt of the knife strapped to her thigh beneath her skirt as she watched Gabbi walk away.

I want to give you a redemption arc.

She got out of the car. Right now, with Gabbi on high alert, a car tailing her would surely send her into hiding. Delaney didn't want that—she wanted to catch Gabbi in the act.

Or . . . before the act would be ideal, really.

Gabbi looked back over her shoulder, but she wasn't used to spotting a tail, that much was obvious. Delaney merely had to duck into the shadows to avoid detection.

Don't do it, Delaney thought at her as she continued on her way toward campus.

But if Delaney had that kind of power, it would have worked on Isabel long ago.

Maybe Gabbi was just meeting someone after classes.

Maybe she had forgotten something on campus.

Maybe she had to turn in an assignment—professors were reverting to handwritten essays now that AI was becoming a popular cheating tool.

Maybe, maybe, maybe . . .

Delaney thought about the beach, the bonfire.

"We have to do something," Delaney had said.

"You think I haven't tried?" Gabbi blowing a ring of smoke.

Gabbi was different from Isabel. She wasn't a psychopath, as far as Delaney could tell. She was just a girl who'd been hurt and whom the justice system had failed miserably. If she killed, it was because she genuinely thought she was ridding the world of villains.

Peter Stamkos had deserved to die, after all, for what he'd done to his daughter.

Lindsey had so clearly been a monster—it was at least a possibility that she'd killed her own father. Delaney wasn't about to mourn her.

Emily . . .

Well, Delaney knew the girl was no prize, but she was probably a victim of Gabbi's psychotic break rather than any kind of noble calling.

Raisa's voice screamed in Delaney's head: *Call the police.*

But Delaney couldn't.

One, she could be wrong.

There was a distinct possibility that Gabbi was actually innocent and all Delaney's evidence was simply confirmation bias. How many college girls talked just like Gabbi—wishing rapists dead wasn't exactly a sign that someone was capable of killing one.

And two, even dead, Isabel could still make sure the rules of her game were enforced. Delaney had no doubt about that. If Delaney didn't follow her rules, she'd go after Kilkenny and Raisa.

Some might think Delaney foolish for fearing a dead woman.

Those people should ask Kilkenny about how serious the threat was.

So as much as Delaney wanted to, she couldn't just ignore the fact that Gabbi was now walking toward a tall, handsome man waiting on the steps of the main hall.

When Gabbi stopped in front of him, her entire demeanor shifted. Gone were the skittish nerves, and in their place was a confident coquette, her pose welcoming, her hand resting on his forearm.

It reminded Delaney of the times she donned the Lana Parker persona.

The man jerked his head toward his car, and Gabbi nodded.

"Shit," Delaney breathed. She wouldn't be able to follow them if they got in. She thought about stopping them in some way, even running over to Gabbi to force an introduction.

Instead she watched helplessly—as she had all her life—as Gabbi climbed into the passenger seat and buckled up.

They drove by only a handful of feet away from where Delaney was hiding, and she could see the suggestion of Gabbi's hand resting on the man's knee.

Maybe this wasn't exactly what she thought it was.

Maybe this was just an affair between a professor and his much younger student. That might not be a healthy relationship, but it certainly wasn't worth calling the cops about.

As she watched the taillights disappear, though, she wondered if she would ever talk herself out of all her maybes and do something for once in her goddamn life.

The police radio app Delaney downloaded on her burner phone crackled to life at 3:00 a.m.

Apparent suicide, over by the harbor.

Male, midforties.

They didn't say, but Delaney guessed he had dark hair and a strong jawline, along with the ghost of a young woman's touch on his thigh.

CHAPTER TWENTY-FOUR

Raisa

Day Three

Raisa couldn't shake the feeling that she was missing a crucial piece of evidence because she hadn't given herself time to truly sit with all the written communication she had from the case.

When she left Roan and the pub behind, the evening was settling in around her. The place had been close enough to forgo the SUV, and she was glad for the walk back now. She would grab everything they'd gathered over the past couple of days and then head to the hospital.

She wanted to see Kilkenny. Even if that meant sneaking past the guard dogs at the nurses' station to do so.

That made her think about Emily's boyfriend, who worked at the hospital. She wondered what he did there, then dismissed him from her mind. It didn't matter.

A block away from the hotel, she glanced in the coffee shop she and Kilkenny had stopped in before his accident, and caught sight of someone familiar.

Mildred . . . something. Raisa didn't remember her last name, but she remembered that she'd praised Essi for helping her get through the loss of her dog.

And now here she was reading a book.

The very one Raisa was eager to get her hands on.

Mildred was pleased as punch—in her own words—to see Raisa.

"Is that Essi's book?" Raisa asked, cutting into Mildred's recitation of her next week's worth of plans. Something about Essi poked at Raisa. She wasn't always good at reading people, and Essi was clearly a master at crafting her own image. But idiolects were harder to mask. Essi was sure to reveal more about herself in this book than she would ever want to. Maybe it wouldn't help the case itself, but maybe it would. Essi was as tangled up in all this as anyone they'd talked to.

Mildred beamed. "Oh, yes. She gave me an early copy. She's always doing sweet things like that. I've already read it through once, but I'm making notations this time around."

"Could I borrow it?" Raisa asked, expecting a fight.

Mildred's fingers tightened around it. "Um, well, dear . . ."

"Please, it's for official purposes," Raisa said. "I'll make sure it's returned to you in perfect shape."

Mildred did not want to hand it over. She licked her lips, her eyes darting side to side, as if she were desperately crafting a good lie to cover why she just absolutely had to keep the thing.

In the end, she surrendered it to Raisa, along with her home address.

"Priority shipping," Raisa promised and then headed back outside.

Raisa ended up packing the thing next to all the other writing samples she had, before heading to the hospital.

The nurse behind the desk—the same one who had been working it when she'd first come in—lit up when he saw her.

"You can go back," he said. "He's not awake, but he's stable. Room 114."

Raisa's rib cage went tight. "Thank you."

Somehow she managed to find the room, and there, for the first time since she'd all but told him to go to hell, was Kilkenny.

She swayed on her feet at the sight of him, reaching out to the wall to steady her.

He looked so small, surrounded by machines with lines coming out of his hands, his arms. A steady beeping filled the room. At any other time it might be grating, but for now it was the sweetest sound she'd ever heard.

His heart beat on.

Raisa exhaled and inhaled, keeping pace with the inadvertent metronome.

Kilkenny was too pale, from what she could see beneath the bruises. The egg on his cheekbone was every color on the spectrum, from a deep violet to turquoise to just a hint of putrid green. His sheet revealed the shape of a cast on his leg.

But the worst part was the white bandage wrapped around his head. She knew that they'd removed part of his skull to relieve the pressure, and she just . . . she couldn't think about the ramifications of something that, in this moment, looked so clean and innocuous.

Raisa sank into the chair beside his bed, her eyes landing on his face, his chest, the bandage, his feet, the rise of his kneecaps, his hands.

Only after the third or fourth pass was she satisfied that she hadn't missed some gaping hole in his chest.

Finally, she relaxed enough to pull everything she'd brought out of her bag. She nabbed a dinner tray so she could spread it all out in front of her.

Despite the fact that Raisa had worked with Delaney before she'd known they were related, she didn't have any writing samples from her. The closest she came were the blog posts submitted to the DA that showed Delaney talking about two different people Isabel had gone on to kill.

Those had been written when Delaney was a teenager, though. While that could provide something of a baseline, Raisa would be hesitant to make any judgments off it.

What she did have were the reviews and the letters from Isabel's Biggest Fan.

They were difficult to run analyses on because they had been written in doublespeak that only one reader was meant to understand. Doublespeak wasn't considered a code in the truest sense, but it would absolutely alter the author's idiolect into something mostly unrecognizable.

Still, both materials were worth working up an analysis on.

One particularly interesting typo in both the letters and the reviews was a missed *t* in *the* so the word became *he*. It happened three times in the reviews and four times in the letters.

It was a small thing, but it was something to build on and gave some credence to her notion that they were the same author.

There were a few other similarities—like the author's tendency to splice a phrase with a comma. But she didn't want to let her biases take over. There were plenty of differences, too, including that noticeable absence of amplifiers in the Biggest Fan letters.

Raisa put those aside and moved on to Lindsey's journals.

She had recently read an article in a research journal about the connection between linguistic choices and psychopathy deviations. The author had found that people with antisocial personality disorders tended to self-reference frequently; use emotional phrases, though not ones connected to anxiety; favor past-tense words, articles, and concrete nouns; and employ shocking language meant to arouse a reaction in the reader.

Lindsey's idiolect fit the model perfectly.

But it didn't reveal much else beyond disjointed fantasies about killing all the people she hated.

Except . . . except for one entry a few days before Lindsey's death.

There was a total cunt ass bitch on the cruise today. Tried to threaten me, something about the dangers of being interested in true crime documentaries. I wanted to kill her right there. Scalp that braid right off her head and shove those hippie rags down her throat until she choked.

Raisa swallowed hard. That description could fit so many people, but it *definitely* fit Delaney. And it matched the one Julia had given her about the woman sitting outside Peter Stamkos's house.

As circumstantial as it might be, the evidence was starting to stack up in ways she didn't want to let herself believe. But Delaney had been linked now to two separate victims in the days before their possible homicides.

It was easy to rule Lindsey out as the author to the Biggest Fan letters and the hiking reviews. Those had been written by someone in control of their idiolect enough to know how to hide it. As she'd thought many times before, that was harder than it seemed.

Delaney would certainly be capable of doing it, though. She was a language genius—had she pursued the study, she'd probably be a better linguist than even Raisa, who was at the top of her field.

Confirmation bias, Kilkenny said.

"Yeah, yeah," she muttered.

The Kilkenny not in her head slept on.

Raisa turned to Emily Logan's essay and blog posts next.

What struck Raisa the most was that Emily seemed incredibly earnest.

Her idiolect was also extremely easy to track between her essay and her blog posts. Written material in formal settings like college tended to be tighter, more grammatically accurate, and contain fewer misspellings on the whole than casual communication like blog posts. But for Emily, her authorial voice remained strikingly consistent over both mediums. Her errors were consistent, which told Raisa that she'd probably read them over the same number of times. Maybe that was once; maybe that was ten times. She also kept the same chatty tone throughout, like she was gossiping rather than defending a thesis statement.

On a whim, Raisa pulled out a tablet and scrolled through a few common social media sites in search of the FreeBell community.

After landing on a pretty niche subthread on Reddit, she poked around for a while until she found a post that was signed "E.L."

Ok it's late, don't @ me if this comes off sounding cray. But. I think IP's case did a lot to shine light on the benefits of the armchair movement, just like "Unsolved Mysteries" and faces on milk cartons did back in the day. Collective knowledge and attention can only be a net positive. I know. I know. Think of the families. But don't you get it? I am. The more eyes on a case, the quicker it will get solved. Just look at Mitchell Johnston's death. It would never have been solved—just another cold case. Do you remember that movie where the activists were fighting against the death penalty and they wanted a foolproof case to show that innocent people could be killed? And one of the characters was dying of cancer? And they staged it so that it looked like the dude killed her even though she was dying anyway? I feel like the armchair community needs that kind of thing. E.L.

Raisa had to read it a couple of times, because it only vaguely made sense, a common trait with this particular author, who didn't always follow through on her thoughts.

Emily seemed to be tightly focused on drawing positive attention to her cause, and in making the argument that there should be more eyeballs on the movement, she took a somewhat nonsensical path. Even the reference to Mitchell Johnston was a bit strange, considering it had been the team at the DA's office who had tracked down that case and not armchairs.

But the actual message was irrelevant. After reading a half dozen samples, Raisa felt like she had a grip on Emily's authorial voice.

Where that knowledge fit into the rest of it all, she wasn't yet sure.

Raisa grabbed for Essi's book. She was curious about how Essi would present herself in the thing when her audience was so wide-ranging. The cover looked like it was trying to be too many things—and landed on the worst elements of an important current-affairs think piece and a celebrity memoir.

The descriptive blurb reflected a similar confusion about what the book wanted to be. Apparently, Essi had talked to experts on the topics of parasocial relationships, grief, and the psychology of cults. But through the entirety of the descriptive text—which would have been written by someone in marketing, Raisa realized—there was an aura of *celebrity talking about her interesting life.*

If Raisa had seen it in a bookstore, she would have picked it up out of sheer curiosity about how they were going to make the thing cohesive.

She supposed that was the point of it all.

"You want honesty?" Essi had said. *"I don't care. I want them looking at me."*

A knock on the door had Raisa looking up from Essi's serious expression on the book flap.

Detective St. Ivany stood there, leaning against the doorjamb. She looked tired and pleased.

Raisa blinked at her, confused in that way of seeing someone unexpected and out of place. "What happened?"

St. Ivany grinned. "I found Delaney."

NOTES FROM FORENSIC PSYCHOLOGIST CALLUM KILKENNY'S PERSONAL JOURNAL

Although I would never diagnose Isabel without having seen her as a patient myself, I believe she has a severe attachment disorder that manifests especially strongly when it comes to her surviving family members, Raisa and Delaney.
We have access to Becks's diary, but my suspicion is that in it she paints a far rosier picture of the girls' childhood than actually existed.
We know that Tim Parker had schizophrenia, and that Becks was so worried about it that she was tracking good and bad days in the weeks prior to their deaths. In the diary, she also talks about how distant she and Tim felt from their children when the girls were babies. She makes sure to mention that Tim only cared about them when they started showing signs of genius.
Their work as mathematicians was paramount for both of them, and Becks was resentful of Tim that he seemed to be getting her pregnant just so that he could handcuff her career.
In all, there are certainly signs that the girls and Alex might have been

vulnerable to reactive attachment disorder.

The signs to watch out for in young children are as follows:

1) Unexplained withdrawal, fear, sadness, or irritability;
2) Not seeking comfort or showing no response when comfort is given;
3) Failure to smile;
4) Failure to reach out when picked up;
5) No interest in peekaboo or other interactive games.

And so on.

We'll never know if Isabel could have been saved from her life of violent, sadistic crime. It's unlikely that she could have been, given her psychopathy. But, when trying to understand Isabel, many people—I'm guessing herself included—describe her childhood as normal. I don't think that was the case. People say Isabel killed her parents because she was a psychopath—that she didn't need a motive.

While that might be true to some extent, they were the ones who had fractured that relationship with their daughter. I believe Tim and Becks Parker's coldness, mental health issues, and distance created attachment disorders in all of their children, some more severe than others.

And while both Delaney and Raisa are successful, well-adjusted and productive adults, the lack of any fulfilling, permanent relationships in their lives are proof that none of the kids were spared.

CHAPTER TWENTY-FIVE

Raisa

Day Three

"Where is she?" Raisa asked, nearly coming out of the chair beside Kilkenny's hospital bed, ready to go confront her sister.

She could hardly believe that St. Ivany really had been able to find Delaney. Maybe she wasn't so concentrated on flying beneath the radar anymore—now that Isabel was in jail and Delaney had been cleared.

Raisa surprised herself with her next question. "Is she all right?"

"Well, I didn't actually find her," St. Ivany admitted. Before Raisa could deflate, she added, "I got her address."

"In Seattle?" Raisa asked. It wasn't far away—it would be worth going to check out, even if they weren't sure she was still there. She glanced outside, and realized the sky had fully darkened while she'd been busy reading. "In the morning, I guess."

"First thing," St. Ivany said, and then knocked against the doorjamb to signal her impending departure.

"Hey," Raisa called. "Someone broke into my hotel room earlier. Ransacked it."

St. Ivany's brows shot up. "And you're just telling me this now?"

Raisa shrugged. She'd been going nonstop since.

"Shit," St. Ivany said, scrubbing a hand over her face. Then she headed directly toward the chair positioned in the far corner of the room and dropped into it. "Fuck, this has been a long couple of weeks."

Raisa huffed out a sympathetic laugh. "Yeah."

"Who broke into your room?" St. Ivany asked.

"The copycat? Protégé, whatever. Whoever killed Peter and Lindsey and Emily," Raisa said. "They left a message on the wall. 'Leave.' No punctuation."

The corners of St. Ivany's lips tipped up. "Ever the linguist. What does that tell you about them?"

"They were raised in the southern part of the United States, born sometime in the eighties, and went to school at an Ivy league university," Raisa said.

St. Ivany's eyes flew to hers. "Really?"

"No," Raisa said on a laugh. "I'm fucking with you, sorry."

St. Ivany made a face at her, but relaxed into the chair.

"It doesn't tell me much except it feels like a show," Raisa said. "Or like an afterthought. They didn't feel any emotion behind it. They just wanted it to look like they were trying to scare me away."

"Why?" St. Ivany asked, seemingly all she could muster.

Raisa thought back to her conversation with Roan, about the fact that he, like Delaney, had contact with at least two of the victims before their deaths. "His heart wasn't in it."

St. Ivany straightened again. "His?"

"Their," Raisa corrected, too late. She decided to just fill St. Ivany in. She didn't fully trust the woman, but they were in this boat together right now.

"I talked to a man named Roan Carmichael," she said, and St. Ivany startled.

"He's the guy who met with Emily for coffee not long before she died," St. Ivany said, now watching her with a new intensity. "He said he was a friend of the family passing through."

"Nope," Raisa said. "He knows her through the true crime community. She wanted to interview him as the brother of one of Isabel's victims."

"Well, Christ," St. Ivany said. "I should have held him."

"He was also Isabel's last visitor," she said, and St. Ivany almost stood at that. Raisa held up a hand. "He says someone faked his identity."

"Not easy, but not impossible," St. Ivany said. "I'll get a warrant for any security footage from the prison. Maybe we'll get lucky."

They hadn't so far, but maybe the tides would change. "Yeah."

"Should we prioritize him over finding Delaney?" St. Ivany asked.

Where Raisa wasn't sure if Roan fit into this investigation, she was now sure Delaney would. "No, we need to figure out the missing pieces. I'm pretty sure she has at least a few of them."

St. Ivany nodded, and then studied Raisa silently.

"What?"

"What if she killed all these people?" St. Ivany asked. "What if she's involved? Would you be able to arrest her?"

"Gleefully," Raisa lied through her teeth. It was what she wanted to be able to believe. She just didn't anymore.

St. Ivany shot her a dubious look.

"Okay, maybe not gleefully," Raisa admitted. "What are you still doing here anyway? Shouldn't you be trying to sleep?"

"Did you see pictures of Emily Logan's crime scene?" St. Ivany asked, in a seeming non sequitur.

Raisa shook her head.

"Yeah, I don't want to ever see something like that again."

It took Raisa a second to realize that St. Ivany was *guarding* her.

"You might not think much of linguists, but I *am* an FBI agent," Raisa reminded her, though she didn't feel as annoyed as she might have.

"Then you can protect me right back," St. Ivany said. "What are you looking at?"

Raisa pulled out Essi's book.

"Who is Essi Halla?" St. Ivany asked after squinting toward the cover.

"Self-help guru. I'm trying to further improve my sunny disposition."

"Think it's gonna take more than a book."

"Don't swing too hard at softballs, it's not a good look," Raisa said. "Her father was killed by Isabel—or she thinks he was. Or she just says he was. I don't know . . . Something about her has my back up."

"You have good instincts," St. Ivany said, staring at the book harder now, as if she could intimidate it into spilling its secrets. "You think she could be our guy?"

"Let me read this and maybe I'll be able to tell you."

St. Ivany waved at her to proceed and Raisa settled in, not letting herself worry about what St. Ivany was going to do to occupy herself.

It turned out Essi had a nice writing voice, which was both conversational and compelling.

Then came a knock, just like so many others in the days before it. I couldn't stomach one more casserole.

But I answered the door, because if I didn't one of the ladies who brought the casseroles would probably call the cops.

Everyone knew I was hanging on by a thread.

It wasn't one of my neighbors at my door, though.

Instead it was a girl. She asked, "Do you know who killed your father?"

And that's when I found something besides the casseroles to make each day worth waking up for.

Raisa wondered how much of the book was real, and then wondered if it mattered.

Oftentimes it wasn't the truth that was important.

It was understanding what story the author wanted to tell about themselves.

———

Raisa woke with a gasp, every part of her achy.

Probably because she'd slept in a hospital chair.

She wiped at her mouth, and blinked the world into focus.

St. Ivany was slumped in her own chair, her head lolling as she softly snored.

Raisa straightened, kicking the book at her feet as she did.

She had barely made it through the first chapter before nodding off.

Next, Raisa's eyes slid to Kilkenny.

No change. She hadn't expected it, but still the knowledge stung. It had been almost forty-eight hours since the accident.

She was no doctor, but she knew that couldn't be a good sign.

St. Ivany mumbled herself awake. "Christ, I haven't slept in a chair since I was in college."

"Yeah, we're not going to feel great," Raisa acknowledged, standing so she could stretch, a hopeless fight against stiff muscles. "But now we can head straight to Seattle."

St. Ivany checked her phone. "It's only five."

Raisa shrugged. "You said first thing."

"That I did." St. Ivany groaned as she pushed herself to her feet.

St. Ivany drove them. Seattle, distance wise, was only an hour away, but with traffic it took them two hours to get into the city and find a parking spot a few blocks from their final destination.

"I looked at the street view earlier this morning—it seems to be an old house," St. Ivany said. "I searched for expired rental listings, and about a year ago, this address had posted about a basement room."

"Impressive," Raisa murmured.

"Don't sound surprised," St. Ivany said.

Raisa shot her a grin, but then sobered as they walked toward the house on the corner.

She swallowed hard and told herself that Delaney probably wasn't there. She would never let herself be found this way if she didn't want to be.

"If she is involved in all this, she won't want us to come sniffing around," Raisa said. "Which means, she probably won't answer if we knock, and then we'll lose her for good."

"What do you suggest?"

"Waiting her out for now," Raisa said.

St. Ivany nodded. "You know her best."

Raisa didn't, but it meant she'd get her way, so that was fine. They walked past the house and then stopped at a coffee shop, where they set up by a window.

The morning passed slowly into early afternoon.

"Do we even know she's there?" St. Ivany finally asked. They'd sat in silence for the past hour. "We can't just wait here forever."

"I'll go check," Raisa said and then had to shake St. Ivany's hand off. "Better me than you. I can say I wanted to check up on her as her sister. You would start getting into dicey territory."

St. Ivany hesitated, but she had to know Raisa had logic on her side. Eventually, she nodded.

Raisa left her bag with St. Ivany and then headed out of the coffee shop. She eyed the house as she crossed the street at a light jog.

She had a feeling there would be windows somewhere near the ground if the basement had been used as an apartment. Most people wouldn't rent something without at least a little bit of light.

Tall bushes flanked the sides of the house, and Raisa headed toward them—after checking to see if there were any passersby about to call the cops on her.

When she felt confident she had the all clear, she ducked behind one of the plants. It was substantial enough to completely hide her from the street.

Right where she expected, there was a window. Only about a foot by two feet, not enough to slip through, but wide enough to at least check inside.

Raisa dropped to the ground and water immediately soaked into the knees of her jeans.

She took a deep breath and then shifted to peer through the window. And there . . . there was Delaney.

Her back was to Raisa, but her long braid and profile were distinct enough that Raisa could tell, even at a glance, at this awkward angle, that it was her sister.

As if she'd heard the thought, Delaney whipped around.

Instinct had Raisa flattening herself to the wall, her breathing tight.

Delaney hadn't seen her, she was sure of it.

But what if she had?

CHAPTER TWENTY-SIX

Raisa

Day Four

Raisa had the question answered quickly. Delaney had, in fact, realized there was someone looking in her window.

Or, at the very least, she'd had the sensation of eyes on the back of her neck, and that had sent her into flight mode.

By the time Raisa risked peeking in the window again, Delaney was already pulling down a go-bag from her closet. The computer on her desk had a thumb drive shoved into the port. She was getting ready to burn the place.

Metaphorically, of course. Delaney was many things, but an arsonist she was not.

"Shit," Raisa murmured and took off, the blood thrumming in her ears.

She nearly skidded to a halt in front of St. Ivany, who was already half-out of her seat, clearly reading the urgency in Raisa's body language.

"She's about to run," Raisa said, grabbing her bag.

St. Ivany didn't need to be hurried along. "Do we confront her?"

"I don't know, I don't know," Raisa muttered as they sprinted back to the SUV. St. Ivany slid in the driver's side and got them to where they could see the door to Delaney's place in under a minute. "She erased her laptop. And there's nothing to arrest her over. I'm not even sure she's done anything wrong, but I can tell you if we approach her now, she's gonna book it."

"Okay, what do you want to do? Just let her go?"

Raisa looked around. "Do you have an AirTag?"

"Her phone will alert her it's there, even if you can get it on her," St. Ivany said, which wasn't an answer.

"No," Raisa said, her eyes locked on the door. *You know her best.* Maybe she did, more than she thought. "She's gonna drop the phone somewhere. Probably as a ruse to lead whoever is following her out of town."

"You think she'll drop it before the phone alerts her there's a strange AirTag near her?" St. Ivany asked.

"I think we should at least try to figure out a way for her not to disappear off to Mexico, yeah," Raisa said, and then looked over when St. Ivany made a sound. She was holding an AirTag up, one she'd pulled from her console. Raisa fist pumped. "Officially, un-invite me from the case."

"You're officially un-invited," St. Ivany said, handing the thing over. Raisa wasn't sure how much of this would hold up as quality police work, but she wasn't about to let Delaney lose them without a fight. They would figure everything else out later.

Delaney chose that moment to step out onto the sidewalk, her bag slung over her shoulder. There were no keys in her hand, so they might get lucky. She was fleeing on foot.

"What do you want me to do?" St. Ivany asked.

"I'm going to get out and follow her. You'll be backup in case I lose her," Raisa said. "Stick with Delaney, not me."

"You're chopped liver. Got it," St. Ivany said, giving her a jaunty salute.

Raisa grabbed her purse this time and left her bag. She had no interest in getting stuck in the middle of Seattle without any money.

She waited until the second Delaney was out of sight and then she hopped out of the SUV, following her at a fast clip. Running would bring attention to both of them, and considering how quiet the street was, she wanted to avoid that if at all possible.

For a brief moment, she considered simply calling out to Delaney. Her fleeing like this wasn't necessarily a sign of her guilt—Raisa was sure she would have run no matter what as soon as she'd seen someone looking in her window. Maybe if Raisa asked, without the Gig Harbor police force behind her, whether Delaney was currently caught up in another one of Isabel's schemes, she'd get an honest answer.

But why would Delaney tell her anything, when for two years Raisa had made her feel like she'd be locked up if she ever stepped a single toe over the line?

What if Delaney had been forced to do something heinous because of Isabel? She had visited Lindsey Cousins and left her "rattled." She had been spotted outside Peter Stamkos's house. Emily Logan had died the same way their parents had been killed, and Raisa had convinced herself that Delaney would never copy that.

But what if it had been a message to Isabel?

I can kill your protégé and get away with it, too.

It would explain the rage.

So Raisa followed her through the streets. She didn't know Seattle well, but she managed, apart from two close calls, to keep Delaney mostly in her sights.

The second one happened when they were in the heart of downtown. She rounded a corner to find only tourists and locals swarming on the sidewalks. Delaney must have ducked in somewhere to try to catch any potential tail off guard. Raisa swayed, feeling vulnerable out in the open.

Raisa didn't know if she course-corrected in time to avoid detection, but when she slid into a coffee shop to regain her bearings, she realized where they were.

Right outside the ferry terminal.

Using the ferry to disappear was smart of Delaney, but Raisa wouldn't have expected anything less. It, also, thankfully worked in Raisa's favor.

Raisa patiently waited in the coffee shop until Delaney finally ducked out of the shadows of a skyscraper and headed toward the terminal.

Following her would be way too risky at this point. Instead, Raisa pulled up the schedule on her phone. The next ferry leaving was in twenty minutes, and it was headed to Bainbridge.

She looked around and found three men shooting the shit outside the furniture store to her right. She flashed her badge but also made sure the fifty she'd pulled from her wallet was visible.

"Gentlemen, may I ask a favor?"

She quickly had a taker. After that, all she could do was wait until he came back out, flashing her a thumbs-up. He must have been able to drop the AirTag into Delaney's bag—or he was lying to her for the money. Raisa would have to wait until St. Ivany picked her up to confirm either way.

Only a few minutes later, St. Ivany pulled to a stop in front of the alley where Raisa had been lingering.

A second later, she was in the SUV's passenger seat.

"She hasn't found it yet," St. Ivany said, handing Raisa her phone, which had a little map of the terminal and the sound beyond it. Delaney—along with the AirTag—was pulling away from the dock.

"Don't jinx it," Raisa muttered, and St. Ivany shut up as she started driving south, out of town.

"Should we head to Bainbridge?" St. Ivany asked.

You know her best.

"I don't think she's in full flight mode," Raisa said. "I think she'll circle back."

"To Seattle?"

Raisa chewed on her lip. It wasn't that she knew Delaney best, she realized. It was just that she knew what someone like her—mainly Raisa herself—would do in this situation.

"She's involved, somehow, in all this up to her eyeballs," Raisa said. "She's going to want to stick around and figure out why someone is following her. What they know, and if it can hurt her."

"Okay," St. Ivany said.

Raisa shot her a look. "You're being very cooperative."

"It hasn't steered me wrong yet today," St. Ivany pointed out.

Which made her wonder . . .

"Did you ever think I was a part of this?" Raisa asked. "Like Isabel had gotten to me. Or that I had killed her myself?"

"I might have landed there eventually," St. Ivany mused. "But I thought you were just being . . . stubborn."

"Diplomatic."

"Always," St. Ivany shot back. "Pretty much up until that little disappearing act Delaney just tried to pull, I was still thinking it was the boyfriend who had killed Emily."

"Delaney leaving convinced you?" Raisa asked, almost surprised. Maybe she was just more familiar with Delaney's paranoia. "She had a go-bag ready; she was able to leave the apartment within five minutes. I think she's guilty of something, but that? She's just like a deer—she catches scent of *something* and goes into *get the hell out of here* mode no matter the level of danger she's in."

"That's quite an analogy," St. Ivany said. "Still on?"

Raisa glanced down. The ferry was halfway across the sound. Delaney hadn't found the tracker, and it was likely she would drop her phone at any second.

"I think we're good."

They both sank back into their seats as some of the tension bled out of the air.

"That was smart thinking," St. Ivany admitted.

"I'm just glad you had one," Raisa said. They could have figured out some way to keep eyes on Delaney, but it would have been so much more difficult.

"So, what's the plan?" St. Ivany asked.

Raisa eyed her and tried to be objective. In her white blazer and with her pretty hair, she didn't read as a cop. "You go talk to her? Wherever she lands?"

"What's the goal with that?" St. Ivany asked. "Do we really want to scare her further?"

They were out of the city now, and Delaney was inching closer to the peninsula. "Delaney is smart, but if she's spooked, she might make an unforced error. We want to keep her unbalanced and anxious."

St. Ivany nodded and then pulled into the parking lot of the next fast-food restaurant.

When she fully braked, she turned to look at Raisa. "You still don't think she killed Emily?"

Raisa hesitated, and St. Ivany pounced.

"You've changed your mind," she said.

"No." Raisa dragged out the denial. "I think if she was angry enough at Isabel for putting her into a bad situation, she might have taken it out on a protégé who was killing people."

"And that protégé might have been Emily?"

Raisa shrugged. "It's a theory. She demonstrated poor coping skills by posting the nudes in her boyfriend's phone. It could indicate she had a broader personality disorder."

St. Ivany shook her head. "What a way to have to live."

"What do you mean?"

"I never wondered what it would be like to have a psychopathic serial killer as a sibling, but it sounds exhausting," St. Ivany drawled.

Raisa stared at her for a long time, until a laugh escaped. Once she started, she couldn't stop it. St. Ivany joined her—probably because laughter was contagious, not because anything was that funny.

"You have no fucking idea," Raisa said when she'd finally gotten herself back under control.

St. Ivany was about to say something, but before she could, Raisa held up the phone.

Right now, nothing else mattered.

Delaney was on the move.

CHAPTER TWENTY-SEVEN

Raisa

Day Four

Delaney drove to a Best Buy in Tacoma and walked out with a laptop-shaped bag.

Then she headed to a hole-in-the-wall bar.

St. Ivany and Raisa parked in a strip mall across the street.

"I'm going to go in," St. Ivany said.

"What are you going to say?" Raisa asked.

"I'll figure it out when I get in there."

St. Ivany shrugged out of her blazer and ruffled her hair. It had already looked soft to start with, but whatever she'd done added some more shape to the cut. She closed her eyes, took a deep breath, and then tossed Raisa the keys.

"In case you need them." And with that, she got out of the SUV.

She was in there for a total of ten minutes, and Raisa counted every second that went by, wondering if they should have called in backup. At least this time, she had her gun.

Raisa had already climbed into the driver seat, so when the door opened and St. Ivany walked out, she was able to pick her up and peel out of the lot as quickly as possible.

"She was looking at a list of Isabel's victims' names," St. Ivany said. "But judging from the photo of it, it looked . . . handwritten. Like the letter you got from Isabel."

Raisa wasn't surprised. She'd assumed that her sisters had been communicating, through the Biggest Fan letters, of course, but through other means as well.

"I gave her my number," St. Ivany said, looking ruffled for perhaps the first time since Raisa had met her. "I don't know what I was thinking. I probably should have planned that better."

Raisa laughed, though it came out a little hysterical. They really should have planned all this better. Delaney had thrown them into chaos when she'd grabbed that go-bag.

That had been a miscalculation on Raisa's part.

"Do you guys have any evidence in Emily Logan's case?" Raisa asked. She knew she should have studied it more by now. Maybe she would have seen an actual connection to Delaney, instead of just her brain constructing webs that were made of nothing but gut instincts.

"Nothing. It was incredibly clean," St. Ivany said. "Weirdly so for such a violent death. It was why we wondered about the boyfriend, who works for the hospital."

"Working around blood doesn't mean he knows how to kill someone without leaving DNA behind," Raisa pointed out.

"Yeah, but it helps." St. Ivany was silent for a beat before asking, "Did we just drive away from Emily Logan's killer?"

"He's got the taste of blood now. It's a tragedy, but you gotta do what you gotta do."

There was a scenario here where Delaney had snapped completely. Isabel had told her to kill Peter and Lindsey and Emily and she'd simply followed orders. That didn't match with the Delaney Raisa knew. That was a strange thought to have, considering how hard Raisa had been on her sister since they'd reunited. But here, facing down a possible situation where Delaney really was a cold-blooded killer, Raisa couldn't see it.

If she had to guess, Delaney had been spotted near Peter's house because Isabel had said her protégé was going to try to kill him. Same with Lindsey.

If that protégé had been Emily, did that mean Delaney had put her down, like a dog with the taste of blood?

Raisa didn't answer St. Ivany's question. She couldn't. Instead, she pulled into another parking lot, this one a grocery store. She jerked her head toward St. Ivany's phone. "Where is she?"

"Still at the bar," St. Ivany said, and then she shifted so that she could look at Raisa. "Can I take a guess at what you're thinking?"

"Sure," Raisa said, though she was slightly nervous about it.

"Let's say Delaney killed Emily," St. Ivany said. "It was because she was looking for someone who was on a murder spree, right? She thought Emily was killing other people, but now that Isabel is dead, she realizes she got the wrong person. There's still someone out there, and she needs to stop them."

"Yeah," Raisa said. That about summed it up perfectly. St. Ivany was more perceptive than Raisa gave her credit for.

"So she must be looking for someone who has a passing interest in Isabel, right? Maybe someone who admires how Isabel went about her business . . ."

"Yeah," Raisa said again, wondering where this was going.

St. Ivany looked sheepish but she shouldered on. "This . . . might not exactly be, uh, by the book, but I have an idea."

"Gabriela Cruz?" Raisa asked, when St. Ivany—who'd retaken the driver's seat—pulled to a stop outside the girl's house. "She's just a college student."

"A criminal justice major," St. Ivany added. "She works for us in the summers, and she'll probably apply to the force once she graduates in the winter. She has some training."

"Some training filing the archives," Raisa muttered. "Did she get a fake badge and everything?"

St. Ivany sent her a look. "I'm serious. She monitors campus safety as well. And you say Delaney will either run or clam up if we try to confront her right now. We have to go in sideways."

That was true. Delaney was too smart for them to break in any conventional way. They needed to apply more pressure, to bait her a little, to get her to act, but to do so recklessly so she'd make a mistake.

She would already be on the alert, just from Maeve approaching her in the bar. If they relented, they would lose the chance to capitalize on that anxiety.

But Raisa was still balking at putting a civilian in harm's way. Especially one she was rooting for.

"If you have other ideas . . . ," St. Ivany said.

"Can you even ask her to do this?"

"We have authority to hire people to go undercover for us," St. Ivany said. "We would have her miked the whole time, and a whole fleet of police hiding nearby to make sure she's safe. It would be like any other sting."

Raisa groaned, but then got out of the SUV, leaving St. Ivany behind. She crossed to Gabriela's door and knocked.

"What do you want now?" Gabriela asked when she answered.

Raisa sighed. "I have a favor to ask."

Gabriela was the one who suggested the party at the beach.

"It's all over Facebook. Anyone who wants to come can just show up. And there will definitely be boys there who toe the lines with the girls," Gabriela said. "If you're looking for someone who is targeting predators—it's the perfect place to go."

"And you're comfortable with this?" Raisa asked for perhaps the thousandth time.

"Yeah." Gabriela's big eyes were terribly wide, and it was obvious she was trying to keep the excitement out of her voice. "She's not hunting *me*."

Maybe. But they were going to make Delaney think that she *should* be.

Raisa studied Gabriela, looking for nerves. There were some, under the rush of adrenaline. But they didn't seem to be crippling.

"Don't do anything," Raisa said. "If she talks to you, great. But don't try to goad her into anything."

Gabriela sent her a look. "So you're sending me in there for no purpose at all, then?"

"I'm serious," Raisa said. "Don't poke her."

"I don't even know what she looks like," Gabriela pointed out.

"You think there will be a lot of middle-aged ladies hanging out with a bunch of college students?" Raisa asked.

"Hey, we're not ageists here."

Raisa rolled her eyes. "She looks like Isabel."

"Does she really?"

"Yeah." Though even as she answered, Raisa almost walked that back. Before Raisa had known Delaney was her sister, she hadn't seen the resemblance. Or maybe she hadn't wanted to see it.

The rest of the day was devoted to prep work. Around dusk, they got Gabriela wired up and then drove as close to the beach party as they dared.

Gabriela sent them a grin. "You guys look like you think I'm about to go get murdered."

Raisa tried to smile back. "Don't do anything to antagonize her. She's more dangerous than she looks."

"As you've warned five billion times," Gabriela said, with an eye roll before popping out of the SUV. "I'm not an idiot, I promise."

And then she was gone into the night.

St. Ivany's mouth pinched tight. They had three of her uniforms stationed around the party, and her partner in another SUV down the road on the other side so they'd be able to monitor everyone who came and went. But St. Ivany wasn't going to relax until Gabriela returned to the back seat unharmed.

Raisa checked to make sure no one could overhear her before turning to St. Ivany. "Do you trust Gabriela?"

St. Ivany made a considering sound. "As much as I would trust any twenty-two-year-old civilian."

"She's obsessed with Isabel," Raisa pointed out. "That could make her the copycat."

"You said the copycat would be erratic, didn't you?" St. Ivany asked. "Does she seem erratic?"

"No," Raisa admitted, shifting to once again look out the windshield. The only reason Gabriela had let them in the apartment that first day was because she'd wanted to know what had happened to Isabel. She didn't seem like some kind of protégé who'd had a rift with her beloved mentor.

Still, Raisa'd had to ask. Delaney was a blind spot for her. Raisa had to steer away from any theory involving her sister, because she was always already sliding toward thinking Delaney was guilty.

And right now, she was worried that she was missing something obvious because she'd been chasing Delaney all day.

St. Ivany was a steadying presence beside her, though. One who wouldn't put up with Raisa's bullshit.

"That's the first time you really asked about Emily Logan in a way an impartial detective would," St. Ivany had said. She wouldn't hesitate to slap Raisa's wrist again, either.

It took an hour before they heard Gabriela audibly inhale over the mic.

"She found her," Raisa murmured.

"No one has cigarettes anymore," Gabriela said to someone, her voice incredibly casual. She was a natural at this.

"They're the leading cause of preventable disease and death in the United States," Delaney replied, and Raisa almost laughed.

St. Ivany huffed out something approximating humor. "Does she always talk like that?"

"Yeah," Raisa said, feeling fond. Kind of.

"She was like that in the bar, too," St. Ivany murmured quickly so as not to speak over the conversation. "I thought she was trying to scare me off."

"No," Raisa said. "That's just how she is."

Gabriela was trying to get info from Delaney and failing. It wasn't exactly poking the bear, but Raisa was tense as she listened to the efforts.

Then Delaney offered, *"It's tough out there for girls these days."*

A pause. Gabriela knew that they wanted Delaney to be intrigued by her. Raisa's heart kicked up as she realized that of course Gabriela was going to try to goad Delaney instead of listening to any one of Raisa's warnings.

"These days? Try at any point in history."

"Anyone I should keep my eye out for?" Delaney asked.

St. Ivany's brows raised when Gabriela actually pointed two guys out.

"Yeah, that's what happens if you send a twenty-two-year-old civilian to deal with a potential homicidal woman," Raisa said, angry—at herself more than anything.

"We'll send uniforms to make sure they're safe," St. Ivany promised. But she looked unsure for the first time since she'd come up with the plan.

"We have to do something," Delaney said. Raisa guessed from the snippets of conversation that the two guys Gabriela had pointed out were cornering a girl at the party.

"You think I haven't tried?" Gabriela shot back.

St. Ivany inhaled sharply, and pressed the mic button. "Gabriela, get back here now, or I'm sending someone in for you."

"Hey, it was nice meeting you, but I gotta pee," Gabriela said, immediately. She must have known if St. Ivany was threatening to

pull the trigger when she'd been on board the rest of the time, then it was serious.

Two minutes later, the SUV's back door opened, and Gabriela hopped back in, her grin wide.

"I definitely made her think I'm sus," Gabriela said. When they just looked at her, she shrugged. "I'll sleep with the lights on tonight."

"You'll sleep with a police officer stationed outside your building tonight," St. Ivany corrected, before she started the SUV. Then grudgingly, she added, "Good work."

When they dropped Gabriela off, St. Ivany pulled up her phone. Delaney hadn't discovered the AirTag yet, which had to be at the bottom of her purse.

She was currently leaving the beach, driving not toward them but south toward the highway.

"Did she get spooked?" St. Ivany asked, but as she did, the AirTag stopped.

A motel.

A motel on the outskirts of town, Raisa heard in one of the many voices she'd listened to over the past few days.

Who had said it, though?

"You game?" St. Ivany asked, and Raisa nodded.

They drove in silence until the motel came into view—a real dump, a pay-by-the-hour type place. St. Ivany parked beneath a broken streetlight.

They waited for an hour or so until a door on the ground level opened.

Delaney stepped out of her room, carrying something.

Raisa tensed, but all Delaney did was sit at the edge of the pool.

About five minutes later, another door opened, this time on the second floor.

It looked like a man, tall and lanky with hair that he'd tied into a topknot.

And just as he moved into the light, Raisa remembered who had said he was staying here.

She and St. Ivany watched as Roan Carmichael joined Delaney at the edge of the unfilled pool.

Then ten minutes later, they watched as Delaney led him back to her room.

CHAPTER TWENTY-EIGHT

Delaney

Day Seven

Delaney stared at the police radio app as if the voice would come on and say the suicide at the harbor was a false alarm.

If it wasn't, Delaney truly did have the man's blood on her hands. She should have called the cops when she'd watched Gabriela drive away with him. She should have called Raisa, at the very least.

And all she'd been able to do was stand by helplessly, like she had all her life.

She closed her eyes, thinking about that evening two years earlier when she, Raisa, and Isabel stood in a loose circle, guns all trained on each other.

Delaney hadn't pulled the trigger. Because she'd never been strong enough to do so.

The story she told about herself was that she was logical, highly intelligent, awkward, but with a strong sense of justice.

After all, she'd been ridding the dark web of monsters for more than half her life now.

But all that had ever taken was anonymous tips to the FBI. She wasn't the one who kicked down doors, who chased bad guys. She wrote an email, made a phone call, all from the safety of her computer.

She was a bystander.

"You're as guilty as me," Isabel had said, and for the first time Delaney believed it.

She waited until the sun came up before packing all her things. She wouldn't be coming back to the motel.

Delaney swung her bag into the beat-up tin can of a fourth-hand Toyota that she was still driving and then nearly screamed when she closed the trunk.

Roan Carmichael stood there, his face all shadows as the sun rose behind him.

"You can't leave." His voice came out strange, wrong.

Delaney huffed a breath and started toward the driver's side. "Watch me."

"No." He lashed out, his hand gripping her arm tight, his fingers pressing into the soft flesh. There would be bruises there tomorrow. "You. Can't. Leave."

CHAPTER TWENTY-NINE

Raisa

Day Five

Raisa and St. Ivany staked out the motel for about an hour after Delaney led Roan Carmichael back into her room. Raisa deliberately blocked any thoughts about what they were doing from her brain. Instead, she tried to find everything she could about Roan, while St. Ivany called her partner for his take on the man.

"Seems straightforward," Raisa said as they drove back toward town, the motel shrinking in the side mirror. "Isabel killed his brother, he met with Emily because she found him through their shared interest in true crime's effects on the victims' families. Did he kill Isabel, then?"

Wouldn't that be strange? If they'd looked into all these other deaths and they hadn't had anything to do with Isabel's.

"Seems like a possibility," St. Ivany said. "We already know he's a liar since he told me he was just a friend of Emily's passing through."

Raisa said, "I don't know where Delaney comes into all this, either."

"Maybe she's next," St. Ivany mused, sounding interested enough in the possibility that Raisa almost wanted her to turn the SUV around. But if they did, if they barged into that motel room, apart from it being potentially incredibly awkward, they would also scare one or both of their suspects into completely clamming up.

They wouldn't be able to arrest them for anything, either. So all they would accomplish was losing their upper hand.

Raisa didn't think either of them was going to die tonight.

She could be wrong, but it was a risk she was willing to take.

"Regroup in the morning?" Raisa asked, when St. Ivany pulled to a stop in front of the boutique hotel.

"Yeah," St. Ivany agreed, though she sounded lost in thought.

"What?" Raisa asked.

"I don't know," St. Ivany admitted. "I can't get a handle on this thing. And you're leading me astray."

Raisa laughed. "Yeah, maybe."

St. Ivany shot her a grin. "Get some sleep. Maybe in the light of day this will all make sense."

Before Raisa closed the door, she threw St. Ivany a salute, though she had no intention of actually getting any rest.

She wanted to make it through Essi's book.

Out of everything she had in terms of writing samples, that was the one she'd barely touched.

Raisa settled into Kilkenny's hotel room—her own had plastic sheeting over the door.

And then she started, once more, from the beginning.

It took only three hours to get through.

When she was done, she didn't feel like she had any answers. She wondered if she'd just completely wasted her time.

But studying words was never a waste.

She went back through, marking key passages that had come across as particularly voice-y, and she started to build an analysis on them.

Essi was conversational. Her use of contractions—which often gave writing a natural feel—became an idiolectic marker. She never used *I am* when she could use *I'm*. She used metaphors and similes so rarely that Raisa wondered if the ones that showed up on the page had been edited in.

Her grammar was harder to judge because she'd likely had several professionals work on the book. But whoever that was had done a nice job.

What was striking to Raisa was that it didn't sound like anything she'd worked on to this point in the case. Narratively, Essi was able to close a circle when she started drawing one—unlike Emily. She never slipped into any of the psychopathic tics that Lindsey did with her writing.

The closest she sounded to any of the players in the case was to Isabel herself. Namely the way they both wrote as if they were addressing the reader.

Do you hate me yet? Essi had asked in one of her opening paragraphs. It was achingly similar to how Isabel had always included *my friend* when writing, even just to herself.

It was something performers did. Not professional performers, necessarily, but people who performed for others as their main type of presentation to the world—which described Essi to a T, if Roan was to be believed. It was a hard habit to turn off, apparently.

Essi did use a few idioms that were slightly left of center, which Raisa assumed were English translations of Finnish originals.

To run with one's head as a third leg.
There are two ends of a sausage.
To pick up one's bones.

The last one—meaning, to finally get around to leaving a gathering—was so interesting that Raisa searched it in a few of the databases she used for her investigations.

The Communicated Threat Assessment Database—the brainchild of Jim Fitzgerald, a prominent agent who worked on the Unabomber case—pinged back a result.

It came in an email written by Mikko Halla, Essi's father.

That wasn't . . . completely strange. Children often used idioms passed down by their parents or grandparents, especially ones that came from their country of origin.

But Raisa slowly toggled over to the software she used to build idiolect analyses, and started one for Mikko Halla.

She then searched his name rather than the idiom itself in the CTAD.

The database wasn't just for threatening messages sent to the FBI; rather, it was meant to hold any kind of written documents that played an important role in *any* investigation.

That meant her request returned dozens of emails and texts all written by Mikko, unearthed in the federal investigation into his business practices.

Raisa glanced at the clock. It was well past midnight, but she wasn't about to put this off until morning.

She pulled a few of the longer emails at random to better get a sense of his authorial voice.

Then she started to read.

All contractions, no metaphors, no similes. A conversational tone sprinkled with strange idioms.

Addressing an audience.

Do you hate me now? one of the emails read. It was in a different tone from the one in Essi's book—snarky and challenging, rather than sheepish and vulnerable.

But it was written by the same person.

Raisa was almost sure of it.

By the time she made it through a dozen emails, she had a profile built that was almost exactly the same as Essi's book.

A fingerprint.

Essi had been running her father's business behind his name.

Raisa whistled long and slow as she slumped back into her chair.

She picked up the phone and called St. Ivany even though it was past 2:00 a.m.

St. Ivany answered on the second ring. "Is someone dead?"

"Mikko Halla," Raisa said.

A pause. "One more time."

"The father of Essi Halla, the woman who is profiting off of saying Isabel killed that very same crook of a businessman father," Raisa said. "She wrote a self-help book about it."

"About getting over your father being the victim of a serial killer?" St. Ivany asked, still sounding mostly like she was half-asleep.

"Pretty much," Raisa agreed. "Only, she's been upfront about it being a performance."

"A grift," St. Ivany said, finally waking up.

"Yeah," Raisa said. "But now I'm wondering if that was all it was."

"What do you mean?"

Raisa explained her work over the past two hours. And then: "I think she might have been running the organization."

"Holy shit," St. Ivany said. "Is that really something your boys would miss?"

"It was a back-taxes case. There was no reason to call a forensic linguist in," Raisa said, defensive of agents who would never defend her in return. "They had the white-collar guys working on it. I'm sure they saw Mikko in the boardrooms and then on email and never once considered he was a figurehead."

"So . . ."

"So did he really die by suicide?" Raisa asked. "Or did Essi kill him so he wouldn't snitch to the feds?"

"Damn," St. Ivany muttered. "Okay, so what does that have to do with either of our homicides?"

Was that the first time St. Ivany hadn't tacked on a *potential* while describing Isabel's death? Raisa couldn't remember, but it sounded newly serious. "Honestly? Maybe nothing. She took advantage of the fact that Isabel had victims in the area, and continued figuring out a way to make money while her other source evaporated."

"I better flag this for the boys down in California," St. Ivany said. There was some ruffling, like she had now fully resigned herself to getting out of bed.

"Sorry," Raisa said, squinting out into the night. "I'll send a note to the lead on the FBI investigation."

"Cool. Let's touch base in the morning?"

"Yeah," Raisa said. "Hey, is Delaney still at the hotel?"

"She found the AirTag," St. Ivany said, with a sigh. "It's disabled. I'll send someone over to keep track of her."

She'll lose them easy enough, Raisa thought.

"See you in the morning," Raisa said.

It would be a long five hours between then and now.

Raisa eyed Essi's book. It had given up a few answers, but she still felt like she was missing something.

Something small, even.

Which meant reading the book in its entirety again.

She finished faster this time and still couldn't put her finger on what had her itching for a third read.

Whatever it was, going through each page, sentence by sentence, wasn't going to shake it loose.

So she showered and thought about sleeping.

Instead, she slipped under the plastic on her old room to grab the box of Isabel's things, everything she'd gotten from the correctional facility. When Raisa had come to Gig Harbor, it had been with the purpose of figuring out who had killed Isabel. Since then, she'd been pulled in a million different directions.

Here were Isabel's belongings, though, and she'd barely made her way through them so far.

She returned to Kilkenny's room and then sorted them out, carefully going through the wallet. Checking every centimeter of the watch for a hidden compartment.

The only thing that really stood out was the landscape painting that Raisa was sure had been done in some art therapy class. But Isabel wouldn't have saved it just because she'd been proud of it.

She wasn't wired like that. She was proud of her victim list; she was proud of how long she'd operated before getting caught. Beyond that, she didn't understand how to feel proud about normal things. Like a painting.

So why had she kept it around?

The landscape was of a ridge of mountains. They made Raisa think of the hiking trails in the Biggest Fan letters.

She touched her fingertip to the canvas, dragging it along the surface until it connected with a thin brown line.

A hiking trail.

It was a visual clue, one Raisa wasn't sure she would have found if she hadn't been up all night existentially contemplating her life.

Raisa followed the trail all the way to the corner of the painting, where it dipped over the side. Instead of ending, it continued on toward the back.

Which was thicker than it should be, she realized.

Raisa quickly unearthed the Swiss Army Knife she kept in her bag at all times—a tradition that felt terribly old-fashioned but had been extremely useful too many times to get rid of it.

The extra layer came off easily in her hand, but it was blank.

Before disappointment could set in, Raisa realized that it had been hiding something else.

A folded-up piece of paper.

One that looked like it had been ripped from Isabel's journal.

Raisa stared at it like the bomb she knew it could be.

It was one page, handwritten.

Everyone always wants me to start from the beginning.
But where is the beginning?

Raisa read through it without thinking like a linguist. She didn't pick up on word choice or grammar or narrative voice. Instead, she read it like a note she wasn't sure she'd been meant to find.

She read it like a true diary, not one that had been written for an audience.

I wanted to make them the same as me.
Broken.
Lana and Larissa aren't broken.
But wouldn't it be more fun if they were?

CHAPTER THIRTY

DELANEY

Day Seven

"Take your hands off of me," Delaney told Roan through gritted teeth. She didn't want to make a scene but she would.

Roan immediately stepped back, holding up his palms. "Whoa. No. Sorry. That was way more threatening than intended."

Delaney stared at him. "I think it was exactly as threatening as intended."

His mouth tightened. "Okay, maybe. Can we talk?"

"No," Delaney said, heading toward the front of the car. He kept pace but on the other side, sliding into the passenger seat before she could get to the locks. "Get out."

"Drive north," was all he said.

Again, she stared at him, incredulous. He was acting like he had some kind of power over her even though he wasn't holding a gun or any kind of weapon. She could simply ignore him.

But then he might draw attention to both of them. That was the exact opposite of what she wanted.

Still, she said, "No. Get out."

"Delaney," Roan said. "I know you don't trust me. But you need to right now. You're about to go do something stupid, aren't you?"

Delaney didn't answer. She didn't say anything, actually.

He visibly swallowed. "Babe, it's a trap. They're trying to draw you out."

"Who is?" she snapped.

"Detective Maeve St. Ivany," he said, and then hesitated. "And your sister."

She blinked at him, hardly able to comprehend that this drifter, this man who'd picnicked with her on the boat, could know about Raisa. And . . . Maeve.

Of course.

The woman at the bar.

Did that mean it had been Raisa hunting her all along?

She closed her eyes, then realized that was giving Roan trust he didn't deserve. When she opened them, though, he was just studying her, his eyes earnest, his hands clear of his pockets.

"Why should I believe you?" she asked.

"Just give me a chance to explain." Roan took out his phone and punched something in before holding out a map to her. "Go to this cove. It has a long road leading down to the water—we'll be able to tell if anyone is following us."

That was a smart move. Delaney thought about her other plan, which he'd been right about. It *was* stupid. She was going to confront Gabriela without much of a plan.

Figuring out what was going on with Roan might be more productive at the moment.

The entire drive she kept her attention equally divided between the road, Roan, and the rearview mirror.

They didn't speak again until they got to the rocky shoreline.

He started to say something when she parked, but she got out of the car, heading toward the water.

"Who are you?" she asked, when they both reached the sand.

"Your sister killed my brother," Roan said. "Mitchell Johnston."

Delaney knew the name immediately. A stabbing outside a bar.

Back when she'd been chasing Isabel, she hadn't been sure the man was one of Isabel's victims. But the prosecutor's team had found photos and receipts linking Isabel to the bar.

"Are you here to take your revenge?" she asked, eyes on the water, giving him the chance if he wanted to seize it. All it would take was a quick strike, and then he could simply dump her body out here.

He breathed out. "I thought about it."

She glanced at him, surprised. She'd thought he'd either deny it or kill her.

Roan nodded. "Not . . . with any intent, really. But Isabel destroyed my family. It wasn't just my brother who died that night—he took my mother with him. Then me, honestly. I've only come back to life in the past couple years, and even then, it was mostly my hatred of Isabel that kept me going."

"I look like her," Delaney said, not sure why she was goading him on. It was almost like she couldn't help herself. She thought of that man last night, the family he must have. She thought of how she'd let him drive away with Gabbi, a woman she suspected was a serial killer on the verge of a complete breakdown. Delaney took Roan's hand, placed it against her throat. His palm flexed against the quick pulse he must feel there. "Don't you want to?"

For one heartbeat, his hand tightened, just a whisper of pressure, really. And then he stumbled backward, appalled.

"No, no. Fuck no, Delaney, Jesus," Roan muttered. "What the hell?"

She turned back to the water as if nothing had happened, despite the fact that she could feel the echo of his warmth against her skin. "Then what do you want?"

"Okay," he drawled out. "Someday we're going to talk about that."

Delaney shot him a look. There would be no *someday*.

"Detective St. Ivany is hunting Emily Logan's killer," Roan said. "I know you know who that is—you're not dumb."

She nodded to get him to go on.

"And she's hunting you," Roan continued. "That night you and I met? I had talked to Raisa the day before. She didn't seem to suspect me of much, but . . . well. I'm not proud of it. But I wanted to see where they were going with their investigation, so I followed them."

No part of this conversation was going as planned. "What?"

"I got into the cold-case community a while back," he said, pacing now. "I'm not saying it was a good idea, but I learned a lot. About police work, about police in general. I knew they were interested in me. They'd already brought me in because I'd talked to Emily before her death. I had a solid alibi, thank god, but then Raisa contacted me."

"You thought they might suspect you, despite the alibi," Delaney said.

"Yeah, so I followed them following you."

She narrowed her eyes at him. "Right."

He snapped his fingers. "You went into a bar. A hole-in-the-wall. St. Ivany went in after you. Raisa sat in the SUV."

Delaney pressed her lips together. "That was sloppy of them."

"And of you," he said, and she had to concede he had a point.

"They dropped an AirTag on me," Delaney muttered, and then realized that letting them do that had been sloppy in and of itself. Best to keep it moving. "Okay, so then you decided to sleep with me?"

"No," he all but shouted. "I just wanted to talk. I knew who you were, but didn't want to scare you off." He paused. "The sleeping-with-you thing . . . well. I just think you're hot."

She stared at him. "My sister killed your brother."

"And no matter what you might think, you're not her," he said, and she realized in that moment he must have been to excellent therapy.

Delaney waved the argument away. "Anyway . . . ?"

"They recruited Gabriela Cruz to provoke you into making a mistake," he finally said on a rush. "I know her from her online presence. She bragged about it in a private chat, and I got sent the screenshot from a friend. The police miked her up to go talk to you on the beach. They want you to think she's . . . I don't know . . . something other than she is. Which is a basic college girl too interested in police work for her own good."

Delaney thought about the beach, the bonfire.

"No one has cigarettes anymore," Gabbi had said.

Delaney had been pleased she hadn't had to approach the girl first. But, of course, she'd been so stupid. Still, she was certain of one thing. "No, she's lying to them."

"How can you be so sure?" Roan asked, like he really did want her to give him reassurance. Her stomach tightened. "Delaney. How do you know that you're not the one being played?"

CHAPTER THIRTY-ONE

Raisa

Day Six

Raisa sat staring out the window of the hotel room, Isabel's journal page on the desk in front of her. She'd read it so many times now, she had it memorized.

Lana and Larissa aren't broken.
But wouldn't it be more fun if they were?

She felt like it was the key to everything, and yet, Raisa couldn't see the few steps ahead she needed to.

Once again, Isabel was winning.

Meet me at the harbor, she texted St. Ivany.

Ten minutes later Raisa found St. Ivany standing across the street from the very coffee shop where Raisa and Kilkenny had stopped the morning of his accident.

Something pulled tight in her chest and she brushed it aside. She took one of the cups St. Ivany was holding. "Isabel hid a page of her diary behind a painting that was included in her belongings." She took a sip of the coffee. "Belongings she wanted left to me."

St. Ivany took her own long gulp. "I'm almost scared to ask, but what did it say?"

"That Isabel wanted to see both me and Delaney broken like her," Raisa said. "It's not a surprise, especially considering she wrote it while rotting away in prison. She would be the last person in the world who would ever want to see us thrive while she was stuck behind bars."

"Broken," St. Ivany repeated slowly. "Okay, what exactly does that entail?"

If she had been in the car with Kilkenny, she wouldn't have hesitated to say what she was thinking. Now she studied St. Ivany. They might not ever be bosom buddies, but the detective was fine enough. There was no real reason not to trust her. They'd come this far, after all.

"Delaney has always maintained a bit of moral superiority over Isabel because she's never actually killed anyone."

St. Ivany made a concerned sound. "Isabel wants to force Delaney into taking a life."

"That's my thought," Raisa said. The hiking trail reviews slotted perfectly into that theory. Isabel had given Delaney a task, and Delaney had *not* wanted to do it.

"And what about you?" St. Ivany asked, sliding her a glance.

"She wants to force me to arrest Delaney after Delaney kills someone," Raisa said, her throat raw from even speaking the words. "Or perhaps she wants me to kill Delaney in the process? That would probably do it."

"Man, she was a sadistic little bitch, wasn't she?" St. Ivany said.

Raisa barked out a laugh. "Yes."

"So maybe Delaney already broke," St. Ivany said. "What if she killed Emily Logan?"

"Then there's nothing left to do but arrest her for it," Raisa said, hating, hating, hating that Isabel would get what she wanted.

"That's . . . frustrating," St. Ivany said as she looked around. "What do you want from the harbor?"

She was about to explain about Essi, when something flashed in the corner of her eye.

"St. Ivany," she said, swiveling to find what had caught her attention. "What's that?"

St. Ivany turned as well. "What do you mean?"

The sun shifted again. "There."

A moment of silence. And then St. Ivany offered, hesitantly, "I don't know. Looks like a camera lens."

Raisa stared up at the curtain, running the calculations in her head. "Did your people talk to that person?"

"What?"

"They would have had a view of the accident," Raisa said, already moving. "They would have had a view of the SUV that hit Kilkenny."

"I don't know," St. Ivany said, keeping pace as Raisa broke into a jog to cross the street. "They should have."

Raisa slowed to a stop, searching for the right door that would take them up to the second-floor apartment. She found it wedged between the coffee shop and the florist. Thankfully, it wasn't locked, and she took the stairs two at a time.

No one answered when she knocked, so she pounded on the door again and then again.

"This is getting close to harassment," St. Ivany muttered from where she leaned against the opposite wall.

"Hello," Raisa called, desperate. "I'm FBI Agent Raisa Susanto. I'm trying to figure out who put my partner in the hospital. I was hoping you might be able to help."

She dropped silent, listening, waiting. St. Ivany leaned forward, doing the same.

Raisa pressed her open palm against the door, resting her forehead against the wood. "Please."

The chain clinked.

Just in time, Raisa stepped back as the door opened.

Standing just beyond the threshold was a middle-aged man dressed in freshly pressed khakis, a blue button-down, and a tan cardigan. He had thick-rimmed glasses and his hair was losing the fight against age.

"I just want to know what happened to my partner," Raisa said, because she was certain that was what had persuaded him to open the door where he probably hadn't to St. Ivany's men.

"You're an FBI agent?" he asked, suspicious.

"A linguist," she rushed to say, because he seemed the type to be put at ease by expertise rather than the idea of some gun-toting G-man. "I'm a forensic linguist."

"You're working on the Isabel Parker death?" he asked.

"Yes," she all but gasped, relieved to find someone who understood without several minutes of explanation. "What's your name?"

"Jameson Ekblad," he said, shoving his glasses up. "I'm a professor at the college. Ornithology."

Raisa glanced over Jameson's shoulder. "You're photographing birds."

"Yes. There's a rare—well you don't care about that," Jameson said, ushering her in. "What do you need?"

"How is your equipment set up?" Raisa asked, crossing to the window. There were two cameras there, pointed at different angles of the street. Or, more likely, the harbor beyond it.

"This is my long range, manual," Jameson explained. "This is the one I keep on video and running for most of the morning."

Raisa didn't want to get too excited. "Do you have footage from Sunday? When there was a hit-and-run right there."

She pointed to the street, where Kilkenny had nearly bled out.

"I do, yes," Jameson said, crossing over to his desk. "I was too distracted to take the manual pictures, but the video captured it."

"And you didn't think to alert the police," St. Ivany said, and Raisa shot her a look.

They weren't going to win favors by slapping him on the wrist.

"I didn't have anything useful," Jameson said, his voice tighter than it had been a moment earlier. "I watched the footage. The SUV doesn't come into frame until the driver is mostly out of view. You can tell it's a woman and that's about it."

He tapped away at his computer, before gesturing for Raisa to come sit. "Here, watch."

Raisa braced herself, but she had hardly any time before Jameson hit play.

And then there they were.

She and Kilkenny.

They had been arguing about Delaney of all things.

Raisa stepped off the curb, and then the rev of an engine cut over the footage. She looked away as the bumper collided with a stunned Kilkenny—the whole thing playing out in the bottom quarter of the screen.

She inhaled, exhaled, concentrating not on the accident itself but on doing her job.

To find the person responsible for putting Kilkenny in the hospital.

Sometimes, when she was bored, she would watch stupid Flik videos to silence her brain. One of the more famous users was a man who could geo-locate anything or anyone on a map of the world by one photograph alone.

The key was taking in all the details and then forcing them into a context that made some logical sense.

With this video, they had way more than one photograph.

Raisa leaned forward and dragged the video back to the first moment the SUV had come into view.

"Can we do this slice by slice?" Raisa asked, as the SUV accelerated toward Kilkenny. It happened in two blinks of an eye, and Raisa wasn't going to be able to concentrate if she couldn't slow it down.

"We can run it at a tenth of the speed," Jameson explained, reaching over her to tap a few keys. "Here."

He hit play and this time Raisa was able to gather her bearings.

She watched it carefully, knowing both Jameson and St. Ivany were doing the same. But it was difficult. There was no good angle of the driver, only of the car. And of Kilkenny and Raisa.

Raisa had to watch her own horrified face too many times before Jameson reached over her and slammed the space bar.

"There," he said, with the confidence of someone who could spot the right markings on a bird a hundred yards away. "That sticker."

He tapped the screen. It was paused on a shot that showed the SUV's windshield. Raisa couldn't tell what he was talking about, and from St. Ivany's silence, she couldn't, either.

Jameson leaned over Raisa once more and tapped at the keys. "Come on. Right there."

He was right. There was some kind of sticker, but of what it wasn't clear.

"Here," Jameson said, and then did some kind of magic with his mouse and keyboard. And there, blown up and pixelated though it might be, was a tag for a local rental place. "They rented the car."

And if the person rented the car, they must have had to show ID.

Raisa nearly pumped her arm in the air but refrained. "Thank you. Can you print this out, and send it to us via email as well? We need to submit it to a judge."

Jameson leaned in for a moment, and then a printer hummed to life. "Done."

"Thank you," Raisa said, as sincerely as possible, when she stood. "I very much appreciate it."

"I hardly did anything," he demurred.

St. Ivany took care of the logistics after that, contacting a local judge, presenting the evidence. Sending the picture of the windshield tag that would lead them back to the local car rental shop that offered better prices than all the chains—in their words.

Meanwhile, Raisa stared at the printed-out picture, trying not to see ghosts in the shadows.

She couldn't deny that it looked like Isabel behind the wheel, even though the rational side of her couldn't help but note that all that was shown was the hint of a profile.

"Let's roll," St. Ivany said, grabbing Raisa by the arm.

"Will we get the warrant?" Raisa asked. St. Ivany didn't even lead them to the SUV. Apparently, the shop was in town.

"Yeah," St. Ivany said. "Our judge is kind of a lovable asshole, but he won't give us shit on this. That picture is a slam dunk, and Kilkenny is an FBI agent. So."

So no one would admit it, but everyone in law enforcement was a little more sensitive to solving cases involving one of their own.

A teenager was working the counter of the rental place, his floppy hair falling into his eyes as he swiped at his phone.

"We need your manager," St. Ivany said, before the door had even closed behind them.

"Jeez, Karen," the teenager mumbled. "You didn't even give me a chance."

St. Ivany flashed her ID. "We need your manager."

The teenager straightened, going a bit pale at the sight of the badge. "Okay, lady. I mean. Sergeant. I mean. Det—"

"Get your manager," St. Ivany cut in.

"Right." The teenager almost fell off his stool in his scramble.

Two minutes later he reemerged from the back, trailing behind a woman with the same no-nonsense expression as the superintendent of the women's prison.

"I'm sorry if Cole—"

"Ma'am, we're about to get a warrant from Judge Iginla," St. Ivany cut in. "We need to see who rented a black SUV from here in the past week."

The woman—whose badge read Letitia—crossed her arms. "Well, we keep impeccable records, so I'm sure we'll be able to help you. But we *will* need to see that order from the judge."

"Of course," St. Ivany said, pulling out her phone. They all waited in semi-awkward silence until the order came through.

Once it did, Letitia shifted her attention to the computer. A few keystrokes later she presented them with a list of three names.

Raisa didn't need to see any others.

There at the bottom was one that jumped out immediately.

Delaney Moore.

CHAPTER THIRTY-TWO

Raisa

Day Six

Black closed in from the sides of Raisa's eyes.

Everything went hazy and distant—like she was a long way away from the car rental shop.

She heard the thump of metal against flesh. Smelled copper in her nose. Delaney had hit Kilkenny. She'd tried to kill him.

Bile rose in her throat. She had thought Isabel had threatened Delaney with Kilkenny's death, but she had been so stupid. Delaney didn't care about anyone but herself—and Isabel.

"Thank you," St. Ivany said to Letitia, who obligingly printed them off the official documents they needed to confirm Delaney had made the rental. Then St. Ivany shepherded Raisa out of the store. "Don't do anything stupid."

Raisa leaned against the brick wall and closed her eyes. That was a mistake. All she could see was Kilkenny hitting the ground. She could feel his cracked skull beneath her fingers.

She took a shallow breath and then a deeper one. She counted to five and then ten and then twenty.

"Agent Susanto." St. Ivany's voice came from a distance, and Raisa stared down at her hands to focus herself.

They were curled into fists, her nails biting into her flesh.

"She should have been in jail," Raisa managed. "This wouldn't have happened if she had been in jail where she belongs."

Any hesitation was gone. Raisa could hardly even believe that she'd thought about hiding incriminating evidence against the woman who had nearly killed Kilkenny. Who, for all they knew, could still be responsible for his death.

Her stomach rolled at that thought, and she had to hum to stop herself from throwing up.

This is your attachment disorder speaking, Kilkenny said calmly, from the hospital.

Raisa shook her head. "It's called fucking friendship, you asshole."

"Uh," St. Ivany said, stepping closer, pausing, and then stepping back.

It was enough to bring Raisa fully back to the moment. "Sorry, I've developed a habit of talking to Kilkenny."

"Oh." St. Ivany didn't seem reassured, so Raisa waved her hand.

"I'm not hallucinating, I know he's not here." This had gotten so absurd, it had actually helped. "Ignore me. Anyway, we must have enough to arrest Delaney now."

St. Ivany sighed. "I'm sorry, but probably not."

Raisa whirled on her. "Why the hell not?"

"Raisa, think like an FBI agent instead of Kilkenny's friend," St. Ivany said, and Raisa wanted to hate her for that. But she didn't. "This is enough to question someone, but there's no definitive proof she was behind the wheel."

Anger coiled tightly around Raisa's rib cage, and she took three deliberate breaths to calm herself down.

"She was spotted outside of Peter Stamkos's house," Raisa said. "It seems like she scoped Lindsey Cousins out at work. She came here—*here*—when she was cornered instead of fleeing to Mexico. Why? Because she had unfinished business."

"Maybe that unfinished business is finding whoever killed Isabel," St. Ivany said. "Exactly like you're doing."

Raisa exhaled again. "No, they were communicating before Isabel died. Whatever Isabel wanted her to do, it's something else."

"Yes, but Isabel is dead," St. Ivany pointed out. "Which means Delaney might disregard whatever the previous instructions were and hunt down her killer."

"Delaney wouldn't do that. She's listened to Isabel all her life." Raisa said. "Where is she?"

St. Ivany's eyes went shifty. "I'm not telling you."

"Why the hell not?" Raisa said, all but vibrating with anger now.

"You need to calm down," St. Ivany said, yelling the last two words.

Raisa wanted to tell her that no one who'd been told to calm down had ever, in the history of the world, actually calmed down. Instead, she walked away.

"This is what Isabel wanted," St. Ivany called. "You said it yourself. She wanted to break you."

Raisa stopped, though she didn't turn around.

"You know, this is the first time Isabel has ever been wrong about us," she said, so softly she wasn't sure St. Ivany would even hear. "She said we weren't broken, like her. But she took care of that a long time ago."

Raisa spent the rest of the day searching for Delaney, with no luck. She also tried finding Roan Carmichael, but there wasn't a trace of him, either.

So, as night fell, she went to the hospital.

"Why did you trust her?" she asked an unconscious Kilkenny after sitting beside him for several hours in silence. They'd had this conversation a million times—she could do his answer by heart.

She didn't want to say *I told you so*. She wanted him to wake up so they could have it for the millionth and one time.

But he wouldn't. He might never wake up again.

Because of Delaney.

A knock on the door pulled her from the well of rage just as she was re-dipping her toes in.

She turned to find St. Ivany standing there, looking as rough as Raisa probably did.

"I haven't had any luck today," she said. "Come get food with me."

Raisa might have been annoyed with her, but she was also hungry. So she went.

St. Ivany drove them to a classic fifties-styled place about as far off the main drag of tourist restaurants as you could get.

The waitress filled their basic white mugs with coffee and then left them alone.

Raisa pulled Essi's book out of her bag.

"Why are you so obsessed with that thing?" St. Ivany asked her.

"I'm missing something in it."

"You think Essi has something to do with Emily's death?"

"No," Raisa said honestly. "I know it's a cliché, but it feels like an itch I can't scratch. Something I read in here lodged in my brain, but it's buried beneath way too much other information."

"And you think reading it again and again is going to shake it loose," St. Ivany said, drumming her fingers on the table. She was all nervous energy, just like Gabriela had been earlier.

"No," Raisa said, before pushing it over to St. Ivany. "You read it."

St. Ivany's brows raised, before she flipped open the cover. Her eyes moved over the page.

"Out loud," Raisa said, kicking her under the table.

"Oh, right." St. Ivany laughed at herself. "'I'll never be able to eat casseroles again.'"

Raisa closed her eyes as she made it through those first few pages.

"'It wasn't one of my neighbors at my door, though,'" she said. "'Instead it was a girl. She asked, "Do you know who killed your father?" And that's when I found something besides the casseroles to make each day worth waking up for.'"

Raisa reached out and grabbed St. Ivany. "Holy shit. It worked."

"What?" St. Ivany asked, staring down at where Raisa's fingers dug into her skin.

This, finally, was the question her brain had been screaming at her to answer.

"Who the fuck was the girl?"

CHAPTER THIRTY-THREE

Raisa

Day Seven

St. Ivany just stared at Raisa. "I don't know who the fuck the girl was. Essi probably made her up to tell a better story."

But Raisa was already dropping her bills on the table. "Let's go ask her."

"It's past midnight."

Raisa didn't care for facts. "Which means Essi will be on her boat."

St. Ivany hesitated one second longer, then pushed herself out of the booth. Raisa took off toward the door.

"Emily?" St. Ivany suggested as she beeped open the SUV.

"Essi said she'd never met her," Raisa said, sliding into the passenger seat. "She could be lying, but then why include the encounter in the book?"

St. Ivany shrugged. "Gabriela?"

"She was trying to exonerate Isabel," Raisa said. "Why would she try to find people who would make that tally higher?"

"Delaney?" St. Ivany offered, though she sounded hesitant.

"No one in their right mind would call Delaney a girl," Raisa said. "Well, maybe a man in his eighties or something. But Essi wouldn't have called Delaney a girl."

"Then I'm all out of girls," St. Ivany said, as she pulled to a stop at the harbor gates. They both leaped out of the SUV and took off toward *Big Deck Energy*.

St. Ivany slowed as she reached the boat. "The rules are different with boats."

"I wonder if she's staying on one because they're harder to search," Raisa said. They had both fallen into a slow walk.

"No," St. Ivany said. "They're actually easier to search."

She leaped on board and knocked on the cabin door. The thin piece of wood flew open beneath the pressure.

A hollow pit opened up in Raisa's belly.

"Is she . . ." Raisa didn't finish the thought.

"No, it's empty," St. Ivany said, and Raisa exhaled. She hadn't necessarily liked Essi—there was something too mercenary about her for Raisa's liking—but she didn't want to see the woman dead.

Raisa dropped down onto the bench near the rudder. It was a full moon, so she could see the disappointment on St. Ivany's face.

"It's strange that she left," Raisa said.

"Maybe Mildred told her she lent you the book," St. Ivany said, plopping down onto the bench across from Raisa. "Why did the girl thing stick out to you?"

Raisa thought about it fully now. "Because . . . because that's why Essi is here at all, right?"

"What do you mean?"

"If we take Essi's book at face value," Raisa said. "The reason she knew why her father died was because some girl—who she never mentions again, by the way, which seems like bad editing—told her about Isabel. And knowing about Isabel is what brought Essi to Gig Harbor at the same time I'm in Gig Harbor and Delaney is in Gig Harbor, and it is too much of a coincidence to think all of that just *happened*. Out of nowhere. Don't you think?"

"Well, Christ," St. Ivany said on a sigh. "When you put it that way..."

Raisa huffed out a laugh and then sank lower, her eyes sliding up to the moon, then back along the masts of all the gently bobbing boats.

And then she saw...

What...

Something...

Raisa straightened.

"St. Ivany," she murmured, already going for her gun.

She didn't wait for the detective to react. Raisa was already on her feet, and then she was on the dock.

The moon was bright, but the shadows were deep, and she stuck to them.

It was probably nothing.

It was nothing.

Raisa crept forward, her pulse steady.

She sensed, more than heard, St. Ivany behind her.

Watching her six.

Raisa ran along the pier lightly, her boots slapping against the wood.

Blood.

She had seen blood.

It was easy to recognize the thick, dark pool of it.

"Here," she murmured to St. Ivany.

They both paused, twenty-five feet from the boat.

They both saw the hand, dangling over the side.

Lifeless.

"Shit," St. Ivany muttered, before she pulled her walkie-talkie from her belt. She was still murmuring orders when Raisa boarded the boat.

And there, lying on the bow, was Declan O'Brien.

The pervy professor, sprawled in all the indignity of death.
One hand was still curled around a revolver.
Raisa dropped her own weapon to her thigh.
There would be a note.
Because Isabel always left a note when she staged a suicide.

CHAPTER THIRTY-FOUR

Delaney

Before Isabel's death

There existed in Jewish folklore a creature called a golem.

It was made of earthen materials such as mud or clay and shaped into a human form. The descriptions of them varied—usually reflecting the hopes and fears of the community where their stories were created.

Many times, though, they were depicted as obedient, created solely to serve their masters.

Delaney sank her feet deeper into the mud, feeling like she was returning to the substance from which she was made.

Because what else was she to Isabel if not a golem? Made by Isabel's hands, forced to carry out her orders.

The mountains rose around her. She hadn't been to Everly since Raisa and Isabel had shot each other in the woods. She shouldn't be here now. If someone could recognize her, it would be these people.

But she'd been pulled back to where it all began, where Isabel had whispered in her ear that she should shove Jackie P. off the monkey bars because the girl had tattled to the teacher on Delaney. Where Isabel had hidden Delaney in the attic, promising that if they didn't stay up there all day, Alex, their brother, would do something horrific to them. Where Isabel had calmly plunged a knife into their drugged parents' bodies and then just as calmly forged a suicide note for their brother.

Where Isabel had assured Delaney that she hadn't seen Isabel carrying a bloody weapon through the kitchen after it all happened.

Living through her childhood hadn't felt all that traumatic, if she were being honest.

Looking back now, she couldn't believe she'd made it out of that fucked-up mess.

Maybe she hadn't.

When she and her sisters had been placed in separate foster homes, Delaney had thought the state was being dramatic. They hadn't known anything Isabel had done, hadn't even suspected it. Yet they must have sensed something was off.

Delaney had long forgiven her younger self. She had been twelve years old and dumb, and Isabel had been the only person who had ever cared about her. She would have run through a wall for her at that age.

If she'd had any concept of what it meant to take a life, she would have killed for Isabel.

She'd never had to.

Until now.

The river ran cold over her legs. Even in the summer like this, with the sun beating down, the snowmelt kept it near freezing. She couldn't feel her feet anymore. But standing in the water itself, the bugs biting, the tourists chattering too loudly on the far bank—all of it made her believe she was human once more.

She needed the reminder.

There were plenty of variations of the golem story throughout the past six hundred years. One of Delaney's favorites, though, was the one where the golem did as he was told, and he saved a community of Jewish people who lived in Prague. But during the fight, the golem's master lost control of him, and thus felt compelled to destroy him before he did any harm.

The master succeeded, but as he did, the golem turned back to clay and then shattered into—heavy, devastating—pieces. Those pieces fell on the master, crushing him to death.

And, so, in the end, they destroyed each other.

CHAPTER THIRTY-FIVE

Delaney

Day Seven

Delaney left Roan of the Carolina mountains at the motel and wondered if she'd ever see him again.

Part of her thought that, if she didn't, it might be because she would simply leave town without checking in on him.

Part of her wondered if it was because she didn't have that much longer to live.

That had always been a possibility, once she'd received that first letter. Now she had to finish what she'd started.

Roan might think her foolish, he might think she'd fallen for St. Ivany's scheme, but Delaney knew now how right she'd been.

Gabbi had inserted herself into the investigation, not the other way around.

Delaney touched the knife at her thigh and realized it wasn't enough. She pulled off to the side of the road into town. There wasn't much traffic, so she simply popped the trunk of her beaten-up, but now sort of beloved, car and found her go-bag. At the bottom was a gun that couldn't be traced back to her.

Let's play a game . . .

She dropped it into her pocket, right next to the AirTag that she'd found in her purse the morning after she'd slept with Roan that first time. She'd disabled it by taking the battery out, but she'd kept it in case it could come in handy later. Perhaps as her own little panic button, if she found herself in a situation she couldn't get out of.

Finally, she pulled out her laptop and brought it around to the driver's seat with her.

She needed to try to get in front of Gabbi.

Delaney's research had been sound. She had lurked on every forum or social media site that hosted conversations about Isabel.

Gabbi was smart and callous and overly invested in Isabel. She pictured both herself and Isabel as vigilantes, not realizing that was antisocial behavior worthy of a diagnosis. The trauma in her past relationship had solidified the rigid moral superiority that had been born into her, and turned it outward. She looked at herself as the only person in the community willing to dole out justice—the way she told herself Isabel had.

Delaney was good at this, she knew she was. It hadn't taken long for her to land on Gabriela Cruz after that. And everything about her speech patterns, her posts, her videos, led Delaney to believe she'd been swept up in Isabel.

The thing that had cemented it all for Delaney, though, was that Gabriela claimed she had actually spoken to Isabel. No one else in the community could say that.

Gabbi didn't make it well known that she had—for obvious reasons now. But she was a bragger; she couldn't help but tell her inner circle of online friends. Just as she had when the police had used her to try to "catch" Delaney.

After that, Delaney was convinced.

Not only was she incredibly dangerous but she was escalating.

Gabbi would have a next target.

Delaney could call St. Ivany and join forces. After all, Delaney *hadn't* killed Emily Logan. St. Ivany might try to arrest her, but Delaney could at least make her case against Gabriela.

But Delaney didn't actually have any evidence. Why would St. Ivany—and Raisa—take Delaney's word on it, when Raisa thought she was no better than Isabel?

If they trusted Gabriela, Delaney would have to offer something real. Like a confession.

Or she would need to stop Gabriela in the act.

Delaney opened her laptop and pulled up the screenshots she'd saved from Gabbi's various postings across different sites. One of the most common themes of her messages was about how much she hated people who had claimed their loved one's death was Isabel's fault with no actual proof.

Several times, she cited a woman named Essi Halla. Apparently, she had a book coming out soon, and it had been enough to send Gabbi into a full-on tailspin that had freaked out even some of her most devout followers.

Halla sounded familiar, and as soon as Delaney pulled up Isabel's full victim list, she realized why.

Mikko Halla hadn't made it into the official charges, but there he was. A bona fide victim of Isabel's.

Delaney laughed at the idea that the honor should come with some kind of sticker for all their loved ones to wear.

It was funny, wasn't it, that Gabbi had focused so much attention on Essi, only for her to have a valid reason to write a book about the experience?

Still, Gabbi didn't know that. Delaney was the only living person who now had the full list.

She pulled out her phone.

"Do you know Essi Halla?" she asked when Roan picked up.

"Yeah, of course," Roan said.

Delaney closed her eyes and breathed out. "Do you have contact information for her?"

"I have her phone number," Roan said slowly. "But I should probably ask why you want it."

"No, you shouldn't," Delaney said. "It's important. She's in danger."

"Danger?" Roan asked, his voice breaking. "Goddamn it, Delaney, just go to the police."

"What's Essi's phone number?"

She had never really had anyone whipped before, but she thought Roan might be on the verge of being so. He rattled off the digits with only a breath more of hesitation. "Thank you."

"Delaney—"

She hung up on him, and punched in Essi's phone number.

It went to voicemail, as expected. No one picked up unexpected calls from strangers these days. She sent a text next.

> It's Delaney Moore—you might know me as Lana Parker. I'm going to call again and you're going to pick up

"I don't like being told what to do," Essi said, though she'd answered on the first ring. She was too eager not to, just as Delaney expected from her online presence.

She was making her money off Delaney's family—she would sure as hell seize the opportunity to talk to the elusive middle sister.

"I don't know why you think I would care," Delaney shot back.

Essi laughed. "Okay, fair enough. What do you want?"

"Where are you?" Delaney asked.

"I'm not just going to give my location to a stranger, especially with your sister sniffing around too close to my personal affairs," Essi said. Her voice went tight, suspicious. "Is that why you're calling?"

"Raisa," Delaney murmured. Of course, it always came back to Raisa. "Why is she after you?"

"You tell me."

With that, Delaney could sense she was losing Essi.

"I haven't even talked to her in months," Delaney said. "I'm calling because I think you're in danger from the person who killed Emily Logan."

"Why would I be in danger?" Essi asked slowly.

"Where are you?"

There was a beat of silence, but apparently curiosity won out. It usually did; it had killed the cat, after all.

"I'm on a boat in the harbor," she said. "Your sister thinks I left, but I just switched to a different yacht."

No way would someone like Essi leave town in the midst of all this chaos.

"But there are tons of police here," she continued. "So I'm pretty sure I'm safe from whatever murderer you've dreamed up."

Of course the police were there, Delaney realized. The "suicide" had been at the harbor. "What is your boat called?"

"*Nacho Boat*," Essi said dryly. "I kid you not."

Delaney stared into the middle distance as part of her soul died a little at that. Then she shook it off. "I'm going to come to you."

"I take it you don't want a police greeting," Essi said, and Delaney realized only then that she was putting a lot of trust in this stranger. Up until now, she'd been counting on the fact that she was a rare commodity for Essi, but depending on her personality, she might very well view calling the cops as the smarter bet for something dramatic to happen.

"I'd appreciate it if they weren't there, correct," Delaney said stiffly, trying to listen for any deception in Essi's voice.

But it came out as neutral when she said, "Okay, well, I'm here. Slip twenty-seven."

Delaney almost hung up before she realized she was falling for a logical trap. Gabriela hadn't talked to Essi this morning. She wouldn't know Essi had switched boats. "What was your other boat? The one you were staying on before?"

"*Big Deck Energy*, slip thirteen. Why?"

"No reason," Delaney murmured.

She hung up and jammed the keys in the ignition. Someone in complete control of themselves wouldn't try to sneak on a boat in the middle of a busy police scene in order to try to kill someone.

But she had no doubt that Gabbi was going to try to do just that.

CHAPTER THIRTY-SIX

Delaney

Day Seven

The police presence at the harbor was heavy. The woman who had talked to Delaney at the bar—Maeve St. Ivany—stood at the far end of the pier overseeing it all.

Delaney parked behind a bakery, then made her way on foot to where *Big Deck Energy* was docked.

If this were a bigger city, the police might have locked down the whole harbor, but they'd concentrated on the one side where the body had been found. Luckily for Delaney, it was on the opposite side of where she needed to be.

Delaney slipped through the dozen or so people gathered just at the edge of the water, thankful Essi's boat was right there.

She leaped aboard the *BDE* and steadied herself as it swayed beneath her feet. If someone was waiting for her, they would know she was there, immediately.

The cabin door was closed. Delaney paused outside it, in a slight crouch. She knew she would be at a disadvantage sliding down into the cabin itself. There would be at least a half minute when she was incredibly vulnerable. But she was hoping Gabbi wouldn't shoot her before she even saw her face.

Delaney took a precious thirty seconds to put the AirTag back together so that it was live, checked her recorder one last time to make sure it was on, and then opened the cabin door.

Gabbi sat cross-legged on the table, empty-handed. She smiled at Delaney. "Hey."

The scene was so unexpectedly different from what she'd been braced for, Delaney nearly wobbled on her feet. She put out a hand to steady herself.

The cabin was tight, especially right at the stairs, before it opened up into a living room / kitchen area.

"Hey," Delaney said, just as easily. "What are you doing here?"

"I wanted to talk to Essi, but it seems like she's left," Gabbi said. "She and I are old friends."

"Oh yeah?" Delaney asked.

"Yeah," Gabbi said.

"I thought you might hate her," Delaney said, carefully.

"Oh." Gabbi's eyes crinkled in pleasure. "You've decided to drop the act. I'm so pleased, Lana."

"How long did you know?" Delaney asked.

"Raisa's right, you look like Isabel," Gabbi said. "But I didn't really know until the beach. Your sister thought I was goading you into being creepy, but you're like that naturally, aren't you?"

Before Delaney could say anything, Gabbi shrugged. "It's okay. No one can go, like, five seconds without realizing how much I want to burn this world down."

"Okay." That was a fairly accurate assessment. "How about you tell me more about you and Essi being 'old friends.'"

"That's a twist, isn't it?" Gabbi asked. "I bet you thought you had me all figured out. But I was the one who figured out Essi's father was killed by Isabel in the first place."

"You wanted to have ammunition about people who made false claims in Isabel's name," Delaney realized. "So you did the legwork for the police."

"I have this really cool formula I developed that figures out the odds of someone's death being linked to Isabel," Gabbi said, looking so young as she did.

Delaney decided she needed to be taken down a peg, if for no other reason than it would be satisfying. "You mean a basic actuarial formula?"

Gabbi's nose wrinkled. "I forgot you're actually smart. I have to say, most people are pretty impressed by that."

"You'll never impress me with statistics." Her parents had invented actual theories, not just silly plug-and-play pattern-finders.

The slap landed, even if it was just a graze. Gabbi looked away. "Anyway, Essi decided to get really annoying with it. So that's where she lost my support."

"You have to dole out justice in your community," Delaney said. "And Essi needs to be punished for her greed."

"I am the moderator," Gabbi said, unironically.

Delaney would have laughed at her had she not been familiar with how dangerous Gabbi was right now. Her mind had to be reeling, awash in unpleasant chemicals for too long. She was probably holding on by a thread, and doing it admirably. Or as admirably as she could, considering she was in the midst of a psychotic break likely resulting in a killing spree, should Delaney not be able to stop her.

"Why did you hit Kilkenny?" Delaney asked.

"Oh," Gabbi said. "You'll see."

"Okay." Delaney wasn't impressed by *any* of Gabbi's posturing. Isabel was her sister; there was no one who came close to touching her in terms of threats. "And Lindsey Cousins?"

"She was a psychopath," Gabbi said. "The world should be thanking me for taking care of that problem." She blinked a few times. Her pupils were the size of dinner plates. Arousal.

"And Emily Logan?" Delaney pressed, forcing her to remember her most gruesome kill. "She was a mistake, wasn't she?"

"Not a mistake," Gabbi snapped. When Delaney remained silent, Gabbi shrugged. "I mean, was she part of a *plan*? No. She was just fucking annoying."

"Where does that fit in with your vigilante justice?" Delaney asked softly.

Gabbi's face went tight with anger and then smoothed out. "You know, it's funny—Raisa kept blabbing on about the fact that Isabel killed some people just because she wanted to, as if I would be horrified about the fact that she wasn't always playing a Good Samaritan. But that's a feeling I relate to more than anything else."

"Killing someone because they're annoying? Like you did with Emily."

"Yes, are you dumb?" Gabbi asked because she had to repeat herself, not realizing that she'd just given Delaney all that she needed. A full confession.

Delaney slipped her hand in her pocket, curling her fingers around the gun. "Okay, Gabbi. What we're going to do is get off this boat and go talk to Detective St. Ivany. Can you do that with me?"

"Uh, no," Gabbi said. "Thank you, though."

Delaney pulled out the gun. "I'm not giving you the choice."

Gabbi's smile went angelic for a moment. Then she got up and crossed to Delaney.

Delaney's finger hovered near the trigger, though she didn't want to pull it.

The unfortunate truth, the one she hadn't wanted to admit to this entire time, was that she saw what she could have become in Gabbi.

Had she and Isabel not been split up—if Isabel had spent the last of both their formative years shaping Delaney into who she wanted her to be, rather than going off to become a true serial killer, Delaney didn't know that she would have been in any different position than Gabriela Cruz was currently standing in.

The boat rocked again, and Gabbi lurched forward, bumping into Delaney.

Delaney tightened her grip on the gun, ready to fight Gabbi for it.

But Gabbi simply shook her head and stepped back. "My bad."

"It's okay," Delaney said, reflexively, and then almost laughed at the ingrained manners. "Gabbi, I want to help you."

"No, you don't," Gabbi said. "You want me to go to jail."

"It'll make you feel better," Delaney said, soothingly. Because it would. Gabbi . . . she didn't want to be doing this, Delaney was certain.

She'd started with people she'd deemed "bad." Likely as a way to prove herself to Isabel. But slippery slopes existed for a reason, and they were especially treacherous when you weren't wired like Isabel had been.

Gabbi laughed at her. "Wow, that was a tactic I was *not* expecting. But do you know what I am expecting?"

Delaney tensed. "What?"

The door that had swung only partially shut behind Delaney opened fully.

Gabbi smiled. "That."

CHAPTER THIRTY-SEVEN

Raisa

Day Seven

Dawn was starting to break over the horizon, and on any other day, in any other circumstance, the view over the water would be literally breathtaking.

Right now, Raisa was just trying—and failing—to make all the puzzle pieces fit into place.

She'd stayed out of the way of the crime scene crew most of the morning. At some point, St. Ivany confirmed it had been Declan O'Brien who had eaten his own gun on the bow of a boat.

Raisa thought about his comfy, messy office, the rug and the plants.

And she wished she'd taken the threat to everyone in Gig Harbor more seriously.

She wouldn't make that mistake again.

Over and over, throughout the morning, her eyes kept sliding back to the boat Essi had rented. *Big Deck Energy*.

What if Essi had only made it look like she'd left?

If she was still there, she might be able to tell Raisa who "the girl" was from the first chapter of her book.

She might also be willing to listen when Raisa told her she was in danger from Isabel's protégé. It was worth checking, at the very least.

Raisa headed toward Essi's boat, weaving her way through the chaos.

Something stopped her from calling out. Boats fell into the category of motor vehicles when it came to unlawful searches. If she had probable cause, she could board and check the cabin. But there was no reason to suspect anything, other than her vague feeling that Essi was in some danger.

That wouldn't hold up in a court of law—in fact, it would probably get her laughed out of a judge's chamber.

Then she heard the voices.

Not Essi's. But she thought she recognized them.

These weren't just the new renters.

As lightly as she could, she boarded the boat. It did sway beneath her feet, but for anyone inside, it probably felt like the natural ebb and flow of water.

She crept toward the cabin door, which was partially open, and her breath caught as she realized what she was seeing.

Delaney.

Holding a gun.

Go, her brain screamed. But the entrance to the cabin was awkward, and would put Raisa in a vulnerable position as she navigated the ladder.

She nudged the door open and then went in gun first.

By the time her feet hit the floor in the cabin, Delaney had shifted toward the middle of the boat.

And she had her gun pointed not at Raisa but at Gabriela Cruz, whose eyes were as big and wet and terrified as Raisa had ever seen them.

"Shit," Raisa cursed beneath her breath. She had no one to blame for this situation but herself. And St. Ivany. This was why she'd never wanted to use Gabriela as bait in the first place—especially with how eager the girl had been to prove herself. "Delaney, drop the gun."

Delaney stared at her for a long moment. It was dark in the cabin, dark enough that Raisa couldn't read much of her expression. "What?"

"Drop. The gun," Raisa said, her own locked on Delaney. She had a moment of déjà vu. A forest that had just as many shadows as this boat.

Gabriela pressed her lips together, but her chin quivered.

Stupid, stupid, stupid. Why had they decided to risk Gabriela's safety? It had been arrogant beyond belief that they'd assumed they could protect her if Delaney got it in her head to kill the girl.

"No," Delaney said.

"I'm not here as your sister," Raisa said. "Drop the weapon, or I'll shoot."

Delaney's eyes narrowed and she lashed out, grabbing Gabriela as she did. She pressed the barrel of the gun to Gabriela's temple. "Raisa, you have to listen to me."

"I really don't," Raisa said, though she couldn't take the shot now, not with the chance of hitting Gabriela. "Delaney, what are you doing?"

"She's the protégé," Delaney said, her arm tightening around Gabriela.

"Apparently I was too good of an actor," Gabriela said with a nervous laugh, seemingly trying to make light of her situation. But her knuckles had gone white where they'd curled into Delaney's forearm.

"I know you think that," Raisa said to Delaney. "We tried to make you think that."

Delaney shook her head. "I'm not an idiot."

"You didn't know," Gabriela interjected. "That I was miked on the beach, right? You didn't know."

Delaney's jaw tightened. "No. But that doesn't matter. I went there looking for you."

"Because we wanted to draw you out," Raisa said. The more they kept Delaney arguing, the better for them. Maybe St. Ivany would look around and wonder where Raisa had disappeared to. Maybe the boat would rock enough to throw off Delaney's balance. Maybe Gabbi could get out of the hold and give Raisa a free shot. "Delaney, Gabriela was the bait. Not the killer."

"She's actually both," Delaney said, sounding more rankled than Raisa had ever heard her. Usually, she was the calm one, the rational one. But she was frustrated. "And she admitted it."

Raisa met Gabriela's eyes, and she shook her head, almost imperceptibly.

"I came here looking for Essi, and Delaney followed me," Gabriela said. "She started yelling about how I'm just like Isabel and I deserve to die."

"Shut up," Delaney snapped, shaking Gabriela. Raisa held her breath, and Gabriela winced but didn't cry out. "You're lying. You're good at it, but not that good."

Delaney met Raisa's eyes. "I have it recorded."

Raisa's quick surprise was tempered by her history with Delaney. "Okay. Why don't we listen to that after you've put down your weapon."

Delaney simply pressed the barrel tighter against Gabriela's head. "Don't move."

And with that, she released her grip on the girl.

Raisa's finger twitched toward the trigger, but she didn't touch it yet.

Delaney dipped a hand into her pocket, dug around for something. But she came up empty.

"What . . . ?" She took her eyes off Raisa long enough to look down at her palm. Again, Raisa ran a quick risk calculation, but it was still too dangerous now to do anything.

"What . . . ," Delaney said again, this time less of a question. Then she huffed out a breath. "You stole it."

"No, I didn't," Raisa replied, before realizing the accusation hadn't been directed at her.

Delaney was staring at Gabriela. And in the next breath, Delaney shifted so that she had her weapon pressed against Gabriela's forehead.

Gabriela was shaking. Her eyes darted, in a panic, to Raisa before returning to Delaney. "I have no idea what you're talking about."

"Oh, ho, ho, little girl thinks she's so clever," Delaney purred, sounding so much like Isabel that Raisa nearly reeled back. Delaney drew a pattern on Gabriela's forehead with the gun. "Little lying girl."

Gabriela didn't say anything, but she was staring at Delaney just like Raisa was.

Like they were watching Isabel's ghost in action.

Raisa's throat went dry, and she tried to swallow. Tried to regain control of her body.

"Little girl thinks she can fill some pretty big boots," Delaney cooed. "But all she's doing is playing dress-up in Mama's clothing."

"Delaney," Raisa said, her voice coming out a croak. She had never realized that Delaney was *so* different from Isabel until seeing her now don Isabel's persona.

Raisa had been struggling this entire time to picture Delaney killing Peter, killing Lindsey, killing Emily in such a gruesome manner. But she hadn't been Delaney at the time.

She'd been Isabel.

Raisa should have realized it, when she'd seen how she was dressed for the bonfire, where they'd sent Gabriela in as helpless bait.

Delaney had looked different. She'd been dressed up as this—a huntress. A sociopath. A killer.

Isabel.

"I didn't . . . I don't . . . ," Gabriela muttered, seeming enthralled by the switch.

"Do you want to know how I punish little girls who lie?" Delaney asked. She caressed Gabriela's face with the gun, running it over her cheekbone, along her chin.

"Are you going to put me in the hospital?" Gabriela said, her voice almost steady. "Like you did with Agent Kilkenny?"

Delaney pulled the gun back and smacked it across Gabriela's face.

Gabriela cried out and crumpled to the floor, holding her cheek. Raisa took a step closer, but Delaney whirled on her. "No."

Then she hauled Gabriela to her feet once more, taking control of the situation. Gabriela had given up trying to be brave, and was openly crying now.

"Gabriela put Kilkenny in the hospital," Delaney said, sounding like herself once more. Maybe because she was talking to Raisa instead of the prey. "Not me."

The anger that had been simmering in Raisa's blood relit at that.

Broken bones, blood. A heart monitor that never varied because Kilkenny still hadn't woken up.

"Delaney," Raisa said, quietly this time. "Drop the gun."

"I didn't hit Kilkenny, you know I wouldn't," Delaney said, and then winced. Because they both knew Raisa would absolutely think Delaney could do that.

"We have a picture," Raisa said, her anger morphing into rage. Maybe Delaney hadn't been in control of herself, maybe she'd been channeling Isabel as she had a moment ago. But that didn't absolve her of the guilt of doing it.

"Then it's doctored," Delaney said, her attention now fully locked on Raisa.

Raisa shook her head. There was literal blood on Delaney's hands, from where Gabriela's cheek had split open. And Delaney was proclaiming her innocence.

This, this was what their family was.

And Raisa wanted nothing more in that moment than to put a bullet into Delaney, thus becoming one of the rest of the Parkers.

No. It came in Kilkenny's voice.

She shouldn't want that.

That would make her just as much of a monster as her sisters.

She hated herself for the impulse, she hated it. She wanted to tear at her own skin and bones; she wanted to trade places with Kilkenny because she was . . .

She was . . .

She was . . .

Broken.

Raisa nearly gasped, and she would have, had Delaney and Gabriela not been watching her so closely.

I wanted to make them the same as me.

Broken.

Lana and Larissa aren't broken.

But wouldn't it be more fun if they were?

"Oh my god," Raisa said. "Did you write Isabel letters?"

"No," Gabriela answered.

"Not you," Raisa snapped, keeping her eyes on Delaney. "Did you write Isabel letters?"

"No," Delaney said, seeming hesitant for the first time since Raisa had entered the cabin.

"Did you write reviews on a hiking trails app?" Raisa asked, knowing she must sound unhinged at the moment.

Delaney confirmed that when she frowned. "No. What are you talking about?"

"Oh my god," Raisa said, her knees nearly giving out. "She never wanted me to solve who killed her."

Her eyes slid to the gun she now pointed at her own sister.

"Did you hit Kilkenny?" Raisa asked, jerking the weapon. "Answer me."

"I was in Seattle," Delaney said. "I got the alert on my phone."

Raisa closed her eyes briefly. Delaney could have driven to Gig Harbor and then gone back to the city. But it had never made sense that Delaney would want to harm the one person who believed in her.

"Someone must have used a fake ID to rent a car in your name," Raisa said. "It was all to push me into being so angry at you I would look for any reason to pull the trigger. Because Isabel doesn't understand that wouldn't have been enough to make me do it."

"Was it Essi?" Gabriela offered.

Raisa tried to remember the still shot of the video, but her brain had told her it was Isabel and then the paperwork had told her it was Delaney and she hadn't questioned it. So she no longer trusted her judgment there.

"Maybe," Raisa said, and Delaney made a sound.

"No, don't you see," Delaney said, shaking Gabriela. "It's Gabbi. It's always been her."

"No." Raisa shook her head. "We made you think that. And . . . And Isabel. She constructed all this. It's her chessboard. We're all playing her game."

"You think Peter Stamkos and that man who shot himself last night both simply killed themselves?" Delaney asked. "Lindsey was in an accident, and Emily Logan . . . ?"

"Her boyfriend killed her," Raisa said, on a humorless laugh. "Of course, it's always the boyfriend."

This wasn't about anyone else. This had been about Raisa and Delaney this whole time.

"That would be nice and all, except Gabbi killed them all," Delaney said, completely back to being the Delaney Raisa knew so well.

"We were the ones who put Gabriela onto your radar," Raisa reasoned. "You think she did it because we made you think she might have."

"No," Delaney said slowly. "I think she did it because she did it."

Raisa shook her head. "Look, we'll get this figured out, okay? Just let Gabriela go, and we'll all go into the police station—"

"And I'll be arrested," Delaney said. "Because you think I've been holding an innocent civilian against her will."

"And threatening her with murder," Gabriela added. "Not to put too fine a point on it, but that is what you're doing."

Raisa shot Gabriela a look, and she shrugged as much as she could, unabashed.

"If you had evidence she'd killed Emily, why wouldn't you just go to the police with it?" Raisa asked. Her gun was now pointed at the floor, an unconscious acknowledgment of trust.

"Because you know she's too good for that," Delaney said. "Isabel was teaching her how to clean up her footprints. You ever wonder how that crime scene was so clean? It's because she had one of the longest professional serial killers instructing her what to do."

"But she never visited Isabel," Raisa said, thinking about the visitor logs. Isabel had three visitors besides Raisa herself. The documentarian, Delaney, and Roan Carmichael.

Gabriela went rigid in Delaney's arms.

"What? Yes, she did," Delaney said.

"No . . . ," Raisa said, but trailed off, her mouth going dry.

Her eyes slid to Gabriela, who was now looking at the floor.

Raisa widened her stance as if to regain her balance, yet the boat hadn't moved at all. It was the reality of the case that had shifted.

Of course Gabriela had visited Isabel. The girl had told them that very first visit that she had gone to talk to her.

But Raisa had lost track of that detail in the aftermath of the attempt on Kilkenny's life. If that hadn't happened, they would have gone to check the visitor logs that very morning. They would have seen Gabriela hadn't been listed.

They would have known she had either lied to them or used a fake name to get in.

Maybe . . . maybe that was why Gabriela had taken a run at them in the first place. She had guessed they would check the logs, and she'd realized she'd misplayed her hand.

She wasn't perfect—she wasn't Isabel. She'd had to clean up her mess, and to do so, she'd nearly killed Kilkenny.

The worst part was that it had worked.

Stupid, Raisa chastised herself, even as she brought her gun back up. This time she pointed it at Gabriela. "You used Roan Carmichael's name as cover for visiting Isabel."

Gabriela looked like she was caught between two impulses. But given another heartbeat, she broke into a smug grin. "I can't believe

Isabel thought *either* of you was interesting enough to fuck with. But people are always weird about family."

Raisa pulled her phone out of her pocket with her free hand, while keeping her gun trained on Gabriela. Taking the shot would endanger Delaney, but the threat of it might keep Gabriela from getting too clever.

"I wouldn't do that if I were you," Gabriela said. "I'm guessing you're calling in the cavalry?"

Raisa knew she should just stop listening to her. But she hesitated.

"You know, aiming for Kilkenny with that SUV served two purposes," Gabriela said, like she didn't have two guns aimed at her head by grown women who outnumbered her. "One, obviously, was to try to make you take out your own sister. How glorious would that have been? Especially when you later found out she wasn't guilty."

Gabriela did a chef's kiss gesture. "I just loved Isabel's big brain. It was my favorite thing about her."

"My favorite thing is that she's dead," Raisa said flatly. "I guess I should thank you for that."

Storm clouds blew in and out of Gabriela's expression. "Anyway, the second purpose it served—along with the reason that I was glad I didn't actually kill him—was it gave me leverage."

"You can't just blindly threaten Kilkenny," Raisa said.

"Is that what I said I was doing?" Gabriela asked. "Have you learned nothing from dealing with Isabel? We don't do anything blindly."

Raisa's stomach lurched, and it had nothing to do with the boat swaying beneath her feet.

Delaney's gaze slid over her shoulder like she was wondering how fast they could get out of the cabin and to the hospital.

"You know that nurse you like so much?" Gabriela asked. "The young man working the desk? That's Emily Logan's boyfriend, and he found her as annoying as I did. If he doesn't hear from me in the next—" She searched out a clock. "Three minutes, he's going to go ahead and make sure Kilkenny never wakes up from the little nap he's been taking."

"Call him," Delaney said, jamming the gun into Gabriela's temple.

But Gabriela's expression didn't change, and all Raisa could think about was what Kilkenny would say here.

Gabriela was erratic. With Declan O'Brien's death, her killing spree was heating up. That usually ended with a flame out to match just how devastating the inferno had been.

A gun to Gabriela's head was not going to save Kilkenny.

Raisa did every quick calculation she could, trying to come up with the best scenario possible.

And then Delaney threw both herself and Gabriela sideways.

The two grappled on the ground for a minute before Gabriela emerged, breathing heavily.

"Psycho bitch."

Delaney sat on the ground, her gun lost somewhere behind her because of the scuffle. "Let her go, Raisa."

"What?" Raisa asked. Delaney wasn't exactly in the position to give her orders.

"She's not worth Kilkenny's life," Delaney said, meeting Raisa's eyes.

They hadn't worked together more than a few days two years ago, yet for some reason, Raisa was able to read her blank expression.

Because Delaney was *hers*.

Family, whether Raisa loved that fact or not.

She hesitated a second longer for show, then stepped aside.

Gabriela glanced between them and then dashed toward the stairs.

They listened to the slap of her shoes against the deck and then the pier.

"You have a plan?" Raisa asked, reholstering.

Delaney grinned as she held up a slim, old-school recorder, the kind of tool journalists in the early aughts had used before smartphones.

"She's not the only one with sticky fingers," Delaney said. "I dropped that AirTag you put on me in her pocket. As long as you have the tracker, we'll be able to find her."

Raisa was already halfway up the steps, already dialing St. Ivany.

"Hey," Delaney called, not following. Raisa paused, looked back. "Thanks for not killing me."

Raisa laughed. "Hey. Thanks for not making me."

CHAPTER THIRTY-EIGHT

Raisa

Day Seven

St. Ivany ran toward her down the long pier, her phone held up to her ear even though she was close enough to hear Raisa in person. "What? What?"

Raisa shoved her phone back in her pocket as she took off toward where they'd parked their cars. "Call whoever is guarding Kilkenny and make sure the guard is on high alert."

St. Ivany was keeping pace behind Raisa, running even without knowing why.

They really had become allies.

Raisa skidded to a stop beside St. Ivany's SUV and held up her palm. St. Ivany tossed her keys toward Raisa, all the while on the phone with her guy at the hospital. Raisa slid behind the wheel and pressed the gas even before St. Ivany's door was closed.

Gabriela had disappeared, and had the advantage in terms of local knowledge of the streets. But Raisa had . . .

"Pull up the AirTag we dropped on Delaney," Raisa said, and St. Ivany did so without question. The dot was moving fast.

"Is this Gabriela?" St. Ivany breathed out. Then without waiting for an answer: "She's heading to the cliffs."

Raisa's heart thudded against her ribs as she thought of that look in Gabriela's eyes when Delaney had threatened to pull the trigger. In this kind of light, it might have been mistaken for relief.

St. Ivany and Raisa glanced at each other, and then Raisa pressed her foot to the floor. There were coves all along the shoreline, but in between those were jagged rocks that dropped off into the ocean. They weren't as dramatic as cliffs in other parts of the country, but they would absolutely offer a way out for a girl looking for one.

They found Gabriela's car first, the driver's-side door open.

"Shit," Raisa muttered. She pulled to a haphazard stop, already running as her feet hit the ground, taking the pine needle–strewn path toward where she could hear the waves slamming into land.

St. Ivany was only a few paces behind her.

Raisa's lungs burned, as did her thighs, but she pressed forward, desperate for a reason she couldn't even make sense of.

The day was almost too clear and lovely for the sight they came upon when the trees finally opened up.

Gabriela stood at the very edge of the world, her arms spread wide. There should've been a storm brewing in front of her to match her clear turmoil.

"Gabriela," Raisa cried, her voice scratchy. "Stop."

Gabriela turned, cocked her head. "How did you find me? Delaney?"

"She dropped an AirTag on you," Raisa confirmed, as she stepped closer, making sure not to pressure Gabriela into shifting back. "Come away from there."

"No, I don't think I will," Gabriela said, with a small smile. "You know, all I wanted was a better world."

"I know," Raisa said, because that was what you did for someone standing at the edge of a cliff. You appeased her. Raisa held out her hand. "Come away from there."

Gabriela stayed where she was, swaying back and forth. "I didn't think killing would feel like that."

"What do you mean?"

Gabriela met her eyes and smiled. "Good."

Raisa inhaled sharply.

"Didn't expect that, huh?" Gabriela said, seemingly pleased. "You wanted me to be some helpless soul, transfixed by the evilest monster you could ever imagine. But I'm just me. And I liked killing Peter and Lindsey and Emily and Declan."

"And Isabel," Raisa couldn't help but point out. Before she shook her head. "Come away from there. We'll talk about all of this some more."

"You don't want to talk," Gabriela said. "You want to lock me in a psychiatric ward."

That was true enough.

"You think you see yourself in me, don't you?" Gabriela said, taunting. But most of the edge was gone from her voice. This wasn't the smug mastermind from the boat. This was just a sad, lost girl. "That's why you chased me here, that's why you want to save me."

"No," Raisa said. She took a step closer. "Come away from there, Gabriela."

"You see yourself in me," Gabriela said, stubborn now. "You were the one who chose law enforcement. You were the one who always wants justice. You're the one who is one bad decision away from burning down the world."

"No," Raisa said, and believed it for the first time in two years. "I've never wanted the world to burn."

"You think that until you get a taste for it," Gabriela said. "And then you'll crave it."

"No," Raisa said again, staring at this terrible product of a monster's hand.

Broken by Isabel.

"You see yourself in me," Gabriela said again, this time sounding so desperate. "You see Isabel in me."

Raisa shook her head. Isabel was nothing like this girl, who would never see that as the compliment it was.

"No, darling," Raisa said softly, so that only the two of them would hear. And she finally admitted to the reason she was standing on this cliffside begging this girl not to throw herself into the ocean below. "I see Delaney."

Confusion and then rage and then betrayal flickered in and out of her expression. "But she's pathetic."

"Aren't we all?" Raisa asked with a smile. "At least a little?"

"No," Gabriela said, and then she screamed it again into the sky. "No."

Then in one quick movement, she whirled.

But Raisa was close enough.

She leaped forward, catching Gabriela by the arm just as she went to jump.

The momentum carried them both forward, Raisa's boots skidding against dirt and loose pebbles, her fingers desperately clinging to the material they'd grabbed. She fell forward, the wind getting knocked half out of her.

Gabriela slid mostly over the edge, and the weight of it was taking them both over.

Raisa tried to get herself to her knees, tried to get leverage.

"Let me go," Gabriela screamed. "Let me go."

"No," Raisa roared, just as St. Ivany grabbed the back of her shirt.

They both pulled until Raisa had better purchase.

They were going to save Delaney.

Gabriela.

Gabriela, not Delaney. They were going to save her. Raisa just needed to pull. Just a little harder.

But then Gabriela began to fight.

"She's going to take us all over," St. Ivany huffed in Raisa's ear. "You have to let her go."

"I can't give up on her," Raisa said, even as Gabriela kicked out against the rock, swinging her body so that she could actually pull against them. "I can't . . ."

She was out of breath, out of energy. Gabriela stared up at her, seeming to sense that Raisa was losing her grip.

"Make the world a better place," Gabriela said. "Let me go."

Raisa would never be able to say if it was a conscious decision. But in that moment her hands failed her. They spasmed, and then . . .

She let go.

CHAPTER THIRTY-NINE

Raisa

Day Seven

Raisa stared out over the harbor, wondering if she should seek out Delaney once more. It would be a long time before she forgot her own mental slip on that cliff, thinking she was trying to save Delaney, even though her sister had never been close to the type of monster Gabriela had become.

Still, it felt like maybe they had said to each other what they'd needed to on that boat.

She was about to head to the hospital—she wanted to check on Kilkenny herself—when Essi Halla strutted toward her, dolled up to perfection.

"Well, this all seems rife with potential for melodrama," Essi said, hands on her hips. "Maybe it will be my second book. *I* was targeted by a serial killer."

"Well, good luck, I guess?" Raisa said, not bothering to mention that she'd already flagged Essi as a person of interest for the white-collar boys at the Bureau.

Essi winked at her. "Don't you worry. I'm a survivor. I always come out on top."

"I'm sure you do," Raisa said, laughing, almost hoping it was true. "So Gabriela Cruz was the one who told you Isabel had killed your father?"

"Yeah," Essi said, brows raised. "Why? Did something happen with her?"

"She was the one who killed Emily Logan," Raisa said. "And likely Isabel, and a couple others."

"She didn't kill Isabel," Essi said. "No way."

Raisa turned to her. "What?"

"I mean, I'm no FBI agent," Essi said, drawing out the acronym. "But she contacted me right after the news dropped. Said I needed to get up here and bring all the attention with me. She was convinced Isabel was killed, but knew she wouldn't be able to get anyone to listen to her. She thought me being here would help."

Raisa pictured that moment on the boat when she'd accused Gabriela of murdering Isabel.

She had been about to deny it, but clearly hadn't wanted to be distracted in that moment.

"Like, maybe she was that good of an actor," Essi continued, "but it does seem weird."

Raisa nodded, staring blankly over the water, trying to figure out where her misstep had occurred. Obsession and hate were two sides of a coin. It had seemed logical to her that Gabriela, who had been losing control, would want to kill the idol who had set her down that path. But Gabriela *had* maintained her hero worship up until the end.

"Well," Essi drew out. "Toodles."

And then she was gone, hips swaying as she went to try to eavesdrop on the police still swarming the harbor.

Isabel had said that she'd wanted both Delaney and Raisa to break. To do so, she'd created a ruse where she'd had an impressionable protégé kill in order to prove her worth to Isabel. She'd then set it up so that it looked like Delaney was putting that very protégé down like a dog who had the taste of blood in its mouth. To push Raisa to the brink, where she might actually have killed Delaney and claimed self-defense, she'd put Kilkenny's life into play.

But Delaney had never planned to kill Gabriela—her strategy had been to get a recording of a confession.

Isabel had thought she could force Delaney into actually, finally killing someone.

Because that had been the difference between the two sisters. Delaney wasn't like Raisa; she didn't think she was a morally upright person. She knew she lived in the gray areas.

What defined her as better than Isabel was that she had never actually taken a life. Not in the real sense of the word.

If Isabel had wanted to push Delaney past the breaking point, that was what she had to get her to do.

Delaney was so smart, though. And Isabel had been in prison.

Isabel had thought she was a mastermind—she'd lived out her little fantasy through those Biggest Fan letters and the reviews she'd written herself. *That* was how she'd seen this all going.

But where Isabel was brilliant at manipulating people into doing her bidding, Delaney was brilliant at being, well, cold. Logical. Isabel could have threatened to kill Raisa and Kilkenny, but Delaney would have found a way around that.

There wasn't a problem out there that Delaney couldn't solve—even if Raisa didn't always like the way she solved it.

In the end, though, she hadn't had to.

Because . . .

Because . . .

Isabel had already been dead.

Raisa laughed.

Delaney was better than Isabel because she'd never taken a life.

Except that maybe she had.

Delaney was sitting on the edge of the motel's empty pool, her legs dangling into nothingness.

"She broke you," Raisa said as she dropped down next to her sister.

The corner of Delaney's mouth twitched. "As intended."

Delaney was smart, but so was Isabel.

She had known that Delaney would figure out a way to avoid killing her protégé.

But Isabel had left Delaney with no choice but to kill *her*.

"Insulin?" Raisa asked.

Delaney shot her a look, and Raisa held her hands up. "No recorder. No wires."

"Right," Delaney huffed. "I'm going to tell Little Miss Goody Two-shoes that I killed our sister."

"I'm sorry," Raisa said.

She was sorry Delaney had been driven to that point—over a line in the sand she'd always refused to cross before.

She was sorry Delaney had to bear the weight of that alone when Isabel had been out for both of their blood.

She was sorry that they were the two left standing. That they were each other's family when Raisa couldn't bear to call her that.

And, technically, Raisa should've been attempting to arrest Delaney.

There would be no evidence, no trace of anything.

"Okay, hypothetically speaking," Raisa said, mostly because she was nosy. "How would someone go about that?"

"*Someone* might have paid off an inmate to try to assassinate Isabel within the prison," Delaney said. "Because that *someone* realized that Isabel was never going to stop trying to kill people. And that *someone* felt like they'd spent their life making a huge mistake in letting her live."

"And when the shiv attempt didn't work," Raisa prodded.

"*Someone* might have researched all the guards until they found one with a personal vendetta against scumbag murderers," Delaney said, kicking her feet out. "The guard easily snuck a syringe of insulin into the prison and then pricked Isabel right before roll call. It took a couple hours for her to actually die in her sleep."

"That guard should probably be fired," Raisa mused.

"And they would be, if this was anything other than a hypothetical," Delaney said with a shrug. "*Someone* might also know that said guard is planning on taking her ill-gotten money and retiring to some island on the other side of the world, if that makes you feel any better."

"It really, really doesn't," Raisa said, and Delaney smirked.

"That's where we differ," Delaney murmured.

"Where did you get the insulin?" Raisa asked, for lack of any better question.

Delaney shot her a pitying glance. "Please tell me you've ventured onto the dark web at least once. It will help you with your career if you get a passing familiarity with what's available on there."

"I've been on it," Raisa said, though they both knew she was lying. "Anyway. When did Isabel know? What you had planned."

"When I went to visit her," Delaney said. "Maybe six months ago. She wanted to play a game. I said I wouldn't do it."

Isabel had never been made for prison, but she wasn't exactly built for suicide, either. Her ego was too dominant—it would have fought tooth and nail to stay alive.

So she'd tried to arrange it to where she could pull the pin and take Raisa and Delaney down with her.

Her ultimate dream. Making them *hers* for eternity.

But not even Isabel could outsmart her own death.

Raisa wondered if she would ever see Delaney again. Isabel was what had held them together, in a strange way.

Kilkenny would tell her that Delaney was family, and that mattered for something. Maybe it did, maybe it didn't. Only time would tell.

But right now, Raisa was just thankful.

Thankful that the rage-fueled fire that burned in her whenever she thought of Delaney had been put out.

Delaney had never been able to stop Isabel when it mattered. Until she finally had.

As an FBI agent, Raisa could never condone someone taking life and death into their own hands. They had a justice system for a reason, and Raisa was staunchly against the government killing people.

As Isabel Parker's sister, though, Raisa would thank the powers that be every night for the rest of her life that the monster had been slain.

"I don't feel broken," Delaney said, sounding like she was confessing something terrible. "It feels like I finally did something right."

Raisa bumped her shoulder, and gave Delaney the one thing she'd always withheld from her. "Yeah, I think you did."

NOTE WIPED CLEAN FROM DELANEY MOORE'S COMPUTER

```
This is the Isabel Paradox.
To prove her wrong, I had to kill her,
thus proving her right.
```

CHAPTER FORTY

Delaney

Day Eight

Delaney had thought about killing Isabel a thousand times.

She'd thought about it while standing in line at the grocery store, and thought about it while on a run, and thought about it while watching a movie. It didn't even have to be a film with a serial killer in it. In fact, Delaney'd had a particularly vivid vision of cutting Isabel's throat once during a romantic comedy's unexpected musical number.

All that planning and fantasizing, and she had never believed she could do it. Not realistically.

But Isabel had known just how to push her over the edge of anything she'd ever thought would be doable.

"I'm never going to stop, you know," Isabel said, when Delaney went to stand up from the table in the visitation room. "I have the taste of blood in my mouth."

Delaney stared at her.

"You know. Like a dog, when they say it breaks skin on a human," Isabel said. "They have to put it down."

For forty years, Delaney had worn Isabel's attention, love, jealousy, adoration, hate, around her neck. The weight of it had pressed down on her chest so that she'd never been able to fully breathe.

As she stood on the pier looking out over the water, she finally filled her lungs to the brim.

That morning, Delaney had called her landlord in Seattle and given her notice on the lease. She scheduled a moving company to pack up her apartment and put it all in a storage container. Maybe she would come back for it; maybe she wouldn't.

The medical examiner had finally come down with a decision in Isabel's death. *Inconclusive.*

St. Ivany hadn't seemed interested in pursuing the case further.

Raisa had been a potential wrench. Delaney should have guessed she would try to figure out who had killed Isabel—even if Isabel hadn't sent her messages to get her curious.

But she didn't seem like she wanted to pursue charges any further, either.

Still, Delaney had bought new clothes that morning—yoga pants without pockets, a tank top. She'd gotten rid of everything but her wallet, which contained exactly two driver's licenses—one with her name and one with someone else's—and the prepaid credit cards she liked to stock up on.

She had also tucked the last note she'd received from Isabel in the coin pocket.

Delaney had thought it sarcastic when she'd first received it. But now, she thought she might understand.

You are the very best of us.

Anyone with half a brain could argue that honor was, in fact, Raisa's. But Raisa would never have been able to kill Isabel outside of self-defense. She wouldn't have been able to logically, coldly, arrange to make the world a better place. And yet, Delaney would never have that taste of blood in her mouth like Isabel did, either—she would never need to be stopped, because she had been born to take exactly one life.

So maybe she didn't deserve to believe that she was the very best of the Parkers. But she believed that Isabel had believed it.

"So you're going to disappear into the wilds?"

Delaney spun to see Roan of the Carolina mountains, standing behind her. "Yes."

He laughed lightly. "You want company?"

"Hardly ever," Delaney said, eyeing him.

"Does that mean you sometimes want company?"

"Yes, that is what it means."

For some reason, that made him smile fully. Then he reached into his pocket and pulled out a set of keys.

"Do you want to spend that sometimes with me on a boat?"

"I thought you were the pauper, not the prince," Delaney said, though she felt an unexpected kick in her belly. Happiness, maybe? She had never been able to make a relationship work before, not with Isabel and all the secrets that went along with her as baggage. But now?

"I may have lied to you on that one," Roan said. "I'm pretty sure you lied to me, though, too. So, even?"

"It won't be the last time," she warned. Because she wasn't perfect. She was the best of the Parkers, but that didn't mean she was the best of humankind. It was a low bar she was passing.

"I think I'll risk it," Roan said.

Delaney studied him and then turned back to the water.

Happiness had been elusive, something she had never wanted to grasp for because it could all be taken away so easily. So she'd buried herself on the dark web, paying for her crime of silence by exposing herself to the worst of humanity in hopes of battling it. She had taken a job as a moderator at Flik for the very same reason.

Anything good in the world could be used against her as a weapon.

But Isabel was gone.

This was just Delaney. No more safety net, no more excuses.
Happiness was a fragile, possibly devastating thing.
Finally, though, she felt ready to try for it.
She glanced back at Roan and studied his face.
"I think I'll risk it, too."

CHAPTER FORTY-ONE

Raisa

Day Eight

The heart monitor beeped steadily, greeting Raisa when she finally woke.

It felt like she'd slept sixteen days instead of sixteen hours. But either way, Kilkenny still hadn't stirred.

"Is it time to start worrying?" Raisa had asked the doctor like she hadn't spent every minute Kilkenny had been in that bed worrying.

"No, I think we'll see progress in the next day or two. The swelling in his brain has decreased dramatically," the doctor had reassured her. "I'm hopeful it won't be much longer."

Raisa knew doctors. He wouldn't have said *hopeful* if he hadn't meant it. They always wanted you braced for the worst-case scenario.

But hopefulness wasn't a guarantee.

"No change, huh?" St. Ivany asked from the doorway.

"Nope," Raisa said, not bothering to stand up. Everything in her body ached. She was getting too old to sleep in chairs, but she would have done far worse if it meant she could be here when Kilkenny came to.

"The DA listened to Gabriela's confession from Delaney's recorder," St. Ivany said, moving around to the end of the bed.

"We're also searching her place now. We've already found some souvenirs."

"Isabel never kept souvenirs," Raisa murmured.

"Yeah, well, Isabel got away with it for twenty-five years and Gabriela Cruz got away with it for six months," St. Ivany pointed out. "With the help of Isabel."

"I hate that she was so good at it," Raisa said, thinking of Delaney, too.

No one would have ever suspected that Isabel had been killed, if the ME hadn't been briefed on the fact that it was a possibility. And that had been Delaney's first try.

Raisa shook off the unease that came with the thought.

She had spent the past two years worrying that Isabel would break one of them, that their Parker blood would come through and destroy the world.

Yet Isabel had thrown her very best at them, and all it had taken was a visitor logbook for Raisa to drop her gun.

Isabel had been obsessed with them, she had studied them, she had tried to understand them.

But she was a psychopath unable to actually do so.

Where her mind had drawn blanks for predicting their behaviors, she had assumed they would do what she did—the most harmful, terrible action possible.

It was in Delaney's and Raisa's humanity that they had finally beaten her.

That knowledge felt comforting.

"Obviously it doesn't matter much, practically speaking," St. Ivany said. "But it's good to have everything on the record."

"Yeah," Raisa agreed. Especially since she had been right there when Gabriela had died.

"We'll keep you updated," St. Ivany said. "I would add to stay in touch, but, well, I didn't like you that much."

Raisa laughed so hard she finally looked at the woman, who was smiling along.

"Yeah, you were terrible to work with, lose my number," Raisa shot back.

St. Ivany saluted her before patting Kilkenny's feet once. Then she turned and left the room.

Raisa's phone buzzed and she almost ignored it. But she glanced down to find an unknown number had texted her.

In case you ever need me.

Raisa stared down at it.

In the past, had she gotten this message from Delaney, she would have deleted it out of spite.

But something had happened on the boat, and then on the cliff with Gabriela. Raisa had realized that not only did she trust the woman Delaney had become—despite the fact that she'd killed Isabel—but she also could more clearly see the girl she'd been.

There was no way her heart could ache for Gabriela and the way she'd been manipulated by Isabel and not acknowledge that Delaney had been molded in that same crucible.

She could have held on, let Gabriela pull her down into the waves with her, just like she'd been letting her resentment toward a young Delaney ruin any chance she had at having family now. Or she could let go of her own hang-ups and live.

Raisa tapped on the screen until the option came up to create a new contact.

This didn't mean she *had* to contact Delaney. They were never going to be the type to call on holidays and birthdays just to chat.

But it felt nice to know that, if she needed it, the number was there.

She toggled back to the text thread, and typed:

Who dis?

Delaney didn't respond, but she liked to think her sister laughed.

Raisa put her phone away and watched the sky outside for a long time as it darkened into evening.

She almost didn't notice when the beeping changed.

Almost absently, her eyes slid toward the bed, only to find Kilkenny staring back at her.

"Oh my god," she whispered, her pulse racing as adrenaline shot through her bloodstream. She blinked against the rush of tears, but they fell anyway while she scrambled for his hand.

She needed to call for someone, right now. But she couldn't.

It was only in this moment, as he squinted up at her, everything probably too bright from so many days in darkness, that she realized she hadn't thought he'd wake up.

Raisa had clutched at the hope offered to her, but she hadn't actually believed it.

A sob caught in the back of her throat, and she brought her shaking free hand to press up against her mouth.

Kilkenny whispered something she couldn't hear.

She took a deep breath, gathering in her silly emotions. "What was that?"

This time it was stronger. His eyes were focused as he forced the words out through cracked lips. "You got your guy."

Warmth flooded Raisa, and she laughed while tears ran down her face. She could hear the commotion in the hall. The staff would be rushing in within seconds. But this moment, right here? It was just for them.

"I got my guy."

ACKNOWLEDGMENTS

For this series I dived into the wonderful and fascinating world of forensic linguistics. These books wouldn't exist without the real-life knowledge shared by experts, including but not limited to Robert Leonard, Jim Fitzgerald, Malcolm Coulthard, Alison Johnson, David Wright, Alison May, and Rui Sousa-Silva. This book was also informed by incredible research into vigilantism by Andreas D. Nehrlich, Jochen E. Gebauer, Constantine Sedikides, and Christiane Schoel. Many thank-yous to all of them and anyone who helps us all understand each other better.

A huge thank-you to my editorial dream team, Megha Parekh and Charlotte Herscher, as well as everyone at Thomas & Mercer who helps make my books into the best versions of themselves.

Thanks, as always, must go to Abby Saul, my wonderful agent, who provides everything from moral support to insightful edits.

And, of course, thank you to my readers, who make all this possible.

ABOUT THE AUTHOR

Photo © 2019

Brianna Labuskes is the *USA Today*, *Wall Street Journal*, *Washington Post*, and Amazon Charts bestselling author of *The Lies You Wrote* and *The Truth You Told* in the Raisa Susanto series; *See It End*, *What Can't Be Seen*, and *A Familiar Sight* in the Dr. Gretchen White series; and *Her Final Words*, *Black Rock Bay*, *Girls of Glass*, and *It Ends with Her*. She lives in Pennsylvania with her puppy, Jinx. For more information, visit www.briannalabuskes.com.